The Leash Around Your Mind

Jeffrey Robert Collins

TABLE OF CONTENTS

Prologue 1

Chapter One 16

Chapter Two 26

Chapter Three 37

Chapter Four 48

Chapter Five 69

Chapter Six 79

Chapter Seven 92

Chapter Eight 116

Chapter Nine 122

Chapter Ten 141

Chapter Eleven 154

Chapter Twelve 158

Chapter Thirteen 160

Chapter Fourteen 170

Chapter Fifteen 175

Chapter Sixteen 181

Chapter Seventeen 188

Chapter Eighteen 192

Chapter Nineteen 200

Chapter Twenty 205

Chapter Twenty-One 209

Chapter Twenty-Two 221

Chapter Twenty-Three 225

Chapter Twenty-Four 246

Chapter Twenty-Five 251

Chapter Twenty-Six...258

Chapter Twenty-Seven 267

Chapter Twenty-Eight...270

Chapter Twenty-Nine 280

Chapter Thirty 282

Chapter Thirty-One 289

Chapter Thirty-Two 292

Chapter Thirty-Three 300

Chapter Thirty-Four...303

Chapter Thirty-Five 316

Chapter Thirty-Six 319

Chapter Thirty-Seven 322

Chapter Thirty-Eight...331

Chapter Thirty-Nine 340

Chapter Forty 344

Chapter Forty-One 348

Chapter Forty-Two...369

Chapter Forty-Three...372

Chapter Forty-Four 379

PROLOGUE

Second Leash

The air in the detention center's training wing was always colder than it needed to be. Maybe that was the point— keep the dogs alert, keep the inmates humble. The chain-link kennels rattled when someone sneezed two rows over. The fluorescent lights hummed like dying bees.

Luna didn't flinch. Not anymore.

She sat like a little shadow on her ragged blanket, paws tucked beneath her like a sphinx, tail curled half-heartedly around her hip. Still. Alert. Watching.

Lucas Santiago sat beside the kennel, back against the cinderblock wall, one knee bent, one leg stretched out, paperback open in his lap. His right hand moved without rhythm, just a slow, idle scratch behind Luna's ear through the mesh. Every so often, her eyes fluttered shut. But only for a second.

The book was Siddhartha by Hermann Hesse. Lucas hadn't turned a page in twenty minutes.

"I think she's training you, bro," Officer Salazar called as he walked past, clipboard in hand, gum snapping between his teeth. "You're the one sittin', fetchin', scratchin'…"

Lucas didn't respond. Not because he was ignoring him, but because he was somewhere else. Not zoned out—held, like a candle flame cupped in invisible hands. Luna's head tilted just slightly, like she could feel Salazar's gaze and chose to disregard it.

McKinnon came through next, heavy boots creaking on the painted concrete. "You want another hot dog for her, Santiago?" he asked without looking up from his keyring.

Lucas blinked, hesitating. "Did I already give her one today?"

McKinnon stopped. Thought. "Dunno. But she's looking at me like I owe her."

Luna didn't blink. Just stared. Calm, expectant. Her ears didn't move, but her tail did—a single wag, like a signal flare.

McKinnon reached into his vest pocket and pulled out a crumpled foil pouch. "Alright, sweetheart," he muttered, crouching in front of the kennel. "But this is the last one, alright?"

She took the piece so gently she didn't even brush his fingers. She didn't chew right away. Just held it, turned it over in her mouth like she was tasting something more than meat. Then she swallowed, licked her lips once, and returned to watching Lucas.

Down the hall, Salazar shook his head. "Damn dog's got you two filing joint taxes."

Still crouched, McKinnon leaned back on his heels, his face slackening—not in fear, but in that dazed stillness people wear when they've walked into a cathedral they didn't expect. He stared through the bars like he wasn't sure how he got there.

"Thought she was shy at first," he said absently. "But it's like she sees through you. Like she's thinking."

Lucas nodded, not looking up. "She is."

And she was. Not scheming—but sensing. Not dominant—but inevitable.

She wasn't the prettiest dog in the program. She wasn't the loudest. Didn't do tricks. Didn't bark. Didn't beg. She had no special story that the volunteers could package with a ribbon. She was just present, in a way that most people weren't. The inmates sensed it. The guards tried not to.

Her body was solid and low-slung, white as a bleached bone with a head too expressive for comfort. One side of her face was marked by a warm tan patch that swept over her eye like a permanent wink. Her nose was pink. Not soft pink—startling pink, like a dropped piece of bubblegum, like something vulnerable that should be hidden but wasn't.

Her eyes were pale and unhurried. Light-colored. Watchful. Not cold. Just… old. Like they'd seen more than her months on earth should allow, and she wasn't in the mood to explain any of it.

She didn't cower, but she ducked instinctively when hands came down from above. She accepted affection better from the side or from below. Lucas learned that without ever being told. He adapted without knowing why.

Sometimes, he'd be mid-sentence in a book, and his hand would shift to rub the exact spot under her jaw she wanted scratched. He'd drop crumbs of peanut butter granola without looking. She'd curl beside him in the evenings, spine to thigh, their breathing falling into sync. Not because she was trained, but because the rhythm felt right.

She didn't dominate the space. She saturated it. Like fog—quiet, shaping everything it touched.

* * *

One night, just after lights-out, McKinnon stood at the control booth, staring at the kennel feed longer than protocol required. The camera was grainy, black-and-white, static-prone. Still, you could make out shapes.

Lucas lay on his back, arms folded across his chest, eyes closed.

Luna lay the same way. Spine aligned. Paws tucked. Not touching, but close enough to echo.

"Jesus," McKinnon whispered to no one. "She's got that boy wrapped around her paw."

Then the feed glitched. Just for a blink. A single line of static jittered when Luna turned her head. Her eyes flashed white for a single frame—washed out by the infrared—but enough to make McKinnon step back like he'd been nudged.

He blinked, shook it off. Just the camera. Old wiring.

Then he opened the small drawer beneath the console and dropped in a fresh bag of hot dogs for tomorrow.

* * *

The yard behind the detention center wasn't much to look at. Patches of dead grass, chain-link enclosures, the sharp stink of bleach on concrete. A few folding tables sagged beneath stacks of paperwork, and a volunteer was trying to tape a "Welcome!" banner to the side of a mobile kennel trailer. The tape kept giving out.

Ted Tompkins adjusted his sunglasses and glanced down at the brochure again. It was the third time he'd read the same paragraph. Something about mutual rehabilitation. Life skills. Second chances. He wasn't really absorbing it.

Gabriela stood beside him, arms crossed, scanning the dogs with a practiced eye. She didn't like decisions that couldn't be unmade.

"You see that little shepherd mix?" she said, nodding toward a pen on the far side of the lot. "She looks sweet."

Ted didn't answer. His head had already turned. He wasn't looking at the shepherd mix.

He was staring at a small white pit bull, curled in a perfect spiral on a blanket inside one of the shaded kennels. She wasn't barking, wasn't pacing. She wasn't even watching the people passing by. Her eyes were half-lidded. Calm. Present.

One tan patch marked the left side of her face, slashing across her eye like war paint. The rest of her was white—bright and matte, like unglazed porcelain. Her nose was a striking pink, like a mistake that hadn't been corrected. She looked both ridiculous and holy.

"She's not even looking at us," Gabriela said, following his gaze.

"She is," Ted said.

He didn't know how he knew. He just did.

The volunteer at the sign-in table was all smiles and structure. "That's Luna," she said, flipping through a clipboard. "She's been in the program for about four months. Came in a little skittish, but she's made amazing progress. One of our inmate handlers really bonded with her—Lucas Santiago. Model participant."

"Does she bark?" Ted asked.

"Rarely. Never without reason. She's calm, very food-motivated. Highly observant."

Ted wasn't listening anymore. He was already walking toward the kennel.

Gabriela hesitated, then followed.

* * *

Lucas Santiago stood by the gate with his hands in his pockets, body turned sideways, head down. When he heard the footsteps, he looked up—just briefly. Then he knelt beside the kennel and pressed his palm to the bars.

Luna didn't move toward him.

She didn't move at all.

But her tail gave one single thump.

Lucas smiled. It was a broken thing. "You got someone good, yeah?"

Luna blinked, then stood—smooth and slow like a tide coming in—and walked to the back of the kennel. She sat facing the rear wall, like she couldn't watch him leave.

Ted watched that too.

Gabriela leaned in to whisper. "She looks... disconnected."

"She's already leaving him," Ted replied, voice flat.

The process took twenty minutes. ID, liability waivers, veterinary records. Gabriela handled most of it. Ted just signed where they told him to.

As Ted leaned over to sign the waiver, a goldendoodle with a crooked grin wandered too close to the edge of Luna's pen—tongue lolling, ears flapping like party flags.

Without warning, Luna snapped once. No bark. No growl. Just teeth—fast and precise—stopping an inch from the chain-link.

The doodle yelped and stumbled back, tail down, confusion in his eyes.

Gabriela saw it.

So did the other dogs.

A subtle shift passed through the yard like wind before a monsoon. A dozen heads turned toward Luna. Some didn't move—but their ears twitched. Their eyes narrowed. For the briefest moment, they held still.

Then, it was gone.

A sneeze. A jangle of keys. The illusion broke, and the dogs went back to their barks, their pacing, their hopeful glances at the gate.

Luna hadn't moved. She was already lying down again, tail curled to hip, eyes half-lidded.

Gabriela watched her for a beat longer. Not with fear, just the quiet knowledge that she'd seen something form and vanish.

Potential.

When they opened the kennel, Luna stepped out without hesitation. No leash, no command. Just a quiet step forward and a long stretch, front legs splayed, back arched.

She didn't run to them.

She didn't sniff or paw or jump.

She just walked a slow arc around Ted, nose low to the ground, then stopped beside him and sat. Her shoulder brushed his leg. She didn't look up.

And somehow, that was worse than eye contact. That was ownership.

Ted crouched, reached out his hand, low, palm up. She leaned into it like gravity had decided for her.

Gabriela stood to the side, eyebrows slightly raised. "You sure?"

"I was sure before I got here."

As they walked toward the exit gate, Ted didn't notice Lucas still standing at the fence, hands now in fists, jaw clenched.

But Luna did.

She didn't look back. She didn't need to.

Behind them, Officer McKinnon appeared with a brown paper bag in hand and caught up with the volunteer at the table.

"I forgot," he said, a blush creeping up his neck. "I meant to send her with these."

He dropped the bag beside the crate.

Inside: a half-used box of training treats, a tennis ball, and three unopened packs of hot dogs.

* * *

The first dog bed lasted eight hours.

Gabriela had found it on sale—orthopedic foam, washable cover, "indestructible" stitching. By morning, it looked like a grenade had gone off inside a Build-A-Bear.

Luna sat calmly in the middle of the wreckage, flecks of stuffing clinging to her ears. Her tail gave a light *thump thump thump* on the bare floor. She blinked once. Then twice.

Ted, still barefoot and half-asleep, stood in the kitchen doorway and stared.

"She doesn't even look guilty," he muttered.

"She's not," Gabriela said, sipping her coffee. "She's proud. Look at her. That's an artist admiring her work."

"I just don't understand why—"

Thump thump thump.

"I mean, it was a bed."

Gabriela shrugged. "Maybe she's not ready to be comfortable."

Ted crouched, scooped up the cover, and started stuffing the innards back in like he could undo it. Luna tilted her head, watching him with something like curiosity. Or amusement.

Like she was evaluating the effort—not the result.

By the end of the first week, two more beds were in the trash, and Gabriela had started calling Luna "The Interior Decorator."

"She has a vision," she said dryly, watching Luna methodically rip a corner seam open with her front teeth. "And it involves the systematic destruction of every soft surface in this house."

Ted chuckled, then opened the cabinet and pulled out a slice of cheese.

Luna dropped the bed and trotted over like she'd been summoned by divine right.

"You're rewarding a war crime," Gabriela said.

"She didn't bark," Ted replied, as if that explained anything.

Gabriela just gave him a look. The kind that ends marriages in some countries. Then came the shoes.

Ted had always kept his sneakers in neat pairs near the back door. Nothing obsessive—just order. System. Two rows of daily drivers. Running shoes. Boots. Loafers for work.

Luna never touched the right one.

Just the left.

At first, he thought it was a coincidence. Then he found the third left shoe gnawed into a leather chrysalis and realized: She's doing it on purpose.

"I don't understand," he said, holding up the chewed husk of a hiking boot.

Gabriela looked over the rim of her book. "Maybe you lean left."

"I'm serious."

"So is she." Gabriela closed the book. "She's off balance without you. You leave, and she punishes the foot that walks away first."

Ted stared at the shoe. "That doesn't make any sense."

"Doesn't have to."

He looked down at the shredded leather—creased, punctured, peeled back in careful layers—and felt a strange chill along his heel. Like the destruction was personal. Intentional. Not a chew toy. A symbol. A warning. A tooth-punched note taped to the back door that said: *I noticed.*

One morning, Ted woke up early. He didn't know why. Just sat bolt upright at 5:16 a.m.

Luna wasn't in her crate.

He found her in the living room, curled on the couch like a pale muscle tucked into itself. One eye was cracked open. Watching.

Not startled. Not guilty.

Just aware.

He stood there for a while, rubbing the heel of his palm into one eye, trying to place the weird weight in his chest.

Eventually, he walked to the kitchen. Opened the fridge. Took out a slice of cheese. Walked back without thinking. Luna accepted it like a queen receiving tribute.

Then he sat down on the floor next to the couch.

The hardwood was cold under his legs. The silence felt thick—like waiting for something to land.

And he stayed there until the sun came up.

* * *

Two months passed, and the house changed without anyone agreeing to it.

The crate migrated to the bedroom. The living room rug had permanent dog prints pressed into the fibers.

There were no more dog beds—just blankets arranged on the couch like Luna was building a nest out of domestic scraps. She didn't chew them anymore. She simply inhabited them, like a queen claiming ruins—not as a guest, but as something reclaimed.

Gabriela noticed it first.

"She doesn't obey commands," she said one evening, chopping cilantro at the counter. "She responds to you before you say anything."

Ted was filling Luna's bowl, one hand already moving to where the cheese slices were kept. He stopped.

"What do you mean?"

"She watches you like you're a thought she hasn't heard yet."

Ted chuckled, shook his head, and gave Luna a piece anyway. She took it gently, like always. No bark. No bounce. Just acceptance. Like it was already hers.

Luna stopped sleeping in her crate.

No one had invited her onto the bed, but one night she'd climbed up silently and curled behind Ted's knees. He'd woken up warm and oddly comforted. When he tried to move, she shifted with him, always keeping contact.

The next night, she was there before he was.

Gabriela didn't say anything until the third night.

"She's getting attached," she said softly, not unkindly.

Ted stared at the ceiling. "It's just a phase."

But even he didn't believe it. He started waking earlier. Not because he had to—but because Luna was always already up. Sitting by the glass door, watching the sky lighten. Some mornings she'd press her nose against the glass. Other mornings, she'd sit perfectly still, ears perked, eyes half-closed like she was listening to a song too quiet for humans.

Ted started joining her.

They'd sit there for twenty minutes without a word, watching the sun climb over the houses. Sometimes Gabriela would come out and find them there—Ted cross-legged on the floor in sweatpants, Luna tucked against his hip, both of them bathed in the orange hush of morning.

She'd pause, coffee in hand, and say nothing. There was nothing to say.

But once—just once—she saw Luna glance sharply toward the east, ears twitching, as if she'd heard something far away. Like a whistle through concrete. The moment passed, but Gabriela didn't forget it.

One night, Ted had a dream.

He was walking down a path he didn't recognize—flat land, no trees, dirt baked into ripples like an old lakebed. Luna trotted ahead of him, never turning back, but always staying just far enough that he had to keep moving.

He wasn't chasing her. He was following her.

There was something in the distance—just a shape. A crooked post. Maybe a sign. Maybe a leash hook. He couldn't read it, but he felt it. Like gravity was weaker near it.

When he woke, his first thought was: *She's leading me somewhere.*

But he didn't tell Gabriela. Didn't write it down. He just looked over at Luna—curled on her side, nose tucked under her tail, one ear flicking in her sleep—and placed a hand gently on her back.

She didn't stir.

But her breathing synced with his. Like it always did. That evening, Gabriela watched them from the kitchen as Ted tossed a piece of banana into his mouth, wiped his hands, and absentmindedly dropped a piece of cheese into Luna's bowl.

Luna didn't bark. Didn't move.

She was just a presence—magnetic and absolute.

Gabriela tilted her head.

And for a second—just a flicker—she wasn't sure who in the house had trained whom.

CHAPTER ONE

Routine

The espresso machine hissed like it disapproved of everyone in the room.

Ted Tompkins stood beside it, watching the brew cycle drag on just long enough to feel personal. Behind him, muted conversations rose and fell in scripted cadences—project updates, weekend plans, some forced joke about someone's dog getting skunked. He offered the appropriate smirk when one coworker glanced over, but dropped it the instant the guy turned back to his phone.

The office was sleek. Modern. Glass walls, dark wood trim, clean angles engineered to look effortless. Metrics scrolled silently on the big monitors overhead—production timelines, cost curves, threat assessments from clients who only spoke in acronyms.

Ted's name was on half the projects. Maybe more. The kind of guy everyone trusted but nobody invited to lunch.

His coffee finished with a strangled burp of steam. He didn't add cream. Just walked it back to his desk like it might turn on him if he looked away.

The ergonomic chair accepted his weight with synthetic indifference. His screen blinked awake. Email.

Prototype updates. Another flagged delay on the magnetic shunt alignment, even though he'd sent specs—twice. He started a reply, then stopped. Deleted it. Rewrote it. Deleted that too.

His fingers hovered a second longer than they should have. His hand felt slow. Like someone else had typed the message before him, and he was just catching up.

He leaned back and looked through the glass wall into the corridor. Two engineers walked past, deep in conversation—one of them gesturing with a stylus like it carried legal weight.

Ted stared at them until they vanished. Not watching—listening.

He turned back to his screen and wrote what he needed with the efficiency of someone who didn't care if it was read—just that it existed. A task fulfilled.

The hours passed in blunted fragments. Meetings, models, a procurement call. At one point he took the wrong hallway—forgetting, even though he never forgot—and ended up in the breakroom where a junior analyst was showing pictures of her kids in Halloween costumes on her phone.

Ted nodded politely.

Then, without thinking, his thumb opened the gallery on his own phone.

Luna on the couch, front legs crossed, head tilted.

Swipe. Luna in the backyard, haloed by the sun.

Swipe. Luna in the passenger seat of the Jeep, ears perked, gaze fixed on something invisible.

Swipe.

Swipe.

Different angles. Different light. Same dog.

Her face didn't change. Always the same solemn composure, like she was holding still for something sacred. One photo caught her in profile, lit gold by the hour. Her nose lifted as though sensing a warning carried on the wind. Her head cocked slightly, tuned to something only she could hear.

Ted's thumb hovered over the screen. Then he clicked it off.

When he looked up, the analyst was still talking. He couldn't remember the last sentence.

The door hissed open behind him, letting in a burst of cool air. That was his chance. He took it.

It wasn't that he disliked his coworkers. They were fine. Smart, even. Decent people living decent lives.

They just felt… tuned wrong.

Every conversation landed out of phase, like watching a dubbed film where the mouths and words didn't match. He nodded at the right places. Spoke when required. But the signal never synced.

When his watch buzzed 5:03 PM, he stood and packed with the muted fluidity of a man who'd done this a thousand times. No words. No goodbyes.

By the time the lobby doors sealed behind him, the only sound left was the wind.

* * *

The New Mexico heat punched him in the chest the moment he stepped outside. Late-day sun warped the air above the asphalt, draping the world in a wavering shimmer. His Jeep sat five rows out, square and proud, white paint flaring against the sky like armor.

He walked in a direct line. Keys in hand. Backpack over one shoulder. No pause, no backward glance.

Just before reaching the door, he stopped.

Not long. A beat. Maybe two.

His eyes drifted to the passenger seat. Empty. Of course. But not forgotten. Something about the vacancy carried… friction. Like a picture hung slightly crooked.

He adjusted the strap on his shoulder and opened the door.

Climbed in. Sat. Didn't start the engine.

The seat beside him was clean. Too clean. Luna's wiry hairs always found a way back, threaded into fabric like memories. But today it looked scrubbed, erased. Like she'd never been there. And yet—

He reached to buckle in, and his fingers brushed a single strand stuck to the edge of the cushion.

Still warm.

He jerked his hand back before he could know why.

He started the engine. The dash flickered to life. A mellow guitar riff slid through the speakers—something queued up weeks ago. Familiar.

He skipped it.

Skipped the next one.

Then turned it off entirely.

The Jeep rolled out of the lot in silence. His fingers tapped the wheel unconsciously, a pattern he didn't recognize. Not Morse. Not rhythm. Just… tapping.

Left on Roadrunner. Right past the Circle K. Red light.

Wait.

His mind rewound to that morning. That strange pause in the living room as he packed his lunch. Luna had been perched on the couch, spine tall, head high, watching.

Not sleepy-eyed. Not playful. Not even alert.

Just… fixed.

He remembered joking—something dumb about her being the breakfast supervisor—but the line felt hollow in hindsight. She hadn't wagged. Hadn't blinked.

She'd just followed every motion he made.

Like she was confirming each step matched what she'd already seen.

He'd reached the door, thermos in hand. Gabriela had called a cheerful goodbye from the kitchen. He'd meant to answer. He usually did. But his hand had already closed the door before the thought landed.

He left.

And it hadn't felt wrong—until now.

* * *

The Jeep moved like a loyal beast under his grip. Firm suspension. Low hum. One hand on the wheel, the other resting loosely on the shifter.

Metro Verde drifted past in heat-haze waves. Trimmed gravel lawns, stucco homes behind tidy ironwork. Golf carts meandered across side roads like retirees on a pilgrimage. Red Hawk Golf Course blinked between lines of mesquite.

He passed a golf cart doing twelve in a thirty. The driver waved lazily. Ted waved back, then forgot the man's face by the next street.

His mind had returned to Luna.

That stare. That stillness. Not animal obedience—something else. Gravity, maybe. Like she wasn't looking at him, but through him, measuring something on the other side.

His shoulders shifted under the seatbelt.

The best part of the day hadn't happened yet.

Not seeing Gabriela. Not stepping into the house.

It was the sound. The ritual. The precise beat between key-turn and claws on tile. A sharp inhale. The sense of something rushing forward from the shadows.

But it wasn't joy. Not exactly.

It was an appointment.

Luna didn't greet him like a dog. She received him like a general checking for wounds—measuring his scent for betrayal.

Sometimes, he swore she could smell his fatigue. The bureaucracy. The ghost of office air on his skin. And she hated it. Not with anger. With certainty.

Gabriela would wave from the kitchen. She always did. A lighthouse, steady and warm.

He told himself he had noticed her first.

He hadn't.

As the Jeep pulled into the driveway, the tires crackled on the gravel with a sound like teeth grinding through bone.

He reached for the ignition—

And froze.

There it was. A bark. Faint. Far off. Not Luna.

Wrong pitch.

Then silence again. Too clean.

He sat motionless, head cocked like a dial searching static.

Nothing.

The engine sighed as he turned it off.

In the rearview mirror, his reflection stared back. A man in his early fifties. Not broken. Not fine. Just… redrafted.

His hand brushed the collar of his shirt. His hair. He adjusted them both with the grace of a puppet rehearsing a scene.

Then he opened the door and stepped out into the brightness.

He paused at the driver's side. Something itched behind his eyes. Not pain—just the ghost of a thought.

He glanced down the street, scanning for… What?

The road was empty. Perfectly so.

He walked to the front door with the feeling that he'd missed something important and wouldn't realize what it was until much later.

* * *

The house was cool. Shaded tile underfoot, faint citrus in the air. Ceiling fan turning slowly, like a clock measured in breaths.

From the back came the thump-thump of the dryer finishing its cycle.

From the kitchen, a rhythmic chop.

"Welcome home, baby!" Gabriela called without turning, her voice warm, ritual-perfect. Like she'd practiced it and filed it for retrieval.

Ted entered with his backpack still slung, the weight unnoticed. The scent of garlic pulled him forward like gravity.

Gabriela stood at the counter in a soft gray apron that read *Yes, Chef.* Her hair was tied up, but a few strands had escaped to curl against her neck.

She didn't look up—just kept slicing half-moons of onion like they were questions with obvious answers.

"How was work?" she asked.

"Fine," he said.

She smiled at the knife like it had told her more than he had.

Then it came.

The pause. The silence.

Luna entered.

Head high. Shoulders relaxed. Each step deliberate, like the floor rose to meet her.

Not a trot. Not a gallop. A procession. She moved like sound tracked her passage, even in silence.

No bark. No tail wag.

Just the click of claws on tile—sharp as piano hammers.

She stopped two feet away.

Lifted one paw.

Demand? Greeting?

Didn't matter anymore.

Ted crouched without thinking. The backpack strap pulled, but he didn't shift it. He rubbed behind her ears, under her chin, then along the thick fur beneath her jaw.

"Evening, Your Highness," he whispered.

It wasn't a joke. Not anymore. He didn't remember the first time he'd said it. It just felt… correct.

Luna exhaled. Then turned. Walked to the fridge and sat.

Perfect posture. Eyes straight. Not begging.

Waiting.

Gabriela's voice floated in, amused. "You spoil her."

Ted stood and opened the fridge. His hand reached—without hesitation—for the Havarti. The good stuff. Wax paper-wrapped. Not the sandwich cheddar.

He peeled a slice. Turned. Offered it.

Luna accepted it like a queen accepts tribute—without greed, without thanks.

Then turned again, prize in mouth, and disappeared down the hall without a glance back.

Ted watched her vanish.

And felt something ease in his ribs. A knot unwound. Something old. Something deep.

Behind him, Gabriela resumed chopping.

"So what sounds good?" she asked. "Chicken fajitas or veggie tacos?"

His eyes were still on the empty hallway.

"Either," he said. "Whatever you want."

Gabriela started listing ingredients—cilantro, salsa, maybe guacamole. Her voice folded into the white noise of the fan and the dull thud of the blade on wood.

Ted stood still.

Smile fading.

He didn't know what he'd do without her.

Didn't want to find out.

CHAPTER TWO

Her Way

The refrigerator clicked shut with the soft slap of suction. Ted stood in front of it for a beat longer than necessary, a slice of Colby Jack in hand, unsure whether he'd meant to reach for it or if his hand had simply moved on its own.

The wrapper was already peeled back halfway.

Luna was sitting in the same spot she always claimed during breakfast prep—three feet from the stove, dead center of the kitchen tile's worn diagonal pattern. Not close enough to beg, not far enough to be ignored. Watching.

Ted tossed her the cheese. A quick snatch from the air, no theatrics. She chewed with purpose, eyes locked on his face the whole time.

"She listens to you like you're the only one with opposable thumbs," Gabriela said, not looking up from the eggs she was whisking.

Ted offered a half-smile, though it faded before it reached his eyes. "She's just food-motivated."

"So are you," Gabriela muttered playfully. "You just don't sit for it."

The coffeemaker beeped behind him. Ted turned to pour a mug, but paused—there was already one beside the sink, steam curling lazily in the morning light. One sugar stirred in, no cream.

Exactly how he liked it.

He didn't remember pouring it.

Gabriela slid a plate onto the table. Scrambled eggs, sliced avocado, pan-toasted bread. No words—just the quiet choreography of people who'd done this dance long enough to know the steps.

Luna circled once and lay near the back door, belly brushing the tile, chin flat, ears forward. Watching.

"Looks like we might get some rain this afternoon," Ted said, pulling out his phone.

Gabriela raised an eyebrow. "You don't usually care unless it's riding weather."

He stared at the screen. "Just thinking about my laptop."

He meant to add, "If I should bring it home," but the sentence never finished.

She didn't push.

Luna blinked slowly, then turned her eyes to the window. Outside, the backyard tree shifted in windless silence—its shadow swaying in a breeze that hadn't arrived.

Ted ate like it was a test. Chewing, scrolling, not tasting. Gabriela picked at her toast, eyeing him sideways between bites.

"You sleep okay?" she asked finally.

"Yeah." He paused mid-bite. "Just a weird dream I can't remember."

Gabriela nodded, unconvinced but too tired to press.

Behind them, Luna let out a long, quiet breath and stretched her paws forward—like a priest resuming mass after a pause. Still watching. Always watching.

* * *

The university office smelled faintly of lavender and toner. Gabriela had opened the window to let in the morning breeze, but it mostly brought dust and the low groan of a maintenance cart turning too sharply.

She rubbed her temples, glancing at the inbox on her screen—eighteen unread emails, none urgent. The desk plant needed water. Someone had used her favorite mug and left it in the sink again.

All normal.

Still, something pressed behind her ribs. Not dread. Not even worry. Just a flick of wrongness—like a single chord struck half a beat early.

She pulled out her phone and opened the hallway camera feed.

Luna was sitting in the exact spot by the door. Not curled up. Not sleeping. Sitting. Spine tall. Still.

It looked like a still image at first. But the faintest ripple in her sides showed breath. Shallow. Measured.

"She does that a lot now?" asked a voice behind her.

Gabriela turned. Dr. Alma Navarro, her colleague in folklore and long-time spiritual mentor, stood with a stack of folders in her arms, one eyebrow raised. She always had that look—like she'd walked into the room already knowing what had happened. "She's been glued to that spot lately," Gabriela said. "Like she's guarding something."

"Or someone," Alma offered, setting the folders down. "You know what they say—when a spirit moves through a house, dogs bark and old people whisper."

Gabriela snorted. "You made that up."

Alma shrugged. "Only the part about the old people."

They laughed, but Gabriela's eyes slid back to the screen. Luna hadn't moved. It wasn't just that she was watching the door. It was how still everything else felt around her. Like time thinned in a circle around her body.

Alma followed her gaze. "She gives me bruja vibes," she said, voice low. "That's not an insult."

"I know."

"She healthy?"

"Yeah. Happy, even. Just… different."

Alma hesitated. "And Ted?"

Gabriela paused. "He's fine. Maybe a little… quiet."

Alma didn't speak, but her expression didn't drop.

Gabriela offered a practiced smile. "I think I'm just watching too many weird shows. Luna's probably bored."

Alma gave a nod, like someone who didn't believe it but respected the ritual of saying it anyway. She left without another word.

Gabriela turned back to the screen.

Luna blinked—slow, deliberate.

The hallway light above her flickered once.

Then held steady.

* * *

The sky had turned the color of week-old bruises by the time Ted laced up his boots. No rain yet, but the air tasted like wet metal. The kind of evening that whispered about storms but never committed.

Ted opened the coat closet. Leash. Flashlight. Poop bags. Each in its place like ceremonial tools. He clipped the leash to the handle and let it dangle like a question he wasn't ready to ask.

Luna didn't move.

She lay on the entryway rug, head down, ears pressed. Not asleep. Not resisting.

Just… paused.

"Let's go," Ted said, same tone as always.

From the kitchen, Gabriela looked up, drying a pan with a striped towel.

"She's not going out in that," she called. "You know how she is with rain."

"It's barely a mist," Ted replied, already reaching for the leash.

"She doesn't negotiate."

He gave the leash a subtle shake. The metallic clink echoed once—then again, a second later, like an audio track lagging behind itself.

Luna didn't blink.

Ted stood there, mind quiet but hollow.

Then—without thinking—he turned to the fridge. Opened it. Reached inside.

A slice of Colby Jack. Already half-unwrapped in his fingers.

Only then did Luna rise.

Not fast. Not slow. Just… with authority. She stretched once. Tail gave a single wag. Not for affection— for confirmation.

She approached the door like it was a gate between dimensions.

Gabriela watched the whole exchange. The towel still in her hands, unmoving.

"She's got you clocked," she said, not quite joking.

Ted didn't answer. Just bent, clipped the leash, and handed her the cheese like an offering.

Luna accepted it gently—never breaking eye contact.

Then she stepped into the dusk like the weather had never mattered at all.

* * *

The bedroom was dark but not silent.

A low hum came from the bathroom fan Ted forgot to switch off. The air conditioner cycled in slow waves, moving the curtain like it was breathing on its own. Gabriela slept curled on her side, one hand beneath her cheek.

Ted lay flat. One arm outside the blanket, fingers twitching slightly in sleep.

Luna was awake.

She rose from the foot of the bed without a sound. Her paws made no noise on the tile. Her breath didn't change. She moved not with stealth, but inevitability.

She padded down the hallway. Past the half-shut guest room. Past the wall of framed wedding photos and vacation shots, Gabriela kept meaning to dust.

In the living room, she paused. Hopped up onto the back of the couch in one smooth motion.

Sat. Watched.

Outside, the street was empty. Porch lights burned on timers. The wind chime stirred once. Then stopped mid-note, as if hushed by something unseen.

Luna's ears twitched. Not left-right. Back—like a receiver tuning itself to an unauthorized signal. Her head tilted.

A sound—or something like it—flickered across the silence. Not heard. *Registered.*

Her nostrils flared once.

Then nothing.

A faint bark echoed from somewhere beyond the cul-de-sac. Too far. Too sharp. Wrong.

She turned from the window, dropped to the floor, and returned to the bedroom.

She did not lie at the foot of the bed.

This time, she settled beside Ted. Not touching. Just there. Head low. Eyes open.

Facing the door.

* * *

Morning arrived like a whisper through a cracked window.

Ted was already dressed when Gabriela entered the kitchen. He moved around the space with too much precision—coffee poured, boots clean, lunch packed.

Gabriela squinted at the bag on the counter.

"You packed your lunch?" she asked, still half-asleep.

"Yeah." Ted didn't look up. "Felt like doing it last night."

"Since when do you pre-pack anything?"

He didn't answer right away. Just adjusted the collar of his shirt like it was the last puzzle piece in a picture he didn't want to see.

Gabriela smiled. "You feeling okay?"

"Yeah," he said. "Just been thinking I should be more on top of things."

Luna entered the room and sat between them. Perfect posture. Eyes fixed—not on Gabriela.

On him.

Ted knelt, scratched her ears. "She knows when I'm leaving," he said softly. "She's been waiting by the door every morning this week."

Gabriela frowned. "No, she hasn't."

Ted looked up. "Sure, she has. I've seen her."

Gabriela shook her head. "I work from home, remember? She's usually sleeping when you go."

Ted opened his mouth—then shut it. "Maybe I'm thinking of a different day."

He leaned in, kissed her cheek, grabbed his bag, and opened the door.

Gabriela went to the window. Luna moved with her, standing up on her hind legs to watch the Jeep pull away.

But she didn't whine. Didn't tilt her head. Didn't wag.

Just watched.

When the Jeep vanished, she turned and walked toward the back door like something was waiting for her.

Gabriela stayed at the window, one hand resting on the sill.

Later that morning, while working at the dining room table, she looked up again.

Luna was lying across from her.

Not dozing. Not relaxed.

Just watching.

Not the door this time.

Her.

Gabriela tilted her head. "You've got a secret, don't you?"

Luna blinked once. Like a photograph with the shutter stuck open.

Gabriela laughed. "I need to stop watching crime shows."

But she didn't look away.

And neither did Luna.

* * *

Alma didn't knock. She never did. The door creaked open, paused, and clicked shut behind her like punctuation.

She moved like someone halfway out of a trance— barefoot in worn sandals, long braid streaked silver, eyes sharp but unreadable. A woman who held silence the way others held knives.

Gabriela looked up from her laptop at the kitchen table, spreadsheets open, brain fried. "You're early," she said, closing the lid.

Alma didn't respond. She placed a small bundle of cloth on the table like it was breathing.

Inside: a disk-shaped charm of reddish clay, strung on a thin black cord. Etched into its face was a single eye— unblinking, off-center, ancient. A bundle of herbs tied with red thread sat beside it, pungent even unopened.

Gabriela picked up the charm. It was warm. No—it was *alive*. The surface pulsed faintly under her fingers, like a heart with a very old memory.

"Fired during a ritual," Alma said. "One I haven't done in years. Took me two days to get it right."

"What does it do?"

"It reminds things that they're being watched."

Gabriela looked up. "You mean the dog?"

Alma just blinked. "Keep it on you. Always. And these"—she tapped the herb bundle—"one goes above the doorway, one under your bed. Don't wait to feel scared. Just do it."

Gabriela hesitated, unsure whether to laugh or lock the doors.

"If she starts licking the corners of the room," Alma added, voice flat, "call me."

After Alma left, Gabriela stood alone in the garage, charm dangling from her fingers, herb packet still warm in her palm.

She didn't believe in this kind of thing.

But she looped the cord around her neck and tied it tight.

CHAPTER THREE

The First Favor

Saturday morning arrived like it was trying not to startle anyone. No loud sun, no wind in the curtains. Just a stillness that hung around the edges of consciousness, waiting to be acknowledged.

Ted clipped Luna's leash to her collar. The snap of the clasp was part of his muscle memory now, like brushing teeth or locking the front door. He grabbed the water bottle, slid two poop bags into his cargo shorts pocket, and scratched behind her ears. She licked his wrist once, then settled into the same starting position by the door as always.

They moved to the Jeep in sync, but it felt less like a habit this time and more like an instruction.

He backed out of the driveway and thumbed the playlist Gabriela had built for him—instrumentals with names like *Skyline Trail* and *Desert Rain*, songs that made him feel like he was traveling even when he wasn't. Luna eased into the passenger seat, calm but coiled, watching the road ahead like a navigator with unspoken orders.

Right on Sonoma Ranch. North on Roadrunner. Then left. Then another right.

It wasn't until the seventh turn that something tugged loose in his awareness.

The GPS glowed on the dash, faint blue lines cutting across the city map—but the trail ahead wasn't their usual one. No Mesilla Valley. No joggers. No shade from the mesquites. This was west. Toward Shalem Colony Road. Toward the Rio Grande levee trail—dustier, wilder. A place they'd visited once years ago and never returned to.

Ted blinked. "That's… new."

He hadn't changed the route. At least, not consciously.

Luna sat upright. Not panting. Not wagging. Still. Focused.

"You pick the hike today?" he asked.

She didn't look at him. Didn't acknowledge the question. Her whole body was trained forward, like the Jeep was following her, not the other way around.

The tires crunched gravel as they pulled into the dirt lot. That noise usually set Luna off with a single sharp bark.

Not this time.

Before he'd even unclicked her harness, she'd slipped out the door. Not a bolt. Not a sprint. Just forward motion—calculated intent.

She wasn't going for a walk. She was going somewhere.

Ted followed, but it felt like following in the true sense—not accompanying, not leading, just keeping up.

She walked with authority. The leash hung loose. She didn't pull. She guided.

He passed the cottonwoods, the uneven trail underfoot like an old scar reopened. His phone buzzed. A text from Gabriela:

Thought you were doing Mesilla this morning?

He stared at the screen for a few seconds too long, then typed back:

We are.

He hit send and tucked the phone away without rereading.

The trail narrowed.

* * *

The house wasn't asleep.

It was paused.

A kind of hush had settled—not peace, not fatigue, just the absence of motion. The fridge didn't hum. The air conditioner held its breath. Even the ceiling fan seemed to whisper, blades gliding in a soft orbit like it didn't want to wake the walls.

Ted lay diagonally across the bed, one arm flung out, one folded beneath the pillow like he was bracing against something in his sleep. His mouth was parted slightly. Breathing slowed. Eyes twitching behind closed lids, but not from dreaming. From reset.

Gabriela shifted once under the sheet. Pulled the blanket up without opening her eyes. Her hand brushed his back, confirmed he was still there. That was enough.

In the hallway, Luna moved.

Her nails ticked the tile once—then again. Not a dog's idle pacing. A count. A signal. Like Morse code tapped by paw.

She reached the doggie door. It swung with barely a sound, like it had been trained to forget it was a door.

Outside, the night air met her like a whisper from something older than wind. A scent moved across the patio—river mud, sagebrush, bone-dry cedar.

She padded to the back wall. Didn't touch it. Just stopped short, a few feet from the sandstone barrier, like she recognized a line drawn not in stone, but in meaning.

She sat.

The sky above her was clean and starless. Not from clouds. From restraint.

And then, as if called to it by some invisible thread strung through the clockwork of the dark—

She barked.

Once.

Not high. Not low. Not in warning or greeting.

Just a single, deliberate note dropped into the middle of night.

She waited.

The silence that followed was too precise to be empty. It felt occupied. Like something unseen had turned to listen.

Then—somewhere to the southeast—a reply. Same pitch. Same interval.

One bark.

Luna didn't turn. Didn't tilt her head. She waited.

Then she returned it.

One bark. Identical weight. Identical shape.

A third voice joined. Fainter. West maybe. Then one more. South again.

It wasn't a chorus. It was a sequence.

A message that used dogs the way a language uses consonants.

Luna lay down—still facing the wall, still facing the source.

She didn't wag. She didn't pant.

She just lowered her head onto her paws like a general resuming sleep after issuing an order.

Back inside, Gabriela's eyes opened.

She didn't know why. No sound had reached her consciously. Just the faint, invisible current that pulses through a house when something realigns.

Her hand reached out for Ted's shoulder. Found it. Rested there.

And then, a whisper.

"Luna…"

Not a call. Not a reprimand. Just a name spoken to the dark.

Luna did not return.

Not yet.

She stayed outside for another hour, spine aligned with the direction of the sound.

Waiting.

* * *

Ted stood in the kitchen, staring at the pantry door like it had just asked him a question.

He didn't remember walking in.

Didn't remember grabbing the mug.

But here he was, barefoot on cold tile, staring at wood grain like it held the punchline to a joke he hadn't heard yet.

He opened the door.

No grocery re-org. No Post-it Note. No reason at all for the pause. But he stared like he was trying to remember what he had come in there for. Like something had been moved. Not an item—an idea.

Behind him, the refrigerator's water dispenser light clicked on.

Not the compressor. Just the light. As if it had flinched.

He turned. Closed the pantry without taking anything. Walked to the fridge.

There she was. Sitting in the space between the dining table and the living room. Not in the way. Not out of the way. Just there—framed in the gap like a comma between two thoughts.

Luna.

Ted opened the fridge.

His hand reached before his thoughts did.

Not autopilot. Not craving. Just inevitability.

He retrieved a slice of cheese.

Luna didn't move. She didn't whine. Her ears didn't perk.

Still, he peeled the wrapper with care, like he was unsealing something sacred.

He crouched. Held the cheese halfway. Luna rose, slow and smooth, like a tide coming in on command.

She took it without sound.

Ted didn't know why he felt like bowing.

Didn't know why he looked down after, eyes tracing the grout between tiles like they might spell something.

"Not a trick," he murmured. "Not even a command."

He wasn't talking to her. Or himself.

Just putting sound in the space.

She licked her lips once. Turned. Walked to the back door and sat again, facing it, but not expecting it to open.

Just keeping watch.

Ted lingered. A whisper in his mind floated up: *She knew you'd be here.*

Not eerie. Not poetic. Just a factual report from somewhere inside his head.

He shut the fridge.

* * *

Ted poured cereal without looking at the box. The milk was already open in his hand, even though he didn't remember unscrewing the cap.

He blinked once. Twice.

Luna sat at the base of the hallway. Just outside the kitchen, framed by drywall. The edge of the world.

She wasn't waiting. She wasn't begging.

She was positioned. Like a puzzle piece set down before the rest of the picture was clear.

Gabriela padded in behind him, still in her sleep shirt. Her hair was tied up, but her face wasn't ready for the day.

"Did you feed her already?"

Ted stirred the cereal like he hadn't heard.

Gabriela moved to the coffeemaker. It was already on. Still warm. Ted didn't say anything, but something about that caught in his posture.

"She was watching you," Gabriela said, pouring. "From the hallway. Like she was waiting to be called but didn't need to be."

Ted kept stirring.

"She does that," he said.

"She does a lot of things."

Gabriela turned and leaned against the counter. Luna hadn't moved. Still at the border of kitchen and hallway. Still watching, but not intruding. Not entering. Like stepping over that line would end something sacred.

Gabriela watched the dog. Then Ted.

"She was on your side of the bed this morning," she said.

Ted glanced at her. "Yeah?"

Gabriela gave a small nod. "Curled up, real quiet. Like she belonged there."

Ted looked at Luna. Still on the threshold. Still as a statue.

Gabriela turned back. "Did you let her in?"

"No."

He looked down at the cereal again. It was soggy.

"Did I?" she asked, quieter now.

Ted shrugged. "I don't think so."

But the answer hung in the air like steam off her coffee—dissipating, but not gone.

Luna got up and walked away without a sound. Not dismissed. Not summoned. Just… done.

Gabriela watched her go.

"Sometimes I feel like we're the ones being trained."

Ted didn't answer. He just let his spoon clink gently against the bowl.

* * *

The toothbrush buzzed low against his molars, and Ted watched himself in the mirror like he wasn't entirely sure he was in there.

45

His eyes weren't bloodshot, but they carried the dull sheen of someone living half a step behind his own thoughts.

He rinsed. Spit. Let the brush die in its cradle with a flat whine. Stared a beat longer.

Behind him, the hallway yawned darkly. The bedroom light cut a wide trapezoid across the floor, its corners feathering into shadow. Gabriela was already in bed, one arm curled under the pillow, the other draped where it used to land on his chest.

Ted reached for the switch.

Paused.

A small thing. A whisper in his gut.

Then—click. The bathroom light blinked off.

He stepped into the hallway and turned toward the bedroom—and saw her.

Luna.

Lying on her bed in the living room. Legs folded beneath her. Head flat to the floor.

Eyes open.

Not blinking.

Watching.

She wasn't asleep. She wasn't resting. She was waiting. Still and square and quiet as architecture.

Ted slowed, just enough to feel it. His footfall softened. Not out of caution, but out of reflex. Like walking near a tidepool you don't want to disturb.

Her gaze didn't follow him. It was already locked somewhere else—*somewhen* else. As if she was listening for something he couldn't hear. Or had heard—and was simply waiting for it to arrive.

He didn't speak.

And neither did she.

Just that cold hum between one thought and the next.

Then he turned away. Slipped beneath the covers beside Gabriela.

Outside, a single bark rang from somewhere past the arroyo.

Then silence.

Luna didn't stir. Didn't flinch.

She just… closed her eyes.

And exhaled.

CHAPTER FOUR

Echoes in the Bark

The morning started out ordinary, which is how the weird stuff likes to sneak in.

Ted clipped the leash to Luna's collar and stepped out under a sky the color of clean steel. Metro Verde was waking up: garage doors yawning, sprinklers ticking life into already-neat lawns, golf carts humming toward Red Hawk like they had somewhere important to be. The desert had that crisp, baked-ceramic smell it gets before the sun remembers what it can do.

Luna trotted a half step ahead—never dragging, never lagging—like a coworker who secretly runs the meeting from the flanking chair. Her ears twitched at the smallest sounds: a mourning dove, a gate latch, the soft scuff of a neighbor's slippers.

Ted held the leash loosely. He liked the rhythm of their mornings. Left at the mesquite, right at the mailbox with the bent flag, across the patchwork of shade where the Palo Verdes try their best.

They passed Dorothy "Dot" Halpern's place first. The paint on her ranch house had given up the fight a few summers ago. The shutter on the south window was still missing. A rusted wind chime hung by the door, clanging like it couldn't find a tune. Dot stood in her robe with a travel mug of coffee, squinting into the day as if it owed her something.

Snickers—the unkempt poodle with the permanent apology in his eyes—was out front on a leash that looked like a thrift-store find. His muzzle had gone mostly gray, and his hips moved with the careful rhythm of a dog who'd learned to pace his own pain. He wagged at everything and nothing, a jittery metronome running a few ticks slow.

Morning, Ted," Dot said, voice gravelly and warm. "And good morning to you, Princess." She meant Luna.

Luna's tail made a single, polite swish. Her gaze skimmed Snickers. She didn't posture. Didn't sniff. She just… noticed him. Snickers noticed being noticed and tried to be three different dogs at once—friendly, cautious, and brave. His paws tap-danced on the concrete.

"It's okay, buddy," Ted said, and meant Snickers more than Luna.

They moved on. The sidewalk turned to a seam of hairline cracks and desert grit. Farther down, the Clarks had already staged their day like a catalog photo. Freshly coiled hose. Newspaper folded precisely on the porch table. David and Barbara wore matching optimism—athleisure and smiles that didn't crack before nine.

Their golden retriever stood at the edge of the perfect lawn, just inside the invisible boundary where a dog understands property law better than most people. He was the color of toast and obedience.

"Morning!" David called.

"Morning," Ted said.

Luna's ears made a slight angle toward the golden, then relaxed. The retriever's tail swept slow, steady arcs, polite as a courtroom oath.

Nothing strange there. Not yet.

At the corner, a sun-faded white fence framed a yard with motorcycle parts strewn like metal bones. Ricky Delmonte—"Smash" to his friends and the handful of people who should've been friends but weren't—was dragging his pit bull, Axel, out to the sidewalk.

Axel was blocky and beautiful in that way pit bulls are when they've survived bad decisions made by the humans above them. He had a chain clipped to his collar—thick and short, the kind you'd use on a small tractor.

Ricky wore a sleeveless shirt and a look that dared the morning to step closer. Tattoos crept out from under his neckline like the world's worst ivy. He saw Ted and gave the tight, neighborly nod men give when they don't want to talk but want you to know they saw you.

Axel saw Luna and paused, the way a fighter recognizes another fighter at the grocery store. His paws splayed slightly. Not fear. Calculation.

"Move," Ricky snapped, and yanked the chain.

Axel flinched forward. A low sound rolled in his chest, more question than threat. Luna stayed where she was, weight centered, head barely tilted. Not a statue—more like a hinge deciding when to swing.

They were close enough now to share the same ribbon of shadow, the same thin line of cool before the sun climbed a notch. Ted felt the leash in his hand as a suggestion, not a command. He took in the geometry of it all: the angle of Luna's ears, the set of Axel's shoulders, the tension in Ricky's forearm, the distance between the Clarks' mailbox and Dot's broken step.

And then it happened.

Luna barked once.

Not loud. Not frantic. A sharp, clean syllable of sound, like a knuckle tapped on glass. It cut across the street, sliced through the air, and sat there—exact, undeniable.

Axel froze. The golden retriever on the Clarks' lawn shut his mouth on whatever breath he'd been preparing and sat. Snickers, two houses back and halfway to a panic attack at any given moment, stopped dancing and set his paws like he'd been told to for the first time in his life.

One house farther down, a chow mix—old, heavy-lidded, leashed to a shady porch—didn't move. Didn't bark. Just stared at Luna with a low rumble in its throat, like a generator running on concrete. Its owner sat in a lawn chair, reading. Neither of them looked up.

The silence that followed wasn't empty. It was crowded with attention.

Dot's wind chime finally found a breeze and gave one soft clink. Somewhere, a sprinkler changed directions with a small hiss. Ricky frowned at the sudden stillness, like someone had rearranged his tools when he wasn't looking.

"What the hell," he muttered, mostly to the day.

Barbara Clark laughed. "Synchronized sitting," she said to David, delighted. "We should enter them in something."

"Dogs will be dogs," David said, like a man filing the moment under Cute and Done.

Axel looked at Luna. Not a stare-down—the old dominance script didn't fit here. He seemed to be measuring a distance he hadn't known existed. His tail didn't tuck, but it didn't brag either.

The golden's eyes were soft and blank in the way of saints and idiots. Snickers panted twice and then—shockingly—remembered how to be still.

Ted's scalp prickled. He didn't believe in mystical anything, but he knew timing. In engineering, timing is the edge where a system either sings or shakes itself apart. This timing wasn't a coincidence. The bark had landed, and a series of switches flipped in three separate heads like they were on the same circuit.

He looked down at Luna. She glanced up with the calm of a creature who hadn't done anything unusual. Her mouth was closed, her breath steady. Her eyes said: *Next*.

Ricky gave Axel another yank, harder this time—the kind of pull you use when the thing resisting you isn't the dog anymore.

"Let's go," he said, and the chain snapped against metal.

Axel hesitated. It was less than a second, but in that second, Ricky's jaw set and his shoulders rolled forward like a storm building. The chain jumped once, sharply. Axel's head dipped under the jerk. It wasn't a whine—Axel didn't whine—but something passed through his body that looked like an insult.

Ted felt the old anger rise—the quick, hot kind that asks to be used. He didn't use it. He wasn't that man and didn't need to become one to prove it. He kept his voice level.

"Morning," he said again, because sometimes you give the day one more chance to behave.

Ricky stared at him a beat too long, something like a dare sitting in the space between them, then looked away and walked on. The chain clinked in small, unhappy bursts.

The Clarks went back to their choreography. Barbara checked the hose's nozzle. David adjusted the newspaper as if precision warded off chaos. Dot sipped her coffee and watched everything with the humane curiosity of someone who has seen enough to know there's always more.

Luna took a single breath through her nose, a tiny intake that felt like a note on a clipboard, then pivoted and led Ted around the corner as if the route had always included this exact turn at this exact moment.

They walked in silence. A roadrunner flicked across the sidewalk, tail like punctuation. Luna didn't give chase. She didn't need to. She was writing a different sentence.

"You're full of yourself today," Ted said. Not unkind. A small joke to keep the edges from getting sharp. "Careful, or I'll have to put 'CEO' on your tag."

Luna's ear twitched. She didn't look back. The leash felt like a formality, a handshake after the deal was done.

They looped the block. The neighborhood sounds layered back in—garage doors, a truck starting, a dog two streets over barking at a passing cat. Normal was busy rebuilding itself.

Ted replayed the moment without wanting to. One bark. Freeze. Sit. Quiet. It wasn't dominance in its usual shape. There had been no bristling, no low growl, no stiff-legged theater. Just… compliance. Clean, immediate, as if Luna had drawn a line and the other dogs had recognized it not as a challenge but as a fact.

He thought about calling Gabriela, then didn't. Saying it out loud would make it a thing with a name, and he didn't have one he trusted. He also didn't want the laugh he'd earned a hundred times—dogs will be dogs—because this didn't feel like that, and he was stingy with words when they didn't fit the hole exactly.

They passed the Clarks again. The golden had resumed his benign surveillance of nothing in particular. He glanced at Luna and then away, an employee who decided to pick his battles. David waved. Barbara offered a bag of tiny bone-shaped treats across the lawn like she was feeding royalty without calling it that.

"She's on a diet," Ted lied easily, because it was faster than explaining anything else. "Doctor's orders."

Barbara nodded like she'd been given a 'task completed.'

"Good girl," she told Luna, and Luna accepted the compliment as rent.

Dot had retreated inside. Her door stood open. The wind chime clinked again, a single note on an empty staff.

At the corner with the white fence and the heap of motorcycle guts, Ricky and Axel were gone. The chain had left a bright scratch on the sidewalk where it had swung. The mark caught the light and flashed—not a scuff, but a symbol. A glyph etched by movement. A little slash of morning violence the concrete would forget by noon, even if Ted didn't.

Back home, Ted unclipped the leash. Luna sat, unprompted, in the spot where she always did for a second before roaming the house like she was checking a perimeter that existed only to agree with her. He rubbed the base of her neck, the soft place where muscle fades to velvet.

"What was that out there?" he asked. Not expecting an answer. Not wanting the wrong one.

Luna blinked slowly. She stood and padded to the water bowl, drank, then looked at the back door.

Ted opened it. She slipped into the yard, the stone wall holding the same morning as everywhere else, but somehow keeping more of it. She sniffed the edges, tested the air, and then came back inside like she'd confirmed what she already knew.

He watched her move and felt it again—that sense of timing, of gears engaging with only one set of teeth doing the work. It wasn't a crisis. Not yet. It was a subtle itch under the bandage: healing or infection, you never know which until you do.

He poured coffee and told himself to get on with the day.

Out on the street, somewhere past the next neat yard and the next, a dog barked twice. The second bark landed a fraction closer to the first than it should have. Ted heard it because he was listening now. He didn't go to the window. He didn't need to.

"Okay," he said to the empty kitchen. "I saw that."

Luna trotted back in and bumped his knee with her head like a signature on a contract he hadn't read carefully enough. He scratched behind her ear and felt the muscle under his fingertips shiften and settle, not tense, not loose—ready.

"Walk again later?" he asked.

Her tail twitched once, a metronome hit, yes. Then she lay down in the doorway like a guard who doesn't doubt the shift will get interesting.

* * *

The place looked like it was built to keep people from worrying.

Bright stucco exterior, cartoon murals of grinning Labradors and floppy-eared hounds splashed across the walls. The front door had paw-print decals spiraling upward as if the dogs themselves had rushed inside. The Pack Station's sign hung above it in cheerful block letters—orange and teal—exactly the kind of branding that told families this was a safe, happy pit stop for their fur-babies.

Ted didn't buy it. At least not completely. He knew "polished" when he saw it. That was his business—products designed to look seamless even when the guts were messy.

Luna didn't hesitate. The glass doors swished open, and she walked through like she was late for a meeting. Ted followed, leash loose, feeling less like an owner and more like a plus-one.

The reception area was bright enough to make sunglasses feel like a good idea. A polished concrete floor, with painted paw prints leading to the check-in desk, and behind it a pair of twenty-something employees with smiles tuned to "over-caffeinated camp counselor." One had purple streaks in her ponytail, the other wore a bandana at her neck like she'd wandered in from a festival.

"Good morning!" Purple Streak said, leaning forward. "And who is this queen?"

Ted gave the default answer he always gave, half-joke, half-truth. "Luna. She runs the place. I just carry the wallet."

Both employees laughed harder than the joke deserved. They crouched a little to make eye contact with Luna. Not the usual cooing or baby talk, though—something sharper. Respectful. Like she might actually respond in words if they asked the right way.

Luna's ears flicked once. She let them look. Didn't wag, didn't shrink, didn't beg. She simply accepted the greeting as if it were overdue.

A man stepped out from a side door, clipboard in hand, and posture like he'd been rehearsing authority in a mirror. Early forties, gym-fit but soft around the eyes, with a Pack Station polo tucked a little too neatly and cologne that hit the air like an exclamation mark. His gaze locked on Luna, and whatever script he had ready stalled in his throat.

"Hey there," he said, blinking. "I'm Rueben—assistant manager here. You must be the Tompkins?" His eyes were drawn to Luna. "Well," he said slowly, smile flattening into something steadier. "She's got presence, doesn't she?"

Ted chuckled politely. "She's a handful."

Rueben didn't laugh. He bent slightly at the waist— not a bow, but close enough that Ted noticed. "We'll take good care of her," he said, tone more like a promise than a sales pitch.

There was a flicker of something else in his posture. Not just courtesy—*reverence*. The kind of adjustment a man makes in the presence of a superior, even if he can't name the rank.

Luna brushed past him into the inner gate without waiting for permission. Her nails clicked once on the floor, a sound that carried farther than it should have in the big bright room.

At the front desk, Stephanie—Purple Streaks—didn't blink. Literally didn't blink. She stood straighter as Luna passed, as if she were receiving an inspection. The girl with the bandana whispered something under her breath, too soft to catch, but her eyes didn't leave Luna.

Ted filled out the intake form while watching her disappear down the hall. He scribbled the basics—diet, vet, emergency contact. Standard stuff. But the form felt like theater; the real paperwork had already been signed the second Luna walked in.

He left her for the day and drove back to work, telling himself he'd check the cameras later, just to make sure.

* * *

That evening, Gabriela asked how it went over dinner. She was plating enchiladas, hair pulled back, the smell of roasted green chile chasing through the kitchen.

"They treated her like visiting royalty," Ted said, still half amused. "Seriously. Rueben looked at her like she was interviewing him for the job."

Gabriela grinned. "Maybe she was. Do you think they do that with all the dogs?"

Ted started to laugh with her, but the question landed harder than the joke. He replayed the morning in his head—the outsized smiles, the strange seriousness in Rueben's eyes. He wanted to say, "No, not like that." Instead, he shook his head and speared a forkful of food.

"Probably," he said. "Dog people are just... dog people."

Gabriela let it go, still smiling, still teasing. But Ted felt the line stick like a burr in his mind. Not all dogs were treated like that. He'd seen it.

Luna padded in from the living room, sat at the edge of the kitchen, and watched them eat. Not begging. Not expectant. Just waiting, as if the day had gone exactly the way she wanted.

* * *

The Pack Station had an app. Of course it did.

Ted sat at his desk that night, bourbon sweating in its glass, laptop balanced across his thighs. Gabriela was in the kitchen rinsing dishes, humming softly to some song she half-remembered from college. The television in the living room murmured a sports recap neither of them was actually watching. The house felt steady—anchored in its routines.

He opened the app and queued up the midday feed from Luna's room. *Just out of curiosity*, he told himself.

The video loaded grainy at first, then snapped into clarity: a wide room floored in soft mats, scattered with play tunnels, rope toys, and those wobbling rubber cones dogs either loved or feared. At first glance, it was what the marketing promised—joyful chaos.

Ted leaned back and let it play.

A shepherd mix was wrestling with a doodle, paws thumping softly against the padded floor. A pug chased a ball and forgot midway what he was chasing. A pair of hounds tugged a rope in opposite directions with the intensity of countries at war. Normal. Perfectly normal.

Then, Luna had walked into the frame.

She didn't bound or strut. She just entered, calm as a shadow changing the temperature of a room. She stopped near the center, nose low, body loose. Nothing dramatic. But the chaos around her began to quiet, as if a volume knob had been turned down.

The shepherd dropped his play mid-wrestle and sat. The doodle blinked, confused, then followed. The hounds dropped their rope, looked at her, and folded into stillness. One by one, every dog—ten, maybe twelve—shifted from motion to silence until the room held a kind of order no trainer could have bought with treats or whistles.

Every eye was on Luna.

She didn't bark. Didn't move. She just was—a presence, magnetic and absolute. The air itself seemed to thicken, like it had taken on weight and memory. Even the dust motes slowed down, unsure of their place in the pecking order.

One terrier lowered into a crouch—slow, belly to mat—not in fear, but something closer to worship.

Twenty seconds passed. Ted counted without meaning to. Twenty seconds in which not a single tail wagged, not a paw shuffled. It was the kind of silence that has weight, the kind that presses on the ribs. Not obedience—*alignment.*

Then Luna blinked, turned her head, and the spell broke. Dogs sprang up again, picking up toys, chasing, barking. The shepherd went back to pinning the doodle. The pug remembered his ball. The rope war resumed with renewed fervor.

Like nothing had happened.

Ted leaned forward, replayed it. Once. Again. A third time, slower. He watched the instant her presence rippled through the room, watched the way dogs who'd never met each other dropped into the same script without rehearsal.

He knew behavior patterns. He liked patterns; his whole job was patterns. This wasn't one. This was something else. Something that bypassed training and hit bone-level circuitry.

Footsteps padded behind him. Gabriela leaned in the doorway, towel slung over her shoulder, hair damp from steam. "What, is she giving them a TED Talk?"

He flinched slightly, thumb snapping the laptop nearly shut.

"Owner cam," he said, feigning casual. Too casual. "Just checking in."

Gabriela grinned. "Well, at least she's popular." She turned back toward the kitchen, the hum of dishes resuming.

Ted sat there, bourbon untouched, screen dark. He could still see it even without the replay—the way the dogs had looked at her, every one of them, like students waiting for instruction.

He told himself not to make it a thing. Not yet.

But the unease was there, quiet and insistent, like the aftertaste of metal on the tongue.

* * *

The house had settled into its nighttime rhythm.

Gabriela was asleep, her breathing steady, hair fanned across the pillow in the faint glow of the digital clock. Ted lay awake, staring at the ceiling, listening to the hum of the fridge and the soft ticks of cooling metal from the Jeep in the garage. He wasn't restless exactly—more like tuned to a frequency he couldn't shut off.

A faint clink of the doggie door.

Luna had slipped out.

Ted rolled onto his side, half-thinking to call her back, but the silence afterward convinced him otherwise. A silence that wasn't empty—more like it was *waiting*.

Then the bark.

Sharp, cutting, bouncing off the stone wall that ran the length of their backyard. The sound was different than her usual bursts at desert rabbits or shadows—less scattered, more deliberate. One bark, then another, and another, spaced evenly, like a code. Not a warning. A signal.

Other dogs answered.

From Dot Halpern's direction, Snickers yipped—a thin, high echo. From farther out, the Clarks' retriever boomed, deep and slow. And from Ricky Delmonte's place, a low growl carried into a bark, Axel's voice hitting the rhythm like a reluctant drummer forced to join the band.

Ted sat up, the sheet falling around his waist. He could feel the pattern in his chest more than hear it—a call and answer, pulsed like sonar. Not noise. Structure. It moved through him like a memory he hadn't earned.

The hair on his arms stood up.

He got as far as swinging his legs off the bed when Gabriela stirred. "Ted?" Her voice was thick with sleep. "Bring her in. She's wound up lately. Maybe too much daycare."

He hesitated, sitting there in the dark, listening to the echoes travel the neighborhood. There was something about the way the sounds overlapped—not chaotic, not random. Almost… organized.

Gabriela sat up a little, rubbing her eyes. "Did you hear me?"

"Yeah," he said, though his eyes stayed on the window. Another bark rolled in, closer this time, as if the rhythm had moved through the walls and into him.

He stood, padded barefoot down the hallway, and slid open the back door.

Luna was at the far end of the yard, her silhouette taut against the backdrop of desert night. The fieldstone wall glowed faintly in the moonlight, each uneven rock a part of some larger, ancient order. She barked once more, sharply, then went still, head lifted, waiting.

From beyond the wall, replies answered in staggered voices, but the timing made them feel less like responses and more like echoes. Ted felt it ripple through the neighborhood like a grid powering up—each bark a live node switching on.

"Luna," he called.

She turned, trotted back, and slipped inside without protest. Her eyes caught a glint from the kitchen light— calm, unbothered, as if she'd been doing exactly what she was meant to do.

Ted shut the door, locked it, and watched her settle on the living room rug. She stretched once, sighed, and closed her eyes.

He stood there longer than he needed to, the sound of that rhythm still working through his chest like a ghost heartbeat.

Back in the bedroom, Gabriela rolled toward him, hair mussed, eyes half closed. "She come in?"

"Yeah," Ted said. He slid under the covers, though the cool cotton didn't erase the echo.

Gabriela gave him a drowsy look—half worry, half annoyance—and muttered, "She's wound up lately." Then she drifted back to sleep.

Ted lay awake, staring at the ceiling, hearing barks that weren't happening anymore.

* * *

Saturday had the easy pace of a day that didn't owe anyone an explanation. The desert sun was already making the stucco bright by the time Ted pulled into The Pack Station's parking lot. Gabriela had come with him this time, riding shotgun with a paperback half-finished in her lap. She slipped a bookmark in, stretched, and followed him inside.

The lobby was busy—weekend drop-offs, owners juggling leashes and excuses, dogs vibrating with the anticipation of reunion. The air smelled like disinfectant layered over wet fur.

Luna came trotting out through the gate when Rueben waved her forward, tail steady but not wagging. What caught Gabriela's attention wasn't Luna's composure—she'd seen that before—it was the way the staff moved when Luna passed.

Cody, the high-schooler with messy hair and too much energy, had been slouching against the counter, scrolling on his phone. The moment Luna appeared, he pocketed it and straightened, shoulders back like a soldier caught out of formation.

Mia, the college sophomore with the wraparound sunglasses perched on her head, had been halfway through stacking folded blankets. She stopped, hands frozen, eyes following Luna as though waiting for a signal.

Even Rueben's tone shifted. "She did great today," he told Ted, voice clipped, formal. Not the usual singsong reassurance of a dog-daycare operator, but a report.

As Luna passed him, Rueben dipped his head slightly —just for a second. Gabriela caught it. It wasn't a habit. It was an acknowledgment.

Luna brushed past all of them and came to sit at Ted's side, calm and centered, like she knew the room was hers.

On the drive home, Gabriela turned the book over in her hands, thumb worrying the corner. Finally she said, "It's like they're afraid of her."

Ted glanced over from behind the wheel. "Afraid? Come on, they're just dog people. They live for this stuff."

"No," she said slowly. "It wasn't just enthusiasm. Cody practically stood at attention when she walked by. And that girl—Mia—she didn't even finish putting down the blankets. She just… froze. Like she was waiting for something."

He smiled, but it felt forced. "It's a dog daycare. Strange is normal there."

She let out a short laugh, though her eyes stayed on the desert rolling past the window. Houses, palm trees, a mountain spine far beyond.

"Maybe. But it was strange."

Luna shifted in the backseat, stretched long, and gave a quiet huff through her nose. Content. Settled.

Ted kept his eyes on the road, but the word echoed anyway. *Strange.* The same burr that had stuck with him since that first morning walk.

Gabriela glanced back, watching Luna stretched across the seat like a queen on a chaise. Her smile faded into something more cautious. Not fear, not yet—but the first genuine chill of wrongness.

There was a moment—barely a breath—where she wondered if Luna had been watching her, too.

She didn't say more. Not then. But the silence she carried filled the Jeep all the way home.

CHAPTER FIVE

Reward Loop

The kitchen carried the same low hum it always did in the morning—coffee maker rattling, toaster ticking, the fridge compressor whispering like a tired old man. Gabriela moved between counter and stove with a rhythm born of repetition. She had a way of filling the kitchen without crowding it, half-singing under her breath in Spanish, a melody with no beginning and no end.

Ted sat at the table with his laptop open, one socked foot propped on the rung of the chair. He was already deep into emails, eyes narrowed at a spreadsheet that didn't need to be studied yet, but habit kept him locked there. He typed, paused, backspaced. Somewhere in the rhythm of work, he registered a quiet weight—not sound, not motion, just presence.

He looked up.

Luna sat by the fridge, still as a statue. Not wagging, not whining. Just looking at him.

Ted's hands kept moving on the keyboard, but the signal had already rerouted his wiring. The motion felt automated, like muscle memory written by someone else.

He pushed the chair back, crossed the tile, opened the fridge. His hand went to the same place without searching:

the plastic-wrapped block of cheddar. He peeled two slices away and set them in front of her. She ate with slow precision, eyes never leaving his. Then he went back to his chair and his email as if he'd only paused to scratch an itch.

Gabriela poured herself coffee and turned. She caught the exchange, the timing so exact it was comical—dog waits, man obeys. She shook her head and smiled, but the smile cooled at the edges.

"She looks at you like you're the one being trained," she said.

Ted chuckled without looking up, fingers resuming their march over the keyboard. "She's just spoiled."

Gabriela sipped her coffee, eyes narrowing at the way Luna had already repositioned herself, back at the fridge, quiet and certain. There was no begging in it, no doggish impatience. Just expectation.

Her skin prickled again—not just because of the moment, but the repetition of it. Like someone rewiring the house in the dark, one wire at a time.

Ted didn't notice.

* * *

The air was still cool enough to trick him into thinking the desert had a gentle side. Early light broke flat across the neighborhood, painting the stucco houses in chalky pastels. Ted clipped the leash to Luna's collar and stepped out, coffee still warming his bloodstream, laptop and deadlines forgotten for the moment.

The walk started as it always did—left turn at the corner, past the golf course wall, the usual loop that made him feel steady, predictable. His head was full of small calculations: which projects to push at work; whether the Jeep needed new tires; what to make for dinner.

Halfway down the block, Luna stopped. She didn't jerk the leash, didn't bark. She just planted herself and looked at him. Then her body shifted slightly, angled toward a side street he rarely took.

Ted frowned. "Alright," he muttered, as if the idea had just bloomed inside his own skull. "Let's switch it up today."

He turned, following her lead without realizing it was her lead.

The new street smelled different—fresher lawns, sharper fertilizer. A shepherd mix appeared on the far sidewalk, straining at his leash. Luna's posture changed in an instant: head high, shoulders forward, body taut as wire. She didn't lunge or growl. She just stared.

The shepherd slowed, his confidence draining out like water through a cracked bowl. His ears dropped, head dipped, tail tucked.

His owner, a man in jogging shorts, forced a laugh. "Guess she's the boss," he said, tugging his dog along.

Ted gave an absent chuckle, not quite sure what he was agreeing to.

They carried on, the leash hanging slack now, Luna's gait measured and satisfied. At the next intersection, she tested something new. She slowed at the curb, fixed her eyes on him again, and stepped forward without waiting.

Ted hesitated. His foot moved before the thought arrived, toes brushing the edge of the asphalt. The cross street was empty, no cars in sight. For a beat, he felt the tug of her will, subtle but insistent, like gravity asking him to ignore the sign.

Then logic broke through—habit, training, whatever pieces of himself were still intact. He stopped. "Hold up," he said automatically, pulling the leash.

Luna froze, eyes narrowed, reading him. Then she stepped back, compliant.

Failure.

But the kind she could use.

Not a setback. Just a calibration.

She filed it away like a scientist noting conditions in an experiment—what worked, what didn't, what needed tweaking next time.

Ted didn't notice. He only felt a faint, inexplicable satisfaction at having done "the right thing."

As if the victory were his.

At the next corner, they passed a quiet yard shaded by a thick mulberry. A chow mix lay on the porch like a weathered statue. It didn't bark. Didn't even blink. Just stared.

Ted recognized her vaguely—Ruby, or something like that. The only dog in the neighborhood that never barked back.

He glanced once, but Luna didn't. She had no need to.

* * *

The house had gone soft around the edges; that post-dinner quiet where everything felt half-settled. Dishes rinsed, lights dimmed, television murmuring low. Gabriela sat curled at one end of the sofa with a book open on her lap, glasses slipping toward the tip of her nose. She turned a page with the same absent grace she used for prayer beads, her body there but her mind somewhere deeper.

Ted sat at the other end of the couch, a beer sweating onto the coaster on the side table. He was pretending to watch the game, but his eyes were glazed, following nothing in particular.

The dog door rattled once, and then Luna padded in, nails clicking against the tile before she reached the rug.

She stopped in front of him. Silent. Steady. Her stare carried the weight of a question already answered.

Ted blinked, set the remote down, and without thinking twice, patted the cushion beside him.

She leapt up, folded herself onto the couch with a sigh, and settled her head on his thigh as if the spot had always been reserved.

Gabriela looked up from her book, frowning. "You swore no dogs on the couch."

Ted scratched Luna behind the ear, eyes still on the television. "She looks comfortable here. Doesn't hurt anything."

Gabriela shook her head, closing the book around a finger. "Until she owns the whole place." The line was light, almost joking, but it landed wrong, like a glass put down too hard.

Ted shrugged, stroking Luna's fur as if the motion were a reflex.

Luna's eyes shifted, her body adjusting with a slow, deliberate press against his leg. Her weight wasn't heavy, but it felt like she was staking a claim. Then she nosed the beer bottle sitting on the table, tipping it just enough to make the glass clink.

Ted reached toward it, starting to rise, the movement half-formed before his mind caught up. His hand hovered, absurd and suspended, like he'd risen for communion without knowing why.

He froze. "What am I doing?" he muttered under his breath.

For a long second, Luna held the stare—too still, too focused. More judgment than instinct. Then she settled back against him, eyes closing, as though she had never asked anything at all.

Gabriela returned to her book, though her gaze lingered a heartbeat too long before dropping back to the page.

Ted shifted in his seat, uneasy without knowing why.

The game went on. The house hummed. And the couch rule was gone, buried without ceremony.

* * *

The house was quiet in that heavy, post-midnight way—appliances silenced, clocks ticking louder than they should. The desert air had cooled, carrying a faint rustle of mesquite through the open windows.

From the hallway came the muted thump of the doggie door. Luna slipped out, soundless except for the tap of nails on tile, then vanished into the backyard.

Moments later, her bark cracked the silence. Not random. Not the scattered outbursts of a dog chasing shadows. Short, sharp, measured. A signal.

The sound carried across the neighborhood, bouncing off stone walls. Within seconds, other dogs answered. One call was half-hearted, quickly silenced by an owner's shush. Another kept pace, finding the rhythm, building something primal between the backyards.

All but one joined in. From down the block, silence held—a void where Ruby never barked.

Ted stirred, sheets pulling away as he swung his legs out of bed. He padded barefoot to the sliding glass door, rubbing his eyes.

Outside, Luna stood with her front paws braced against the fieldstone wall, her body outlined in silver by the thin moonlight. Head raised, ears pitched forward, she barked again—two beats, pause, one more bark. The cadence had the precision of language, though he couldn't have said why.

He felt it in his chest—not sound, but resonance, like sonar bouncing through soft tissue.

Ted didn't tell her to be quiet. He didn't reach for the door to pull her inside. He just watched, entranced, hand pressed lightly against the glass.

Gabriela rolled over, voice muffled in the dark. "You spoil her."

He didn't answer.

Another bark ripped through the night, sharper this time. Luna twisted her head, eyes scanning the sliding door. She wanted him out there. With her.

Ted's hand drifted higher on the glass, drawn without command, his breath fogging a small circle. The cold seeped into his skin like an invitation. His body leaned forward an inch, and then he stopped.

He shook his head, whispered to himself, "Not tonight."

Luna barked again, the sound edged now with frustration. She paced once along the wall, tail stiff, then froze in place. The rhythm broke, but only for a moment. She recalibrated, adjusting her stance, watching the house as much as the horizon.

She didn't blink. She just waited—for compliance, for connection.

Ted lingered another breath, then slid back into bed.

Luna remained at her post, the night folding around her.

* * *

Morning light pushed into the kitchen, soft and yellow, the kind that made the tile look colder than it was. The routine unspooled the same way it always did: Gabriela at the counter buttering toast, the coffee maker chuffing, Ted half-distracted at the table with his laptop open.

Luna was already in place. She sat squarely in front of the refrigerator, silent and unblinking, her body carved out of patience itself.

Ted felt her before he saw her. His fingers slowed on the keyboard, the rhythm of his work unraveling under the weight of that stare. He looked up, caught the line of her gaze, and knew what it meant.

For the first time, he hesitated. His hand stayed on the trackpad. He told himself he wouldn't move. Not this time.

Luna didn't blink.

The silence stretched. Gabriela clinked a knife against a plate. Somewhere outside, a lawn sprinkler hissed to life. Ted's chest tightened with something that felt embarrassingly like pressure.

Don't move, he thought. *Don't feed the loop.*

He sighed, pushed back the chair, and crossed the tile. Each step felt like a surrender in slow motion. The fridge door opened with a suctioned pop, cold air spilling out.

He opened it like a man giving a confession.

His hand went to the cheddar without searching, pulling free two slices as if they belonged to her.

Luna took them, slowly and deliberately, eyes never leaving his.

He returned to his chair, trying to bury the twitch of irritation at himself. It wasn't guilt. It was gravity. And Luna was the center of mass.

Gabriela had turned, watching. Her brow pinched. She didn't say a word, but her silence carried more weight than if she had.

The ritual was complete. The loop closed tighter.

Luna didn't ask. Didn't wait. She simply existed, and the room bent around her like an orbit around a dark star.

CHAPTER SIX

Conditioned

Ted woke to the sound of nails tapping against hardwood. Not the alarm. He didn't remember setting the alarm at all.

Luna stood by the bed, motionless except for the steady rhythm of her tail thumping once, then twice. No whine, no bark. Just expectation radiating from her like heat off asphalt.

He swung his legs over the edge before thinking. By the time his feet hit the floor, she was already pivoting toward the kitchen, sure of the outcome.

Ted fed her first. Kibble, measured, scoop sliding through the bag in one automatic motion. He didn't even make coffee—his hand had gone straight for her bowl.

Behind him, Gabriela leaned in the doorway, robe tied loosely, eyes sharp. "Since when do you put her breakfast before yours?"

Ted poured the food, shook the bag closed. "Since she's the one who pays rent," he said, smiling without humor.

Gabriela tilted her head, unconvinced. She had a way of looking at him as though she were waiting for the real answer.

Ted avoided it. He crouched and set the bowl down, Luna already sitting, patient, pupils fixed on him like she'd trained him. The second he released the bowl, she leaned in, eating with quiet ferocity.

Only then did Ted realize his mouth was dry, bitter with sleep. Coffee. He should've made coffee first. He always made coffee first.

But his brain smoothed the wrinkle: dogs needed structure, didn't they? Priorities. He was just being responsible.

That's what he told himself, anyway.

* * *

The Jeep idled in the driveway, exhaust ghosting in the cool morning. Ted clipped Luna's harness without thinking, the leather straps worn smooth where his hands had traveled the same path too many times.

He intended to drive to the usual trail—closer, convenient, efficient. But his hands turned the wheel before the thought fully formed, tires pointing toward the park on the far side of town.

Halfway there, it hit him: *I didn't decide this.* The steering column hummed under his palms, the faint rattle of coins in the console keeping time with his pulse. He could have corrected course, turned left at the next light. Instead, he stayed the path, as if the decision had already been signed in ink.

Luna rode shotgun, head out the open window, ears slicked back in the wind. She wasn't looking at the scenery—she was watching the road, each turn anticipated before he made it. Queen on parade.

He passed up the quicker route through Rio Grande Terrace. Too many yappy dogs. One in particular—some kind of chow—always watched their Jeep like it knew something. Luna had tensed once when they'd stopped at that corner. Never again.

A man crossing the lot at the park smiled as Ted parked.

"She driving today, or you?" he said, nodding at Luna like she was the one behind the wheel.

Ted laughed because it was expected. But the words lodged in his chest uncomfortably, like they fit too well.

He threw the Jeep in park, cut the engine, and scratched Luna between the shoulders. "Guess this is your show, huh?" he muttered.

Her tail wagged once, slowly, as though confirming.

Later, when Gabriela asked why he'd gone all the way across town, Ted reached for the first excuse that came to hand. "Just felt right," he said. The phrase felt flimsy even as it left his mouth.

And yet—it was the truth, wasn't it?

At least, the version of truth Luna allowed.

* * *

Breakfast was quiet, except for the scrape of forks against plates. Gabriela studied Ted across the table, her eyes tracing the small hesitations—the way he lingered over each bite, chewing as though stalling for time.

He used to fill the mornings with small talk. A complaint about traffic, a joke about work. Now it was silence, and not the comfortable kind.

She cleared her throat softly. "You seem tired," she said, keeping her voice light.

Ted looked up, smiled in a polite, almost automatic way. "Didn't sleep as well as I wanted. Nothing unusual."

Not true. You slept hard, almost heavily. I could feel it in the bed. Like you'd sunk too deep to hear me breathing beside you. Like you were buried in something I couldn't reach through.

Under the table, a faint shift pressed against her ankle. She stilled, then adjusted her foot, but the pressure remained—not sharp, just insistent. She glanced down, saw nothing in the shadows. Still, the sensation lingered. *Like being nudged by a thought that isn't yours.*

Ted set his fork down, folded his napkin once. "I'm fine, Gabby. Honestly. Probably just distracted with work stuff."

The explanation was neat, plausible. Yet his eyes flicked down—just for a second—as if anchored elsewhere.

Work doesn't hold you like that. I know the weight of it. This is something else. Something I can't name because you won't.

A flicker moved behind her ribs. Not panic. Not yet. But something older than logic. A kind of mourning for a version of him she couldn't summon back.

Gabriela nodded, picking up her coffee. "Okay," she said, letting the word stand there, a marker.

She didn't press, though the silence felt thick. *If I push, he'll only defend it. Better to wait. Better to watch until the shape of this thing shows itself.*

Across from her, Ted's hand drifted under the table. The sound of fur shifting followed, quiet but unmistakable. He smiled faintly, as if soothed.

Gabriela's fingers tightened on her cup. *Even here, in my kitchen, it feels like I'm the one intruding. Like I walked into the wrong room wearing the right face.*

* * *

The Pack Station smelled of disinfectant and dog biscuits, a polished façade over the musk of fur and bleach. Ted pushed through the glass door with Luna at his heel, her nails clicking like a metronome across the tile.

Three employees looked up at once. The receptionist's smile spread wide. "Luna! Back again." She didn't greet Ted first.

A young man in a Polo crouched low, hand out like he was meeting royalty. "There's our girl," he said, scratching her chest.

Ted tightened the leash out of reflex. "Morning."

The room buzzed with noise—dogs in kennels, in playpens, tails thumping against wire. But as Luna stepped farther inside, the sound shifted. A shepherd mix froze mid-bark, ears flattening. Two terriers dropped their chew bones in unison. Even a Labrador in the corner slunk back against the wall, gaze lowered.

Ted caught it, unsettled, but the staff didn't blink.

One woman, clipboard in hand, spoke softly—not to him, but to Luna. "Still setting the pace, huh? That's what we like to see."

Ted laughed lightly. "She's stubborn."

"Leaders usually are," the woman replied, her voice tinged with something new—something just a little too reverent.

He moved to the counter, but noticed one of the kennel techs—a teenager in oversized scrubs—pause mid-mop and mouth the word *boss* under his breath as Luna passed. Then he blinked, like he hadn't realized he'd said anything at all.

The sign-in process moved quickly. Feeding notes. Scheduled playtime. Efficient, polite. And yet every phrase bent toward Luna, the way staff in a luxury hotel bowed without quite bowing.

When Ted unclipped the leash, Luna didn't even glance back. She walked through the gate like she owned the place, head high, tail a steady flag. A pit bull rolled onto his back as she passed, paws tucked, offering up his throat.

Ted chuckled, brushing away the unease. "Guess she's popular."

One of the handlers gave a small nod. "She's the kind others follow."

Ted carried the words with him to the Jeep. But by the time he turned the key, they'd already softened into pride.

Nothing more than a dog owner's glow.

Still, when he reached the corner of the lot, he glanced in the rearview mirror—not at the building, but at the absence she left behind. Like stepping out of orbit.

* * *

Evening settled over the house, filtering through the blinds in thin amber bands. Ted dropped his keys on the counter, kicked his shoes halfway under the bench, and thought vaguely about the garage. The bike still needed work. He'd told himself all week he'd get to it.

But somehow he was on the couch instead, Luna's head heavy in his lap, his hand idly tracing the curve of her skull. He couldn't remember the choice that had put him there. One minute he was standing in the kitchen, reaching for a glass of water, the next he was seated, TV glowing, the room shaped around her.

The thought slipped through him like a draft: *When did I sit down?*

Luna's breathing slowed, deliberate, her ribs pressing warm against his thigh. She didn't move otherwise. Just was. A steady weight that pinned him like an anchor dropped in shallow water.

From the doorway, Gabriela's voice cut through. "Weren't you going to fix the bike?"

Ted blinked, hand still on Luna's head. "Yeah," he said automatically. "I will."

Hours slipped past, indistinct. He didn't move. The garage stayed dark, tools untouched.

Gabriela passed through the living room once, carrying a stack of folded laundry. She looked at him, then at Luna, then back again. Her mouth opened as though to speak, then shut. She set the clothes down with more force than necessary, the sound sharp against the quiet TV.

Something about the stillness of the house felt wrong— *too* still. Not peaceful. Smothered. Gabriela paused with a sock in hand, halfway to the basket. She sniffed the air. Fabric softener. Dust. And something else she couldn't place.

Ted lifted his eyes from the screen, about to say something—an excuse, maybe. But Luna shifted just enough to press harder against him, eyes still closed, and the words thinned out before they left his mouth.

By the time Gabriela had disappeared down the hall, Ted couldn't remember what he'd meant to say.

* * *

The kitchen hummed with its usual evening sounds: the tick of the cooling oven, the faint hum of the refrigerator, the muffled static of the TV two rooms away. Ted leaned against the counter, nursing a glass of water he didn't remember pouring. Luna lay stretched across the threshold, her body a barrier that made the kitchen feel smaller than it was.

Gabriela dried her hands on a towel, then folded it over the sink. She didn't speak right away. She studied him—his posture, the absent way he stared at the condensation sliding down the glass, as if it held more meaning than it should.

He's here, but not. He used to fill this space with chatter, or at least small movements. Now he waits, like she's given him orders he doesn't even hear.

She crossed to the table, pulled out a chair, and sat with the care of someone easing into a decision. "You've been different," she said, her voice quiet, cautious. Not an accusation. A feeler in the dark.

Ted glanced over, a polite half-smile tugging at his mouth. "Different how?"

Her eyes dropped to the grain of the table. *If I say it too plain, he'll retreat. If I soften it, maybe he'll meet me halfway.*

"Your days revolve around her now. Feels like you've changed your routine."

Ted shifted his weight, rolling the glass in his hand. "Dogs need consistency. Structure. I'm just… making sure she gets it."

His tone was gentle, not defensive. But it was too smooth, like he'd rehearsed the answer.

The problem with practiced lines is that they leave no room for truth to leak in.

Gabriela nodded slowly, pretending to accept it. Inside, the unease thickened. *That's not all it is. I've lived with you long enough to know the difference between habit and surrender.*

Her fingers tapped once against the table, then stilled. "It just… feels like she's the center now. More than before."

Ted chuckled softly, aiming for disarming. "She's always been the center. You know that."

The words should have been harmless, but they carried a weight she couldn't shake. *Always? No. Not like this. Not at the cost of everything else.*

She meant to let it go. To swallow it. But the words slipped out sharper than she intended: "Feels like you're not the one making choices anymore."

The silence that followed stretched tight, every appliance hum suddenly louder.

Ted froze, his smile lingering just a beat too long. Then, carefully, he said, "Of course I am. You don't have to worry." His tone was calm, polite—so polite it felt brittle.

But something cracked behind his eyes. The phrase echoed in his head, brittle: *Not making choices. Not making choices.*

And for the first time, he wondered if she was right. A flicker, quick and dangerous, the sense that he'd drifted too far off course. That maybe he wasn't steering at all.

The thought startled him. He leaned toward it instinctively—then felt the faintest brush against his ankle.

Luna, under the table, silently pressing her paw onto his foot. Her eyes were half-lidded, watching without watching.

The pause broke. The thought slid away, untraceable, like a dream dissolving in daylight.

Ted cleared his throat, the sound small in the charged air. "You're reading too much into things," he said softly, almost apologetic.

Gabriela didn't answer. She lifted her coffee instead, sipped, eyes on him over the rim. Her restraint was deliberate now, her silence a choice. *If I push again, he'll close the door completely. Better to let him think I didn't notice the crack.*

Ted drained his glass and set it carefully in the sink. He smiled at her, gentle, composed.

But the sharp corner had already been taken. Neither of them could pretend it was a straight line anymore.

* * *

The bedroom was dark except for the dim wash of a streetlamp cutting through the blinds. Ted lay on his back, the sheets twisted at his waist. Gabriela's steady breathing came from her side of the bed, a rhythm that should have grounded him.

But his focus was elsewhere.

At the foot of the bed, Luna sprawled across the blanket, her body heavy against his ankles. She didn't stir, didn't twitch her ears at the night sounds outside. She simply existed there—warmth, weight, inevitability.

Ted stared into the ceiling's shadows, his hand sliding absently to the blanket near her flank. His fingertips pressed the fabric as though tracing her through it. He didn't notice the strangeness of the gesture. It felt natural, even necessary.

"You did good today," he whispered, the words more breath than sound. "Kept things steady."

Gabriela surfaced just enough to crack her eyes. In the dim light, she caught the outline of Ted's hand resting on the blanket at Luna's flank, fingers splayed like he was making sure she stayed. The words rose to her tongue and died there. She turned onto her side, facing the wall, and let the room keep its secret.

Luna's tail gave a single, lazy thump against the bedspread—an acknowledgement, nothing more. Her eyes stayed closed, but her presence was absolute.

Ted smiled faintly in the dark, though he didn't know why. A ripple moved through him—his fingers tightening once against the blanket, his brow drawing the smallest line. It wasn't a thought, wasn't a choice. More like a reflex, as if some hidden nerve had been touched.

At the foot of the bed, Luna shifted just enough for her weight to press harder against his ankles. The pressure was subtle but final. Not discomfort. Not affection. Something closer to a seal being set.

Sleep crept in behind it, and Ted drifted without ever noticing what he had given.

CHAPTER SEVEN

Good Dogs

The morning had a faded quality to it, like an old photograph that had been left too long in the sun.

Ted turned the corner with Luna at his side. The leash was slack in his hand, almost unnecessary, but he held it anyway. The streets of Metro Verde had their rhythms—sprinklers hissing, golf carts humming toward the course, the desert light sharpening by the minute. He knew the walk by muscle memory. Luna knew it better.

The Halperns' house sat crooked on its lot, a squat ranch-style from the late sixties, still wearing the same beige paint it had worn when the neighborhood was new. Time had gnawed at the edges. A shutter hung by one screw, the roof sagged like it was tired of trying, and the chain-link gate leaned inward as if waiting for gravity to finish the job.

The front yard had no grass, just patches of dirt where weeds came up and died in the same season. A rusted mailbox sat open, last week's circular curling like a dead leaf inside.

Dot stood in the doorway wearing a robe patterned with faded roses. She held a plastic mug of coffee in one hand, Snickers' leash dangling from the other. Her gray hair was uncombed, floating around her head in loose strands that caught the light like cobwebs. Her eyes carried a warmth, but it flickered—the kind of warmth that could forget why it was burning.

"Morning, Teddy," she called. Her voice was gravel wrapped in honey. She squinted, as if trying to make sure she had the right name.

Ted forced a polite smile. He'd learned not to correct her. "Morning, Dot."

Snickers, the apricot poodle, shuffled out behind her. Age had stiffened his gait, but there was still a twitch of energy in his movements. His fur was uneven, matted in places, brushed too vigorously in others, like someone had tried but lost the thread halfway through. His eyes, clouded with cataracts, still managed to gleam with something sharper—an alertness that seemed wrong for a dog so old.

The leash clipped to his collar sagged like a forgotten thought. Dot's hand trembled lightly as she held it, fingers fluttering as though she couldn't remember why she was holding it at all.

Snickers wagged his tail, a frantic metronome. Then, as Luna passed, the wag slowed, shifted, and stopped. His posture stiffened. Not a threat, not even a challenge—more like a sudden awareness, a dog recognizing a stronger frequency in the air. His cloudy eyes locked on Luna, and for a flicker of a moment, he was still.

Luna gave him a single glance. Not a bark. Not a growl. Just… acknowledgment.

And Snickers responded. His tail gave one short, hesitant beat, then he tugged the leash forward with more force than his small body should have mustered. Dot stumbled a step, coffee sloshing from her cup.

"Easy there, Snick," she said, laughing as though it was all a game. She shuffled after him, slippers dragging.

Ted watched, a small frown creasing his forehead. "You okay, Dot?"

"Oh sure, sure," she said. She smiled at him—sweet, confused, full of misplaced cheer. "He likes his walkies."

Ted nodded. It was easier than explaining what he saw: the way Snickers wasn't so much asking as insisting.

Luna moved on, her head high, tail calm. She didn't look back to check if Snickers followed. She didn't need to.

Later that week, Ted saw Dot again. Evening this time. The sky was bruised purple, streetlights buzzing to life. He was walking Luna a few blocks from his house when Snickers dragged Dot out of the doorway, leash taut, her slippers scuffing the concrete. She looked bewildered, as if she'd just woken from a nap and wasn't sure how she'd ended up outside.

"Where are we going, Snicky?" she asked, half to herself.

Snickers pulled her toward the street, cloudy eyes brightening as Luna appeared. He didn't bark. He didn't whine. He just tugged until Dot's thin frame lurched after him.

Snickers positioned himself at the curb, body angled toward Luna, tail low but steady. It wasn't obedience. It was something else—something close to ritual.

Luna paused, ears forward, head tilted just slightly. The silent exchange lasted only a breath, but it was enough. Snickers sat, stiff and deliberate. Dot blinked down at him, confusion clouding her face.

"Well, that's new," she said softly, as if Snickers had just recited a prayer.

Ted tugged Luna along. His scalp prickled. He didn't want to linger.

Behind them, Dot's voice carried, uncertain and small: "Did I already feed you, sweetheart?"

The question floated into the air unanswered.

Inside her house, Dot's neglect revealed itself in pieces. Unwashed dishes stacked in the sink, a calendar from last year still pinned to the wall, sticky notes with half-finished reminders stuck to the fridge:

"Call doctor Tuesday?"

"Buy more…?"

"Snickers med??"

Some days she remembered. Some days she didn't. Snickers ate irregularly, sometimes not at all until he pawed hard enough at her shin. His water bowl often went dry, refilled only when he dragged her attention to it with insistent yips.

Yet when Luna called in the night—one sharp bark, echoing across the neighborhood—Snickers always heard it. Always rose, tail twitching, claws scrabbling at the door until Dot, half-asleep and bewildered, stumbled after him into the dark.

She didn't remember those walks. She'd wake in the morning, robe dusty at the hem, shoes by the door, and assume she'd simply gone outside to get the paper. Sometimes she'd find "WALKIES?" written on the bathroom mirror—traced faintly through steam. No memory of writing it.

But Snickers remembered.

And Luna remembered.

For Ted, the moment would come later, when Luna planted the thought in his head like it was his own: *This isn't right. Someone should do something. Report it.*

And he did.

The call to the ASPCA was made, though Ted would never remember holding the phone, never remember saying the words.

What he would remember—what haunted him—came later in dreams.

In one, he stood on the cracked sidewalk outside Dot's house. The evening light was harsh, throwing long shadows across the yard. A white van idled at the curb, side door yawning open. Two uniformed workers led Snickers toward it.

Dot wept on the porch, her voice trembling. "Snicky? Where's my boy?"

None of them saw Ted. He was invisible in the dream, a ghost in plain sight.

But Snickers saw him. Even as the leash pulled him forward, the old poodle turned his cloudy eyes on Ted, sharp for just a moment, as if recognizing the hand behind it all.

Somewhere in the van, an engine revved—not mechanical, but familiar. Like a bark caught in a fan belt. Luna's bark. Echoing inside metal.

Then the van door shut, and the dream collapsed into silence.

Ted would wake with his chest tight, unable to tell if it was guilt or something colder.

That was the shape of it. The way Luna worked: never directly, never loudly. Just a nudge. Just enough.

Snickers was proof.

Dot was collateral.

And Ted? Ted was the tool.

* * *

Vera was the kind of dog you couldn't pin a breed to. Something terrier in the wiry fur, something shepherd in the ears that never quite stood up straight, something anxious in the eyes. She was a patchwork mutt, the sort that should've been forgettable, but wasn't—because she carried herself like she expected disaster.

Her house sat three blocks east of Ted's, at the quiet end of a cul-de-sac where the desert sand pressed up against the asphalt. A sagging chain-link fence enclosed the entire lot, wrapping both front and backyard like a cage. Rust showed through the silver in patches; the gate latch held shut with a strip of fraying bungee cord. Inside, the yard was bare dirt, dotted with tufts of dead grass and one sun-bleached lawn chair tipped on its side. The only green came from weeds threading through cracks in the driveway.

Ted noticed Vera most mornings on his walk with Luna. She patrolled the fence line with obsessive precision, paws carving grooves in the same loop. Nails clicked when she crossed concrete, then shifted to a soft scrape in the dust. The moment Luna came into view, Vera froze. Then she trembled—not with fear, but with recognition, like she'd been waiting for a signal.

Earl was her owner. Fifty-something, pot-bellied, a man who still wore his work shirt even though he'd been retired from the utility company for a decade. The blue fabric was faded thin, the name patch crooked. He sat heavily in a folding chair on the porch, cigarette between his fingers, eyes not on Vera but on some middle distance. A man slowed down so far it was hard to tell if he was moving at all.

Earl never raised his voice to Vera. Never struck her. But there was a vacancy about him, a slackness in the way he responded. He fed her, yes. Let her inside when the heat climbed too high. But he moved as if each decision took effort, and Vera—twitchy, calculating—had learned how to move him.

Ted had watched it happen more than once.

A sharp whine from Vera, just under the register of annoyance, and Earl would push himself up with a sigh, walking stiff-legged back into the house. Moments later, he'd return with a biscuit, dropping it on the concrete without looking at her.

Or Vera would scratch once at the door, stop, then scratch again—measured, deliberate. Earl would grumble but open it, letting her slip past him like smoke.

It wasn't affection that passed between them. It was something else. Dependence in reverse. Earl didn't command her; she nudged him, rewired his reflexes so that her small demands became habits.

Like she was programming him.

Like she was erasing old functions and installing her own.

This morning was no different.

Ted slowed as Luna's ears twitched, catching Vera's pacing before they rounded the bend. The mutt's body stilled when she saw them. Her gaze slid past Ted and locked onto Luna. Her trembling eased. She sat down abruptly, posture awkward but deliberate, as if waiting for instruction.

Luna barely looked at her. Just a tilt of the head, a narrowing of the eyes. Enough.

Vera whined once. Earl sighed, flicked his cigarette into the dirt, and pushed himself up with a groan. "Alright, alright," he mumbled, shuffling inside. When he returned, a biscuit dangled from his hand.

As he approached the porch, he muttered something under his breath: "Good girl, Luna."

Then he blinked. Frowned. Looked down at the treat like it had appeared there without his knowledge.

He tossed it onto the step without meeting Vera's eyes. Like someone leaving a tithe on the threshold of a chapel they didn't attend.

Vera didn't eat it. Not right away. She kept her gaze on Luna, posture taut. Only when Luna turned away and resumed walking did Vera move—nose to the biscuit, crunching fast and low, like she'd been granted permission.

Ted frowned. He didn't know why it unsettled him, but it did.

Earl slumped back into his chair, already lighting another cigarette, oblivious.

Or maybe not oblivious.

Maybe resigned.

Ted tugged Luna's leash. "Come on." His voice was too sharp, and he heard it. But Luna didn't break stride.

Behind them, Vera started pacing again, back and forth along the chain-link, her loop worn deeper into the dirt each time she passed.

Later that week, the pattern sharpened.

Ted and Luna passed by in the evening. The yard was dim, porch light buzzing with moths. Earl wasn't outside this time. Vera was, her wiry form pressed against the fence. She let out one short bark, clipped and direct.

Inside, a shadow shifted. Earl appeared in the doorway, shirt untucked, face blank. He looked at Vera, then at nothing. His hand went to the treat jar on the counter before he seemed to realize it.

He stood there for a second, frozen, holding the lid in one hand like it had teleported there. Then he completed the motion. One biscuit, one throw. Ritual complete.

Ted's stomach knotted. He couldn't explain why it looked wrong—the way Earl moved like a puppet on an old string, the way Vera's body loosened only once the treat hit the ground.

Luna didn't look back. She never did.

But Ted did. And the sight clung to him, sticky and sour.

* * *

Brian and Lissette Corley's place looked like it had been designed for a magazine. White stucco walls, sharp roof tiles, iron fence out front. Where most houses in Metro Verde bore the scuffs of desert wind and time, theirs was scrubbed clean. Gravel was raked into even patterns. Agave and yucca were spaced like chess pieces. No clutter. No softness.

Behind the house stretched the real operation. Ted saw only glimpses in passing, but they stuck with him. Chain-link runs laid out in perfect rectangles. Concrete pads scrubbed daily. Stainless steel bowls polished until they caught the sun. It wasn't cruel. It wasn't kind, either.

The dogs were products.

The Xoloitzcuintls themselves were flawless—sleek bodies, skin like burnished leather, eyes that seemed too knowing. One adult male, regal and taut as wire. Three females, muscled and sharp. A scattering of pups in the nearest pen, all awkward limbs and oversized paws. They were healthy, immaculate, everything the breed standard called for. But there was no softness in their world, no affection.

Ted saw it one Saturday morning when the Corleys were working in the yard together.

Lissette wore latex gloves as she measured kibble into stainless steel bowls, each scoop leveled with a knife edge. Brian followed behind, placing the bowls in each run with practiced precision. Not a word of encouragement, not even the absent-minded hum most people gave when feeding their pets. Just the rhythm of the routine: scoop, measure, place.

The dogs ate hungrily, but none wagged. They didn't press forward with the messy joy Ted was used to seeing in Luna. They waited. Sat in taut silence until the bowls were down. Only then did they eat—quick, efficient, like soldiers on rations.

Later, Lissette bathed a female in the yard. She crouched low, sponge moving over the dog's sleek body in smooth, methodical strokes. The dog stood still, tolerant, resigned. There was no baby talk, no cooing, no "good girl." Just the swish of water and the squeeze of soap. When the rinse was done, Lissette dried her briskly with a clean towel, hands working like she was polishing a car. Then she moved on to the next.

Brian photographed the puppies that afternoon. He crouched with a DSLR, adjusting angles, coaxing the pups into position with bits of cheese. His voice was clipped, functional. "Sit. Hold. Good. Stay." Shutter clicks punctuated the commands. Each picture was another entry for their website, another promise of heritage and purity for potential buyers scrolling online.

Not once did he kneel to stroke their heads just because. Not once did Lissette tuck a pup against her chest.

They weren't cruel. They weren't neglectful. But they were absent in a way that mattered.

Ted slowed at the sidewalk as Luna stopped. She stood perfectly still, watching through the fence.

The male Xolo froze first, eyes sharp. Then the females followed, three shadows folding in symmetry. Even the pups, restless seconds before, sat with clumsy obedience.

But it wasn't fear.

It was attention. Alignment.

Brian didn't notice. He was bent over his camera, reviewing shots. Lissette was coiling the hose, lining it neatly against the wall.

But Ted noticed. The way the dogs' bodies tilted toward Luna. The way their stillness felt heavier than noise.

Like the space around them had shifted density.

Like their skin remembered something older than commands.

Luna gave the smallest flick of her ear. A command without words.

Every Xolo held their position, eyes locked. Silent. Waiting. It wasn't submission—it was staging. As if they were being counted for something. Positioned for deployment.

Ted's heart gave a single offbeat thud. He tugged at the leash, pulse quickening. "Come on," he muttered.

Luna allowed herself to be led away, calm, deliberate.

The spell broke as she turned the corner. The pups toppled back into play, clumsy bodies colliding. The females stretched. The male shook himself, as if dusting off unseen cobwebs. Brian snapped another photo. Lissette stacked bowls for washing.

Business resumed.

Ted exhaled slowly, though he hadn't realized he was holding his breath.

He didn't look back.

That night, he dreamed of the Xolos again. Not in cages, not behind chain-link, but moving across the desert in perfect unison. A pack without a master. Their silence louder than howls.

The stars overhead blinked like signal lights. He tried to call out, but no voice came. Only the rhythm of paws on sand.

He woke with Luna at his feet, her breathing steady, deep.

And he wondered—if dogs had souls, could they be bought and sold? Or only borrowed…

Until someone stronger came along?

* * *

Ricky Delmonte's yard looked like a prison camp dropped in the middle of suburbia. Chain-link fencing boxed in every angle of the property, front and back, reinforced with extra posts like he expected a siege. A dented Harley leaned against the porch, oil staining the concrete below it. Beer cans littered the steps, sun-bleached and crushed flat.

The grass was gone—what little there was had been replaced by hard-packed dirt. A length of chain lay coiled near the porch, heavy links glinting in the sun. At the far corner of the yard sat a pitiful plywood doghouse, roof tarped with a strip of corrugated tin.

The smell hit Ted and Luna as they passed: ammonia, sweat, the sour tang of unwashed fur.

Axel lay chained near the doghouse. A pit bull, broad-shouldered, brindle coat dulled by neglect. His body was strong, but there was a thinness to him, an edge of underfeeding. His eyes tracked Luna immediately, sharp and desperate. His ears folded back, tail rigid.

He didn't wag. Didn't whine. He just stared.

There was recognition in it—not just of another dog, but something older. Something elemental.

Smash staggered out of the house then, leather vest hanging open, a Devil's Stallions patch stretched across his back. His jeans were torn at the knees, grease ground into the fabric. A cigarette clung to his lip, ash dangling until it fell on the porch. He squinted against the daylight, scratching his beard.

"Shut it, Axel!" he barked before the dog had even made a sound.

Axel flinched. Not a whimper, not a growl—just the twitch of a muscle along his jaw.

Smash stepped off the porch and swung a boot sideways, not hard enough to break bone, but hard enough to slam Axel's ribs and roll him half a body length across the dirt. The chain rattled, taut, then clanged back against the stake in the ground.

Ted's chest tightened. Not from the sound, but the *absence* of one.

Luna made no noise. No growl. No whine. Just a stillness—so deep it felt like static.

She watched Axel not as another dog, but as a ledger entry. Pain received. Noted. Stored.

Axel scrambled upright, crouched low, tail tucked tight. His gaze never left Luna.

Ted felt his stomach coil, bile creeping up the back of his throat. His fists flexed at his sides before he realized it.

"C'mon," he muttered to Luna, pulling her away. He didn't want Gabriela to see him shaking when he walked back through the door later.

Smash spat into the dirt, muttered something about "worthless mutt," and stomped toward his bike. The Harley coughed to life with a ragged roar, spewing exhaust as he gunned it down the street.

The silence afterward felt worse.

Axel didn't move from his crouch. His eyes burned through the chain-link at Luna, not pleading, not commanding. Just transmitting one raw frequency: fear.

Luna returned the stare calmly, as if cataloging it. Not pitying. Not intervening. Just… remembering.

Her tail lifted slightly, then lowered again. A marker dropped.

And Ted felt the strangest thing: a chill, sliding down his spine, settling in his bones.

He tugged harder at the leash, eager to turn the corner, to leave the stench and the scene behind.

That evening, Gabriela stood at the kitchen counter, slicing tomatoes for dinner. The smell of cilantro and lime drifted through the room. Ted leaned against the doorway, arms folded, Luna sprawled at his feet.

He cleared his throat. "Saw Delmonte out front today. He was kicking that pit bull again."

Gabriela's knife froze mid-slice. Her jaw tightened. "Axel?"

"Yeah." Ted rubbed the back of his neck. "Dog just crouched there, didn't make a sound. He… He looked at Luna the whole time. Wouldn't look away."

Gabriela set the knife down, palms flat against the cutting board. When she spoke, her voice was low, steady, but edged like glass. "That man. You know what he is?"

Ted hesitated. "An asshole?"

She gave a sharp laugh without humor. "He's worse. He's the kind of man who mistakes fear for respect. That's poison, Ted. Pure poison. You can see it in the way his dog looks at him. No loyalty. No love. Just terror. And men like that? They rot everything around them."

Her eyes lifted, locking on his. "That poor pit bull deserves better than him. Any dog would. If there's ever justice in this world, it'll be that dog walking away and never looking back."

Her words landed with a thud, and Ted found himself nodding. It wasn't opinion—it was truth, spoken with the clarity of a verdict.

Luna shifted then, lifting her head. Just a flicker—her gaze touched Gabriela for a moment, slow blink, tail-tip twitch. A rare signal of approval, subtle but unmistakable.

Gabriela caught it and drew a slow breath, steadying herself. She went back to slicing tomatoes, but her words lingered, filling the kitchen long after the silence returned.

Ted's eyes drifted to Luna. He thought about Axel chained in the dirt. About the way Smash's boot had slammed into him.

He thought about rescue.

Nothing else.

* * *

The desert neighborhood was hushed under a brittle sky. Night had stripped the heat but not the weight; the air still clung to Ted's skin as he walked Luna along the quiet streets. The leash lay loose in his hand. It wasn't a leash anymore—it was ceremony, an object meant to suggest control where there was none.

It started with Vera.

Somewhere behind her chain-link pen, the mutt gave a jittery yap, sharp and nervous, the kind of sound that came from bone-deep vigilance. It wasn't random—Ted knew it in his gut. The noise carried too cleanly, and it was too well-timed, like a flare shot up into the dark.

Then the Xolos answered. A layered chorus—one deep, three sharp, high-pitched yelps folding in over the top, then the tumble of puppies squealing and rattling at their enclosures. It was less a bark than a chant, a sound that seemed to unspool across the blocks like a rope being pulled taut.

Ted slowed. His scalp tingled.

From the Clarks' house came Samson. One bark, low and certain, a golden retriever's voice meant for fetch and guard duty but now repurposed, absorbed into something larger. The sound made Ted's stomach twist—it wasn't hostile, but it wasn't friendly. It was acknowledgment, compliance.

Last came Axel.

The noise was ugly, a bark that broke against steel, half-choke, half-threat, dragging across the night like barbed wire. Ted imagined the pit bull straining at the chain, muscles trembling, ribs flaring with each pull. The sound didn't fit with the others, yet it belonged—it was the closing of a circuit.

One by one: Vera, the Xolos, Samson, Axel. Every voice accounted for. Roll call.

Ted waited for more. But none came. Not from the arroyo. Not from the northeast hill. Not from the quiet edge of the map.

One voice didn't answer.

Not refusal. Not defiance. Just… distance.

Ruby remained silent.

Ted stopped walking. His hand tightened on Luna's leash, though she hadn't moved. She stood poised, eyes forward, body language steady. She wasn't listening—she was leading.

There was a tension in the air, like sound had just been vacuumed out of the atmosphere. The night held its breath around her.

He swallowed. "It's nothing," he muttered. "Dogs bark. That's all."

At the house, Gabriela was waiting on the porch, sweater draped over her shoulders, book folded in her lap. She looked at him before she looked at Luna.

"You heard it," she said flatly.

Ted froze, halfway up the step. "Heard what?"

"Them. One at a time. Like a roll sheet." She tilted her head, studying him with the same suspicion she used when grading student papers. "That wasn't a coincidence."

Ted forced a shrug, his laugh brittle. "Babe, every yard has a dog. Sometimes they get each other going."

Her eyes narrowed. "Not like that. That was order. That was a call."

Luna stepped past Ted and sat neatly at Gabriela's feet, her gaze steady, her body pressed against the porch wood as if staking a claim. Gabriela stared down at her. Luna blinked once, slow and deliberate.

Gabriela's jaw tightened. She looked up at Ted. "You think you're walking her." She gestured at the leash dangling in his hand. "But you're part of her walk. Don't you see it?"

Ted opened his mouth, but nothing came. His mind scrambled for the easy explanations—coincidence, dogs being dogs—but the words dried before they left his tongue.

The neighborhood was quiet again. Too quiet. Attendance taken. Silence restored.

And Ted, for the first time, felt like he was the one being counted.

Back inside, the house felt off-balance. Too clean, too staged, as if their life had been nudged a few inches out of alignment and they were the only ones pretending not to notice.

Ted rinsed a glass at the sink, staring at the water as it swirled away. Gabriela lingered in the living room, not reading, not moving, just watching Luna stretch out across the rug like a monarch settling into her throne.

No one spoke.

Through the window, the neighborhood hummed again—sprinklers ticking, an engine turning over some-where down the block, the faint bleat of a television laugh track drifting from an open window. Normal sounds. But they felt thinner now, like someone had pulled the stuffing out of them.

Ted climbed into bed later that night beside Gabriela, who pretended to be asleep. He told himself nothing had happened. Just dogs barking. Just a coincidence.

But lying there in the dark, he felt the lie like a lump under the mattress.

* * *

It was the middle of the night when Ted walked out the front door without a thought in his head. His face was a mask of vacancy, not peaceful, not troubled—just empty. Luna padded at his side, her nails clicking softly on the concrete. At the end of the driveway, he stopped, as if he'd reached the border of some invisible map.

Luna tilted her head up at him, waiting.

Ted bent, unclipped the leash, and set it on the ground. He turned without a word and walked back into the house. Thirty seconds later, he returned, crouched, slipped a square of cheddar into Luna's mouth, and scratched behind her ears. She licked her lips, satisfied. He clipped the leash back on, stood, and resumed walking, blank as a mannequin.

They moved through the dark streets until Smash's yard opened before them—a patch of dirt fenced with rusting chain-link. Axel was there, straining against the collar, ribs showing through his hide, his chain rattling in metallic bursts.

Ted walked straight to him. No hesitation. He unclipped the collar with a smooth, deliberate motion, chain still coiled in his fist. Axel blinked, startled, then sat six feet back, silent now, as if he knew what was coming.

When Ted turned, Smash was already there, weaving slightly, a bottle hanging loose in his hand. His eyes narrowed, words brewing on his tongue, but they never left his mouth.

Ted swung the chain.

The first hit landed with a flat, brutal crack—like someone turning off a television with a hammer. Static exploded behind Ted's eyes.

Smash reeled, dropped the bottle, and staggered.

Ted stooped, scooped the bottle up, and turned it into a weapon.

The beating was merciless. The blunt end came down again and again, a percussive rhythm of wet thuds and groans. Smash clawed at the dirt, tried to crawl away, but Ted pinned him with a boot and hammered until teeth snapped, cheekbones shattered, and breath came in broken gasps.

Ted was calm through it all, breath steady, face impassive. He might as well have been sanding a piece of wood. Tightening a bolt. Cleaning a drain.

No rage. No noise. Just the cold mechanics of removal.

Smash tried to scream, and Ted jammed the broken bottleneck into his mouth, grinding until blood spilled, teeth cracked, and the sound turned into a wet choke. Then, with surgical cruelty, Ted gripped both sides of Smash's jaw and pulled until tendons tore and bone cracked. The scream died in his throat. His body slackened, ruined.

Axel didn't move. He only watched, silent and still, as if the violence itself had finally given him peace.

When it was over, Ted let the body fall. He turned, walked inside Smash's house, and washed his hands in the sink. Red swirled into pink, then to clear, and then there was nothing at all.

The next morning, the house smelled of frying eggs. Gabriela hummed to herself at the stove, hair still mussed from sleep. Ted sat at the table, posture neat, face unreadable.

She slid a plate in front of him and smiled softly. "How'd you sleep?"

Ted lifted his fork, paused a beat, then gave a small nod. "Fine."

And that was all.

CHAPTER EIGHT

Indifferent Ted

The conference room smelled like dusted-off carpet and yesterday's coffee. A half-smeared whiteboard behind the screen still bore a faded diagram from a past sprint review—something about handshake protocols and adaptive filters. Ted noted the ghost of his own handwriting. He didn't bother erasing it.

Everyone was seated except him.

He had entered ninety seconds late, laptop under his arm, a single AirPod still in. No one said anything, but Emi Takahashi—his division director and former mentor— gave him a long, silent look from the far end of the table. Just a flicker of calculation, then gone. She turned back to her tablet, stylus tapping like a slow metronome.

Marc Shevlin, the senior systems engineer Ted had worked with for over a decade, cleared his throat. "All right, let's jump in."

The Kestrel project, codename Echo Nail, sat five months into a fourteen-month plan and was already limping. Ted had led tighter projects with half the budget and a third the runway. But somehow, this one dragged—firmware bottlenecks, signal crosstalk, unexplained interference

in the AI filtering layers. None of it was catastrophic, just…
sticky.

"Prototype three still fails handshake at boot," Marc
said, nodding toward the screen. "We think it's firmware
race conditions. Arjun's model throws inconsistent outputs
when comms are disrupted mid-packet."

Arjun Mehta, the AI specialist who'd architected the
model's decision layer, adjusted his glasses. "It's not the
model; it's the fallback loop. When the RF disruptor hits
static, the buffer gets flushed too early. The AI thinks it
succeeded because the error handler returns a zero code."

Ted looked at the code snippet projected on the screen.
He blinked. He knew this bug. Had diagnosed it three
weeks ago, in theory. Why hadn't he fixed it?

His voice came out flat. "So patch the handler to delay
flush by two cycles. Add a confirmation ping before zero
return."

Marc nodded slowly. "Right. That's what we assumed.
But your last commit rewrote the timing logic in the
opposite direction."

A pause. Not hostile. Just… factual.

Ted stared at the table for a moment, searching his
memory like digging through someone else's inbox. "I
must've been exploring something else. Roll it back."

Renee Calderón, the project coordinator who tracked
every deadline like a sniper watching a clock tower,
scribbled something in her planner.

Across the table, Lani Reyes, the team's UX designer and human-factors specialist, clicked open her Figma window. "UI feedback came in from Kestrel's trial team. They're asking for fewer nested menus during field ops. I mocked a simplified UX path—less taps, clearer icons."

Ted leaned forward, squinting at the screen. "Looks fine."

"Just fine?" she asked, half-joking.

"I mean—it works. Ship it."

Lani tilted her head. "It's not ready to ship, Ted. I just built this draft yesterday."

"Then don't ship it," he said, too flat to register as sarcasm. "We'll keep iterating."

Jonah Stein, their contract security consultant and resident cynic, arms crossed, said nothing—but tapped a knuckle against his notebook like someone marking a rhythm.

Harris Kim was bouncing slightly in his chair, waiting for permission to speak. "Um—so—I added some custom UI states to the sandbox build," he offered. "And I dropped in a placeholder mode toggle… just for fun."

Ted's eyebrows lifted. "Fun?"

"Yeah, it's… It's like a joke mode. Not live, obviously. Just kind of an Easter egg."

Renee shot him a look. "Please tell me it doesn't affect compiled output."

"No! Totally separate. Just a graphic. There's this little pixel dog that shows up when you press 'L' three times in a row. Says 'Luna Mode.' I thought—"

"You thought it was funny," Renee snapped.

"It is funny," Lani muttered.

Ted's mouth twitched. Not a smile. Not not a smile either. "Let it ride. Just flag it before demo builds."

Marc glanced over. "We doing Easter eggs in defense prototypes now?"

"We're not," Renee said.

Ted waved a lazy hand. "It's harmless. Unless Kestrel's got a problem with humor."

Emi didn't speak. Just watched him again. Then tapped her stylus twice—on rhythm, offbeat.

After the meeting, Ted stayed behind while the others drifted out. Renee led the pack, muttering about demo timelines and liability exposure. Marc hung back a beat longer, hesitating just long enough to feel like a question was almost asked—but he left without speaking.

Only Emi remained. She stood, closed her tablet, and didn't sit back down.

"I'm adding a second check-in with Kestrel this week," she said calmly. "Colin Narvez is circling. He's not happy."

Ted nodded once. "We'll get back on track."

"We need to do more than that."

Her voice was even. Controlled. Like pressure behind glass. She held his gaze just a breath longer than professional norms required.

"You feeling okay?" she asked finally.

Ted wanted to say yes. But what came out was, "Define okay."

A pause.

"You've always had strange hours," she said. "But your commits are erratic. Meeting notes are incomplete. And your prioritization flow has—shifted."

It wasn't an accusation. It was a diagnosis.

He looked down at his laptop, still unopened. The sleep light pulsed like a tired breath.

"I've just been distracted," he said.

She gave a soft nod. "Clear the noise, Ted. Before Kestrel clears it for you."

Then she walked out.

Ted didn't move for a while. The room emptied itself. The screen blinked back to the home screen. The projector hummed, then clicked off automatically.

Luna Mode.

He hadn't laughed when Harris said it. But part of him... wanted to chuckle. Because that's exactly what it felt like. Like some other mode had been activated. Not possession. Not hypnosis. Just... re-prioritization. As if someone inside him had adjusted the sliders:

- Empathy: 30%

- Urgency: 20%

- Alignment with Luna's comfort: 100%

He didn't feel guilty. Not really. Just… unbothered.

The hallway lights outside flickered once. He heard the distant tap of dog claws echoing on tile, but when he looked through the glass, the corridor was empty.

Still, he waited before standing. Just in case.

CHAPTER NINE

Rain Breaks the Spell

The desert doesn't ease into weather. It makes a decision.

By late evening, the Organ Mountains wore a storm-hardened edge, a hard purple line against a sky that couldn't shut up. Lightning stitched across the ridges—flash, count, rumble—closer each time. Wind came first, lifting the grit off Metro Verde in little ghosts and shouldering at the stucco. Then the rain hit as if it remembered every dry month at once.

Gabriela worked at the dining table, the good one. Laptop open, glass of water sweating a ring onto a coaster she pretended would help. Her hair was up, pencil tucked behind one ear, Track Changes blooming on the screen like a rash. She didn't look up when the first thunderhead cleared its throat. She'd lived here long enough to know a bluff from a swing.

Ted was in the garage with the big Beemer, pretending to be busy. The R1250GS Adventure didn't need much. Shaft drive meant no chain to fuss over; he knew that, but he needed something to do. He wiped dust out of the radiator guard with a toothbrush, dotted a drop of oil into the side stand pivot, checked tire pressures he already knew were fine. Busy work is still work if your hands need it. The garage smelled like old rubber, clean steel, and the faint medicinal bite of ACF-50. Outside, the first fat drops slapped the stone wall in the yard—Las Cruces fieldstone, darkening in blotches before surrendering to a sheet.

Luna hated storms. She'd heard the same low growl Gabriela had ignored and had been shadowing Ted for ten minutes now, pacing the hallway, pausing at the back door, nails ticking a nervous code on tile. Ears flat. Mouth closed. Tail a tight line. Her head twitched once before the thunder—like she flinched in advance. Every time the wind got its hands under the eaves and shook the house, she cut a glance at the ceiling like it might come down and accuse her.

The rain found second gear. Water hammered the roof like a thousand small, mean ideas. A white vein of lightning split somewhere behind the Organs, and the garage fluorescents hiccupped. Ted froze, toothbrush poised over a grille. He felt the sound in his molars more than he heard it.

That did it. Luna bolted.

One heartbeat, she was a shadow at the kitchen threshold; the next, she was muscle and motion. She drove through the flap of the doggie door with her shoulders and vanished into the yard, barked once at nothing, then looped hard along the stone wall that split their space from the neighbor's. Ted heard the side door to the garage work against a lazy latch and then slam wide. She shouldered through, damp and raw, and skidded on the concrete, claws scraping for purchase.

"Hey," Ted said on reflex, half a hand out.

Luna didn't come to him. She didn't nose at his hand or lean that heavy head into his knee like a lever. She went small. She tucked herself under the steel workbench, where the vise lived and the boxes of old screws pretended to be organized. She curled tight enough to make herself a question mark and trembled in neat, efficient shivers.

Ted crouched. The GS threw back his reflection in the black paint—ghosts of a man doubled in the tank's curve. The storm had a pulse now. Every flash lit the garage like an interrogation, and the thunder arrived before the count even started. The smell changed, too—petrichor punching through the back door, creosote waking up outside like something ancient remembering its name.

"Gabs?" he called.

"In here," she answered, voice thin with distance.

Another crack, closer, a sound with edges. The house seemed to duck. Gabriela came to the garage doorway with her pencil still behind her ear and her mouth already forming a smile she didn't get to finish. She saw Luna first.

"Oh, baby," she said, her voice soft. "She's shaking."

"Yeah." Ted's voice sounded like it belonged to someone who hadn't slept. "She's not... herself."

Luna tucked her nose tighter, the way a dog hides from fireworks or a vet. The whites of her eyes showed in the quick flashes. She didn't meet anyone's gaze. The alpha act was gone—no stance, no silent pressure. Just fear. It didn't fit her; a queen in a paper crown.

Rain turned the world outside into a single moving surface. Down the driveway, the street ran shiny and useless, a narrow river carrying leaf fragments and someone's glittering receipt to a drain that never learned how to keep up. The side of the GS wore a fine mist where the wind had reached it. Drops like silver fish scales clung to the crash bars and saddlebags.

Gabriela squatted, two fingers extended past the bench's lip. "Luna, mi amor. It's okay."

Nothing. Luna's chest heaved quick-quick, then held.

Ted set the toothbrush on the bench and wiped his hands on a rag out of habit. He didn't reach for Luna. Something about the direction of her fear said: Don't. Not dangerous—just fragile. He stood and looked at the storm through the open side door like it was a thing you could negotiate with.

New Mexico rain has two settings: off and punishment. Tonight, it chose punishment. A sheet of water beat the gravel flat, and every time lightning stitched the Organs, the mountains looked a step closer, like they were walking their way into town.

"It'll pass," Gabriela said. She spoke to the dog, but Ted heard the pitch aimed at him too.

He nodded.

The garage light flickered and stayed. Ted shut the side door partway to keep the spray from pushing in. The rain found whatever dust he'd missed and drove it to the floor in muddy commas. A puddle crept under the threshold and made a cold map around the floor drain.

Luna's tremors eased, then surged again on the next thunder roll. She made a small sound—barely there, a swallowed whine. Powerless isn't a word he'd ever use to describe her. Tonight, it fit.

"Do you want me to get her blanket?" Gabriela asked.

Ted shook his head. "If we move too fast, she'll try to be brave about it and break."

"That a diagnosis?" She gave him a sideways look, testing his temperature.

"A guess," he said.

Another flash lit the garage, hard and flat. It washed the color out of everything—bike, bench, hands, fear— leaving only shape and shadow. The sound that followed didn't crack so much as it shoved. The air thumped. For a second, the rain wasn't noise; it was pressure. It pressed on the roof, the walls, his chest. And then, very simply, something in the room shifted. No gesture. No cue. A feeling like static bleeding off a sweater. The hair on his arms went down.

He didn't name it. Not yet. He only noticed that the space between his thoughts had changed size.

The storm kept doing what storms do—cleaning what it could, breaking what it couldn't, moving on. Gabriela eased to her feet and touched his elbow on the way past.

"I'll make tea," she said. "She'll settle."

"Yeah."

He stayed where he was, halfway between the door and the dog, rag in hand like he'd forgotten to put it down. Lightning drew another line on the mountains, and the thunder chased it like a debt collector. Under the bench, Luna squeezed her eyes shut against both.

Rain is just water, he told himself. But the desert had made it into something else—something that scoured. Out in the yard, the stone wall ran slick and dark, every seam leaking a narrow waterfall into the rock bed. The smell coming off it all—wet dust, creosote, iron—felt like an old room getting aired out.

Under the bench, the dog that usually ran the house shook and tried to disappear into her own ribs.

First time he'd seen her lose the script.

He didn't say it aloud. He just stood there and watched the rain do its work.

* * *

Ted didn't notice it at first. He only knew the storm had weight, and the dog didn't. Then something slipped.

It wasn't an event, not really—no flash, no voice, no broken thing to point at later. It was an absence. A sudden, clean subtraction. Like a fan shutting off in the next room, and only then realizing you'd been living with the hum.

He blinked. Stood straighter. The rag in his hand hung loose. For weeks—months maybe—he'd moved through his days with a taut string in the back of his skull, tugging, tightening, setting his pace. Now the string was gone. His shoulders eased down, and his jaw went slack, and he felt stupid for not noticing how clenched he'd been until this second.

Static gone. Radio clear.

Like someone had yanked a plug he didn't know was powering him.

He turned toward the workbench. Luna hadn't moved. She was still folded tight, ribs rising in quick drafts, eyes too wide, whites showing with every lightning flash. Not watching him. Not commanding anything. Just cowering. Just a dog.

But the words felt too light. *Just a dog.* It was like calling a disabled bomb a paperweight.

He crouched, and his knees cracked. She didn't even flick her ears in acknowledgment. She was busy trying to vanish into the concrete.

Gabriela padded in behind him, mug of tea steaming between her hands. She leaned against the doorframe, watching him, then followed his gaze.

"What is it?" she asked.

Ted rubbed the heel of his hand against one eye. "Feels… different."

"Different how?"

He searched for the shape of the thing and came up empty. The words hid from him, scattered into the shadows where he couldn't reach. "Like… Like I woke up. Like there was… something on me, and now it's gone."

Gabriela's eyes narrowed, not in suspicion but in study. She'd been cataloging him quietly for weeks: the missed beats, the half-hearted smiles, the way his presence in a room felt dimmed. And now—suddenly—the brightness was back. He looked ten pounds lighter, as if the storm had scrubbed something from him. His eyes had the clarity she remembered from before.

Her stomach flipped, because clarity is proof. Proof that the fog was real. Proof that it hadn't just been her imagination.

Ted lifted both hands, palms open, frustrated at his own lack of vocabulary. "I don't know how else to say it. It's… quiet. Up here." He tapped his temple once.

The storm cracked again, but softer this time, muted by distance. The rain kept drumming, relentless but almost rhythmic now, and the garage seemed washed in a silence he hadn't felt in a long while.

Gabriela glanced at Luna again. The pit bull hadn't budged. No claim to the center of the room, no magnetic stare, no unspoken push-and-pull. Just an animal hiding from thunder.

"Feels good," Ted said, half to himself. His chest expanded as he breathed in the smell of wet creosote, that desert incense rising through the storm. For the first time in months, his breath felt like his own.

Gabriela didn't answer right away. She just sipped her tea, watching her husband, feeling a mix of hope and dread. Because if the storm had given him back to her, then it meant something else had taken him away.

*　*　*

The storm carried them back inside.

Gabriela set her mug on the dining table and flipped her laptop shut, work forgotten. Ted followed, slower, like a man testing new legs. He left the garage lights on and the Beemer still propped, Luna hidden under the bench. For once, he didn't feel compelled to wait on her.

The house sounded different too. Rain flattened the world outside, muting the constant buzz of sprinklers, AC units, and distant freeway growl. Inside, it was just the drum on the tile roof, steady and protective, like they'd been sealed in a cocoon.

They ate leftovers at the counter—enchiladas Gabriela had made the night before, reheated until the cheese blistered again. She got two beers out of the fridge without asking. Ted took his bottle and clinked it against hers. The sound was small, swallowed by the storm, but it carried weight.

"How are the papers?" he asked.

She shrugged. "Most of them… not good. One kid compared the French Revolution to a soccer game. I think he meant it as a compliment."

Ted grinned, real and unforced, teeth showing. He even laughed, a quick, rough bark that startled her before it warmed her. She realized she hadn't heard that sound in weeks.

"What?" he said, catching her expression.

"Nothing. Just—" She shook her head, smile curling. "You seem… lighter."

He didn't argue. Just sipped his beer and let the moment breathe.

They talked about safe things. Her students, the neighbor who never pulled his garbage cans in on time, the company Ted swore was running their new project into the ground. Normal conversation—like a warm coat borrowed from someone else's closet. Familiar, but slightly off in the sleeves.

Gabriela leaned her chin into her palm, listening, watching his face move with animation again. She felt him in the room with her, truly present. It was like a part of her marriage had been returned in the storm's downpour, soaked free from whatever grip had dulled it.

But not all of him.

Every few minutes, Ted's eyes flicked toward the garage door. Quick, almost unconscious. Like he couldn't help but check the shadow under the bench. He tried to cover it, but Gabriela noticed each time.

And then once—just once—he tilted his head slightly, as if listening for a sound no one else heard. Nothing followed. But the look passed across his face like a cloud's shadow.

She didn't call him on it. She let him talk, let him laugh. She let herself laugh too. For a little while, they both pretended they were just a husband and wife riding out a storm, sharing food and beer while the desert scrubbed itself clean outside.

But in the quiet beats between words, Gabriela felt the weight of it pressing again. A question she wasn't ready to ask: If this was borrowed peace, who would come knocking to collect?

* * *

After dinner, the storm sagged into its slower rhythm, thunder drifting farther off, rain thinning to sheets that broke into softer patter. The house felt insulated, wrapped in wet cotton.

Ted leaned against the counter, bottle in hand, staring at the way the condensation ran down the glass in crooked lines. His thoughts had edges again—sharp, distinct. For the first time in weeks, he felt like he could step back and see himself. The clarity startled him—like stumbling out of snowblindness into bright sun.

Gabriela sat sideways on a barstool, elbow hooked on the counter, chin resting on her hand. She was watching him without hiding it. He caught her eyes, and looked away too quickly.

"What?" he asked.

"You're thinking hard."

"Yeah." He dragged a thumb across the bottle's label. Peeled a corner loose without meaning to. "Something's… different. In me."

She straightened a little. "How?"

He tried to line up the words. They slipped. He tried again, slower. "I feel like… I've been walking around underwater. Not asleep, not awake either. Just… blurred. Tonight it lifted. Like the rain pulled me up."

The confession hung there. The only sound was the rain peppering the back patio, ticking off the stone wall in rivulets.

Gabriela's fingers tightened around her beer glass. She forced her voice to be steady. "Fog from what?"

Ted's brow pulled together, searching for a reason. "Stress? Work's been heavy. Or maybe—sleep, I don't know. Could be age catching up." He shook his head, frustrated. "But it doesn't feel like any of that."

He rubbed the back of his neck, a nervous gesture she hadn't seen from him in years. His eyes weren't dull now. They were too clear, too bright.

Gabriela felt a slow chill creep down her spine. She didn't say the word forming in her throat. Didn't say *Luna*. But the thought was there, glaring.

Her eyes tracked toward the garage. The dog still hadn't emerged. From where she sat, she could just make out the shape—Luna crouched under the bench, ears pressed flat, muscles twitching with each roll of thunder. Not prowling. Not demanding. Not staking her claim. Just small.

Still—but not relaxed. Like a statue carved for worship, not comfort. Something ancient in time-out.

The inversion unnerved Gabriela more than the usual dominance ever had. Fear made Luna look ordinary, and ordinary was wrong.

"Maybe it's nothing," Ted said finally, almost apologizing.

Gabriela didn't answer. She just took another slow sip of her beer, gaze shifting between her husband and the dog that, for the first time, seemed to have lost the script.

* * *

That night, the house exhaled.

The storm lingered, steady rain keeping its grip on the desert, though softer now, a lullaby for the restless. The gutters sang in trickles, and the stone wall out back shone slick and black, rivulets chasing each other into the rock bed.

For the first time in weeks, Ted didn't pace. He didn't find himself standing at the refrigerator with Luna at his side, hand reaching automatically for the cheese drawer. He didn't sit on the couch with the television murmuring nonsense he couldn't remember afterward. He didn't feel compelled to step into the yard and stare at the darkness like it was calling to him.

He just went to bed.

Gabriela lay beside him, eyes open in the dark, listening. The rain played percussion on the roof, irregular and soothing. She felt the bed move with Ted's breathing—slow, even, heavy. His body had melted into the mattress, slack in a way she hadn't seen since before the fog took him.

She turned onto her side and studied his silhouette, faint against the window's silver wash. Relaxed brow, unclenched jaw, the faintest whistle at the edge of each exhale. Her husband, unburdened. A simple thing, but tonight it felt like a miracle.

She whispered a prayer she didn't expect him to hear. *Thank you.*

Her mind should have rested with him, but it didn't. Couldn't. Because if the storm had freed him, even briefly, then something had been holding him. She'd sensed it for weeks—Ted drifting like a man underwater, never fully breaking the surface. Tonight, the water had drained, and what returned to her was proof.

She closed her eyes, but her body stayed taut.

In the living room, Luna shifted restlessly on the rug. Every few minutes, the dog's nails clicked against the tile, a pacing rhythm too light to be comfortable. Once, she let out a sharp, muffled whine—then went still, ears twitching like she was dreaming.

And for no reason she could name, a thought blinked through Gabriela's mind: *Ruby—the calm chow mix down the street, unshaken even by Fourth of July chaos.*

Why that popped into her head now, she didn't know. It left her uneasy.

Gabriela lay awake, staring at the ceiling, listening to both rhythms: Ted's calm breathing beside her, and the unsettled movements of the animal in the dark.

When sleep finally claimed her, it wasn't gentle. It felt like slipping through the crack in a door you hadn't meant to open.

By dawn, the storm had moved on. The desert carried its scent like a badge—wet creosote, iron in the air, dust pressed flat. The mountains wore a hard, clean outline, as if the rain had sanded them overnight.

Ted woke before his alarm. He lay there for a moment, listening to the stillness, then rolled out of bed with a kind of ease that startled him. His joints felt looser, his mind uncluttered. His body moved as if he'd been unshackled. He hummed an old tune under his breath—something he hadn't realized he remembered—while he pulled on his robe and padded barefoot to the kitchen.

Gabriela stirred awake at the sound. She blinked at the space beside her: warm, empty. For once, it wasn't because

Luna had dragged him somewhere. She wrapped the blanket around her shoulders and followed.

Ted was already moving around the kitchen, measuring out coffee grounds, filling the carafe. He had a bounce in his step, a rhythm she hadn't seen in months. When he turned and saw her, his smile was easy, unguarded.

"Morning," he said.

She leaned against the doorway, studying him. "You're cheerful."

"Feel good today," he admitted. "Clear. Like the storm washed something out of me." He said it without thinking, like it was just weather-talk.

Gabriela nodded, tucking the observation away. She didn't want to scare it off by probing too hard. She settled at the table, watching him move, savoring the return, however brief, of the man she recognized.

The smell of coffee filled the kitchen. Outside, puddles on the patio reflected the sharp blue of the sky. Birds shouted louder than usual, drunk on the freshness.

Ted poured two mugs and set one in front of her. He sat down, humming again, drumming two fingers on the table. For a split second, his hand drifted toward the fridge—then stopped. Gabriela saw the hesitation. He didn't notice it.

For a moment, she let herself believe it might last.

Then the dog came in.

Luna padded through the doggie door, paws damp, fur smelling of wet dirt. She shook once, droplets scattering onto the tile, then fixed her gaze on the room. Her eyes locked on Ted.

Gabriela saw the shift instantly.

His sentence broke off mid-word. His brow furrowed, just a flicker, but enough. The brightness in his eyes clouded. His fingers stilled against the table. A small slackness returned to his face, like a curtain being drawn.

It was subtle. Barely there. But she felt it happen. Like a room losing air.

It was the leash—not clipped on, but coiled around him again, tightening with every second he held her gaze.

She sipped her coffee, hiding the knot in her throat. The storm's gift was already gone.

* * *

After Ted left for work, the house was too quiet.

Gabriela sat at the kitchen table with her hands wrapped around a cooling mug of coffee. The storm had rinsed the sky clean; sunlight poured through the windows in crisp rectangles, sharp enough to show every streak on the glass. The world outside looked fresh, remade. Inside, nothing felt new.

She stared at the back door. Luna lay on the tile just beyond it, chin on her paws, eyes half-lidded in a picture of serenity. The dog's body was loose now, calm, as if the night of trembling under the workbench had never happened. No fear. No weakness.

Gabriela felt the weight of the contrast like a hand on her chest. Last night she'd watched Ted come back—watched his shoulders relax, his eyes sharpen, his laugh return. She'd seen it with her own eyes, felt it in her own skin. It hadn't been a dream. The rain had given him back to her, if only for a handful of hours.

And then this morning, she'd watched Luna step into the room, dripping rainwater, and pull him away again without a sound.

It was real, she thought. *I saw him come back.*

Her throat tightened. Saying it aloud felt dangerous, like naming a ghost in the dark, but she whispered it anyway.

"It was real. I saw him."

The dog flicked an ear at the sound, nothing more.

Gabriela pressed her palm against the table until her knuckles whitened. This wasn't imagination, or paranoia, or the slow erosion of routine. Something unnatural was at play, and it lay sprawled on the patio as if it owned the house.

No growl. No threat. Just that quiet, arrogant stillness —like a god resting between commands.

She forced herself to stand. Took her empty mug to the sink, washed it, dried it, and placed it neatly on the rack. The movements were crisp, deliberate—a ritual of resistance. Something to anchor her spine.

If the storm could break the spell once, it could break it again. And until she understood why, she would have to watch. Quietly. Carefully. Without tipping her hand.

Behind her, Luna stretched long across the tile, a slow, confident sprawl. No trembling now. No trace of fear.

The leash hadn't been removed. It had only gone slack.

And Gabriela was the only one who knew it.

CHAPTER TEN

Proof in the Mirror

Ted sat in the garage with the door cracked just wide enough to let in the dawn. The air was still cool, touched with desert night, but already humming with the promise of heat. Muffled doves called from the roof. The house behind him remained still.

The notebook lay open on the workbench next to a cold mug of coffee. The handwriting didn't look like his. It was, technically. Same pressure, same slope—but the spacing felt off. Like the hand that wrote it wasn't entirely convinced it should have.

He stared at the most recent line:

She gets what she wants before I even think about it.

He hadn't meant to write that.

Above that, the rest of the page was worse. Half sentences. Repeated words. A paragraph scratched out so viciously that the paper tore.

He turned to a fresh page and picked up the pen. Then paused. His hand was trembling—not dramatically, just enough to make the ink wander when he wrote.

Dreams again. Too vivid. No plot—just motion and sound. Woke up sweating. Felt like I was running without

141

moving. Or sinking while standing still. Like the dream kept writing itself on me, line by line, even after I woke.

He blinked at it. Something itched in his chest, low and hot, like he was remembering a nightmare he couldn't quite recall. He'd had these dreams before—over the past few weeks—but they were picking up speed. Always the same flavor: something chasing, something pulling, no violence, just inevitability. And always the same aftermath—like his brain had been walked across during the night.

He uncapped the pen again.

I keep waking up with my jaw clenched. Last night I bit the inside of my cheek hard enough to taste blood. Luna was already in the room, sitting at the foot of the bed. I don't remember her coming in. I don't remember hearing her.

He let the pen hover. His gaze drifted toward the open gap in the garage door. A hummingbird flitted past and was gone.

Ted exhaled. Not fear—something else. Weariness without a cause.

He wrote:

She watches me like she knows what I'm about to do. No commands. No barking. Just presence. She just… is.

He scratched his temple. His skin felt too tight there.

From behind him came the faintest sound—claws on tile, a low thump. Luna, moving through the house. He didn't turn around. He didn't need to. He felt her.

The leash is for show. I think I know that now. I just don't know what to do about it.

The words sat on the page like a confession he hadn't signed.

The pen dropped softly onto the page. Ted stood. Stretched. Rolled his neck until something popped. The notebook stayed open.

Luna didn't come into the garage. But she sat at the threshold of the laundry room, watching. Her ears weren't perked. Her tail didn't wag. She didn't make a sound.

Ted looked at her for a long time.

Then he nodded, just once, like he'd come to an agreement he couldn't name.

And left the journal behind.

* * *

Gabriela found the notebook in the garage by accident.

It sat on the edge of the workbench, next to a crusted socket wrench and a half-empty cup of coffee. The kind of thing Ted would never leave behind unless he was distracted—or unraveling.

The pages were open. Not laid flat, but deliberately open. She could feel it in the placement. The spine just barely cracked. A subtle angle. Like something meant to be seen.

She glanced back into the house. Quiet.

She read.

"Dreams again. Too vivid. No plot—just motion and sound. Woke up sweating."

Her brow pinched. She turned the page.

"She gets what she wants before I even think about it."

The breath caught in her chest. It wasn't fear—not yet. It was recognition. The kind that starts in the teeth and works down the spine.

Ted didn't keep journals. He hated the idea of leaving thoughts behind. Once, years ago, she'd caught him deleting a half-finished email mid-sentence—paranoid that even drafts could betray him. He believed in context. In control.

This wasn't that.

This was a man charting his own drift. A log from a boat slowly losing sight of shore.

Footsteps. She turned. Ted stood in the doorway, backlit, blinking like he hadn't slept.

He saw the journal.

Didn't flinch.

"Is this…" Gabriela hesitated. "Is this yours?"

Ted's eyes lowered. "Yeah."

"Are you okay?"

He nodded. Too fast.

She tilted the journal toward him. "You're writing about dreams. About… her."

He scratched the back of his neck. "Just trying to make sense of things. Been having these weird nights. No big deal."

"That's not what it sounds like." Her voice was soft, but edged. "Ted, this line—'The leash is for show'—what does that mean?"

He opened his mouth. Closed it.

"I don't know," he said. "It just came out."

"That's not how you write."

"I know."

There was a pause. Not awkward. Tense. Like the room itself had taken a breath and was waiting to see who would exhale first.

Then came the sound—soft nails on tile.

Luna padded into view from the living room, her white coat catching a shaft of morning light like it had been staged for her. She didn't bark. Didn't nudge. Just walked between them and sat, slowly, facing Gabriela.

That presence.

Gabriela felt her pulse rise. The conversation had been a current. Luna was a dam.

Ted's posture changed—barely. A shift in the shoulders. A softening of the eyes.

"She just wants attention," he muttered, his hand already lowering before his mind caught up.

Gabriela stared at him. "We were talking."

"I know. I just—" He paused, petting Luna's head absently. "It can wait."

Gabriela's mouth tightened. The moment had fractured. She could feel it. Like a thread pulled too hard.

She closed the journal without another word and placed it on the workbench.

Ted scratched behind Luna's ear. His touch was automatic, like muscle memory. Like service.

She didn't say what she was thinking.

But she thought it hard enough for the windows to feel it.

* * *

Ted sat on the couch, flipping absently through an unread book. Not reading—just moving pages. The sound of paper against paper was empty, like trying to turn silence. Luna lay at his feet, body long and silent, her head between her paws, eyes trained on the hallway.

Gabriela entered slowly, barefoot. Her earrings chimed once as she moved. In her pocket, the small pouch of salt and rosemary—freshly replaced—rested like a stone.

She held the journal. Not accusing. Just present.

"You never used to write like this," she said quietly.

Ted didn't look up. "What?"

"The notebook. What's in it—it's not just sleep problems, Ted. You're describing control. You're describing her."

He closed the book in his lap, still not making eye contact. "It's just thoughts."

"It's more than that." Her voice didn't rise. It settled deeper. "You're saying things you won't say out loud."

Finally, he looked at her.

And she saw it—that flicker of something trying to surface. A question half-formed. A man trying to feel the edges of his own mind.

Luna moved.

She rose without sound, and climbed onto the couch beside him. Not in his lap. Not playfully. She sat parallel, her flank touching his, her gaze locked not on him—but on Gabriela.

She didn't blink.

Gabriela took one step forward. The salt in her pocket warm against her thigh.

Ted's arm moved reflexively, wrapping around Luna like an old instinct. His hand settled on her ribs, thumb brushing in slow, circular strokes.

It was automatic. Almost devotional.

"You see what's happening, don't you?" Gabriela asked. "She didn't ask. You didn't choose. She moved, and you answered."

Ted blinked. A strange stillness took hold of him—like fog rolling over something warm.

"It's easier when she's here," he murmured.

"No," Gabriela whispered. "She claims you."

Luna shifted her weight, pressing closer into his side. Gabriela saw it—saw the moment when Ted disappeared. Not physically. Not all at once. But like someone falling asleep with their eyes open.

His shoulders dropped. Jaw softened. He turned toward Gabriela, and the person behind his eyes wasn't fully there.

"I think you're overreacting," he said. Soft. Reasonable. Disarming.

And completely false.

Gabriela stood her ground.

The small ceramic charm around her neck, shaped like a closed eye, twitched under her shirt. Not visibly. Not loudly. But she felt it.

A warning.

"I'm not afraid of you," she said—not to Ted. Not exactly.

Luna did not move. But something cold passed between them—like a scent Gabriela couldn't place, or a silence that arrived too fast.

Ted turned back to his book. The sound of the pages now was different—too slow, like his hands belonged to someone else.

Gabriela stepped back. One pace. Then another.

She didn't cry.

She didn't scream.

She turned and left the room, closing the hallway door behind her.

Then she lit a candle. Not for peace—but for clarity.

And whispered, not to the air—but to something older:

"I need your eyes now."

* * *

Gabriela sat at the kitchen table with her laptop open, the screen dimmed to its lowest setting. Outside, the desert morning was surrendering to heat, but the house stayed unnaturally cool. Still. Like the walls were listening.

A white candle burned beside her keyboard. The flame didn't flicker. Not once.

She reached into her pocket and touched the charm pouch—salt, rosemary, a sliver of obsidian—and set it beside the candle. Then she cracked the window an inch. Not for air. For movement.

The first tab she opened was scientific: articles on canine cognition, behavioral mimicry, owner-sympathetic routines. Rational, clinical. Useless.

She scrolled. Her eyes moved fast, but nothing stuck.

Then, faintly, behind her—a smell.

Burnt cedar. Earth after rain.

She turned.

Nothing.

She closed the psychology tab. Opened another.

"Dogs in Mesoamerican mythology."

Gabriela scrolled deeper. Her spine straightened without her noticing.

"In Aztec belief, the Xoloitzcuintli guides the dead through Mictlán. But not all dogs lead with honor."

"The Nahual is a dual-spirit. Sometimes protector. Sometimes predator."

Another gust—impossible but clear—wet fur and warm stone.

She blinked. The air was dry.

Her fingers hovered over the keyboard. Something in her bones tensed—ancestral memory brushing awake.

"Some spirits take form not to guard—but to guide the soul into servitude."

She copied that one. Pasted it into a new document. Labeled the file:

Luna—Patterns

Then she reached for the small clay charm around her neck. A gift from her mentor, Alma. Fired during a ritual, etched with an unblinking eye. When her fingers touched it, the vibration was faint but alive, like a pulse passed down through centuries.

The candle flame bent, as if reacting.

Gabriela didn't flinch.

She opened another tab.

"Milagros para la protección del hogar—"

The search auto-filled with miracles for home protection before she finished typing.

Her laptop fan kicked on for the first time all morning—but the air stayed cold.

She paused.

Then typed faster.

Outside the window, a wind chime rattled once and went still.

Her email pinged. A message from the university—department updates.

She ignored it. But the sender's name caught her eye: Alma Navarro.

Gabriela stared at it for a long moment.

Not because it was rare.

Because it was right then.

She reached for her phone.

Stopped.

Instead, she whispered—quiet, sure, spine straight:

"I'm not alone in this."

The candle flame dipped, steadied, and the room seemed to breathe with her.

The air felt lighter after she said it.

And somewhere, behind the walls or beneath them, Luna shifted.

* * *

The house was too quiet.

Ted stood at the sink rinsing a glass, moving slowly, like he wasn't sure why he'd picked it up in the first place. His shoulders sloped. His eyes were half-lidded. He didn't speak.

Behind him, Luna sat at the edge of the hallway, her body perfectly still. Not lying down. Not wagging. Just… poised. Watching the kitchen.

She blinked once.

Then turned.

Her paws made no sound on the tile as she moved toward the bedroom. She passed the living room without pausing, passed the office, passed the corner where the sun spilled through the blinds in familiar golden angles.

She stopped in front of the closed hallway door.

Gabriela was on the other side—still researching, still whispering fragments of prayers into the flickering candlelight. Still thinking her thoughts were her own.

Luna didn't growl. Didn't scratch.

She simply sat.

Tilted her head once.

Then stood again and walked a few paces down the hall. She lifted her nose. Sniffed once. The air was different. It smelled like salt and cedar and something older than either.

A sound—so faint it didn't reach human ears—shifted beneath her ribs. It was not a growl, but a frequency, a note waiting to be answered.

She turned her head slowly toward the front door, toward the desert beyond.

A new presence was forming.

Not a threat yet.

But not hers.

It pressed at the edge of her awareness like a mismatched signal trying to tune into the same station.

She padded back toward the kitchen. No hurry. No fear.

She would wait.

She always did.

CHAPTER ELEVEN

Detective Nia Wallace ducked under the sagging chain-link gate and stepped into Ricky Delmonte's yard.

The grass was dead. The air smelled like rust and piss and dry rubber. A deflated basketball sat near the back steps, split open like a dropped melon. Overhead, a swamp cooler hummed and clicked like it was trying to die.

She scanned the yard slowly. No clipboard. No partner. Just eyes and memory.

The scene had been cleared a week ago, but it still clung to the dirt. Blood doesn't linger in smell—just in shape. In silence. In a stain, the sun can't bleach out.

Ricky "Smash" Delmonte had been found slumped near the shed, on his back, head tilted, mouth ruined. The medical report described "trauma consistent with forced insertion of a rigid object into the oral cavity, resulting in mandibular dislocation and catastrophic dental injury." Which was the long way of saying: someone shoved something inside his mouth and kept going.

A beating? Maybe. But the precision told a different story.

Nia crouched beside the outline.

Glass fragments had been collected, logged, and marked "inconclusive." Not enough of them. No neck. No label. Just slivers.

She imagined the scene—Smash yelling, stumbling, maybe drunk, maybe high. Something in his yard pissing him off. A bottle in hand. A dog nearby. Or something worse.

The dog was gone.

Nia stepped over to the doghouse.

It leaned against the concrete like it had been shoved—not toppled, but moved with intent. The anchor bolts were torn from the concrete, chain still attached. Not pried. Not chewed. Ripped straight out, as if the slab itself had given way.

Inside the doghouse, she found claw marks. Fresh. Not frantic, but deliberate—like the dog was bracing itself. Or watching.

Under the shredded fleece, something metallic caught her penlight.

A collar tag. Smooth. Circular.

Axel

No address. No number. Just the name. Simple. Sharp.

She slipped it into an evidence bag and stared at the blood trail again. It was localized—splashed, not sprayed. Most of it had pooled in the dirt by Smash's head. But some had run between his shoulders. Gravity-defiant. A position that didn't match a fall.

The image landed in her mind too clearly: a man forced down, knees in the dirt, head wrenched back. The scream gagged before it was a sound.

"You knelt," she murmured, imagining him mid-scream. "Or were put down."

Behind her, a gust kicked up. The chain-link gate rattled once.

She turned.

No one.

Just heat and dust and silence.

"Ma'am?"

She didn't jump. Just turned.

A patrol officer in mirrored sunglasses stood at the perimeter, holding a file.

"Coroner's final came in this morning. No foreign DNA. Blood alcohol high. Some meth traces. No defensive wounds. Nothing under the nails."

Nia nodded. "Weapon?"

"None recovered. They're guessing a bottle, but… no glass fits the pattern."

She looked back at the yard. At the doghouse. At the tag in her hand.

"What about the dog?"

"Axel?" the officer asked. "Gone. Neighbor says he vanished same night."

"Right," Nia said on a breath.

The officer hesitated. "You want canvass expanded?"

"No." She crouched once more. Brushed the edge of her glove against the chain's bolt. Felt the heat.

"Start pulling veterinary calls," she said. "Two-mile radius. Ten-day window. Emergency visits only."

The officer blinked. "You think the dog attacked him?"

"I think something did."

Behind her, somewhere blocks away, a dog barked.

Not a frantic bark.

Not lonely.

Just one sharp, declarative note.

It carried through the heat like a signal, too clean to be an accident, too precise to be ignored.

Like a message.

CHAPTER TWELVE

Ted stood in the backyard with his hand on the stone wall, palm flat against its warmth. The sun had risen fully now, spilling across Metro Verde like a poured promise, but the light didn't reach him. Not really.

He couldn't remember walking outside.

Couldn't remember waking up.

There was a moment—maybe a dream—where he'd been kneeling. Dirt in his teeth. A taste like iron and citrus. A broken rhythm pounding behind his eyes.

Now... silence.

Luna lay in the grass a few feet away. Head up. Ears back. Watching the same spot on the fence she always watched. Nothing moved there.

Ted looked down and realized his hand was bleeding—just a little. A crescent-shaped cut across the meat of his thumb, still fresh.

He didn't remember doing that either.

From across the neighborhood, a dog barked once. Sharp. Distant. A perfect match to the one Nia had heard moments earlier.

Ted flinched.

Not from fear.

From recognition.

Like a sound he used to know—once.

In the other room, Gabriela heard it too. Only she didn't hear one bark—she heard two. The second trailed the first, faint and discordant, like a mismatched echo trying to break free of the rhythm. The hairs on her arm lifted before she could name why.

Luna turned to look at Ted, slowly and precisely.

Ted didn't speak.

He just nodded.

Once.

And somewhere in the dissonance between the barks, a countercurrent stirred—faint, but not hers.

And the leash around his mind pulled one inch tighter.

CHAPTER THIRTEEN

Celeste

The Pack Station smelled like lavender and industrial sanitizer—same as always. Dogs paced behind frosted kennel glass, tongues lolled out, tails flicking like metronomes. Somewhere in the back, the piped-in guitar music hiccupped, skipped, then looped again.

Celeste Rojas stood with her hand on the mop handle, watching the camera in the corner.

She wasn't smiling. Not frowning either. Just standing still. Like she was waiting to see if the camera blinked first.

She was maybe eighteen. Brown skin, high cheekbones, and short dark hair that didn't quite obey gravity. Her black apron read The Pack Station in neat green lettering, but the embroidered paw print above the logo had been carefully covered by a silver charm safety-pinned into place. A milagro charm in the shape of a heart.

She'd been hired three days ago, but already there were whispers.

Not gossip. Just silence that hung too long when she entered a room. The dogs noticed her before the people did.

Some cowered. Others stared. One had peed the second she touched its collar.

Rueben called it "first-week jitters."

Luna didn't have jitters.

She walked into the main room without fanfare, silent as an opened letter. Her paws clicked once on the tile, then stopped. She didn't bark. Didn't tilt her head. Just sat—motionless—in the middle of the walkway. Directly in Celeste's path.

Their eyes met.

The air in the room seemed to thicken, like someone had turned the oxygen knob down a notch.

Celeste didn't flinch. She didn't smile either. She just looked. And something in the way she looked suggested this wasn't new to her. Like she'd met the devil before, and it hadn't impressed her.

She bent slightly, hand resting on her thigh, and said, "You don't want anything. You just... want."

Luna didn't move.

Behind her, four dogs shifted inside their kennels—synchronized, sudden. As if a cue had been given.

Celeste noticed. Her fingers went still on the mop handle.

"Thought so," she whispered.

Reuben's voice broke the spell. "Hey, Celeste! Can you take Luna out to the courtyard?"

He was holding the door open with his hip, clipboard in one hand, coffee in the other. Didn't notice the tension. Didn't see the way the dogs had gone stiff.

Celeste turned without responding and walked to the gate. As she reached for Luna's leash, Luna rose—slow, deliberate—and backed away a single step. Not fear. Not resistance. Just calculation.

The leash clicked anyway. Celeste didn't yank it. She didn't tug or encourage. She just started walking, and Luna followed.

Not because she wanted to.

Because she was watching.

* * *

The lunch break crowd at The Pack Station gathered under the patio awning out back. Fold-out chairs. Plastic containers. The scent of microwaved enchiladas and dry kibble.

Gabriela hadn't planned to be there long. She came to drop off Luna's new health paperwork—vaccination updates and a note about a dietary allergy Ted had insisted was "probably just gas." Rueben had been busy, so she stayed a minute. Then five.

Now she sat alone at the far table, sipping from a Styrofoam cup of bitter coffee, watching the workers.

She liked dogs. She liked their honesty.

But this place had started to make her itch. And it wasn't from the fur.

The door creaked open. Celeste stepped outside.

She didn't carry food. Just a small canvas pouch tucked under one arm and that same silver milagro charm pinned to her apron. It winked in the sun like an old secret.

She saw Gabriela and crossed the patio without hesitation.

"Mind if I sit?" Celeste asked.

Gabriela shook her head. "Please."

The girl settled beside her, resting her forearms on the table. "You're Luna's owner."

It wasn't a question.

Gabriela smiled politely. "She owns us most days. But yes."

Celeste didn't laugh. She nodded once and looked out across the gravel lot.

"You ever get the feeling she's not asking for things?" she said. "She just makes people realize they already said yes."

Gabriela's fingers stilled on the paper cup. "Yes."

A beat passed between them. Not silence—more like a hesitation in the air. Like the space between a held breath and an answer you already know.

Celeste continued, her voice low. "Some dogs beg. Some dogs bark. Others… they wait. They wait for your soul to sit still. Then they take the part you weren't using."

Gabriela turned to face her fully now. "Why are you telling me this?"

Celeste didn't answer. Her eyes drifted over Gabriela's shoulder.

Gabriela followed her gaze.

Luna stood behind her.

No footsteps. No jingle of tags. Just there—a white shape in still-frame. Tail low. Head slightly dipped. Eyes locked on Celeste like a weight that never blinked.

Gabriela's throat tightened.

Celeste didn't move. She didn't look away. Her fingers closed over her pouch, then released. Her voice dropped to a whisper.

"She's testing you too. Not just him."

Gabriela started to speak, but her voice snagged on something that wasn't there.

Luna stepped between them.

No growl. No sound at all. She simply inserted herself—smooth as a shadow—and sat facing Gabriela, her back to Celeste. A velvet blockade.

Gabriela felt a pressure behind her eyes. Like heat. Like someone was pushing from the inside with a finger made of static.

Then—just as suddenly—it faded.

Celeste stood up.

"I need to finish mopping," she said, already walking away.

Luna stayed seated for one more breath. Then she turned, smooth as glass, and followed the girl back inside.

Gabriela remained at the table, coffee forgotten.

The scent of lavender drifted from the door.

And behind her ribs, something old stirred.

* * *

The break room at The Pack Station always felt two degrees too warm. The microwave beeped at random intervals, and the mini-fridge leaked just enough condensation to soak the heel of your sock if you weren't careful.

Rueben Castillo sat in the corner with his phone in one hand and a protein bar in the other, watching footage from the security monitor on his desk. His smile had gone soft around the edges. That was happening more often lately. Like his face couldn't decide what it was supposed to do.

He rewound the tape.

Wrong bowl. Wrong kennel. Twice. Gate left unlatched. A scuffle between boarders.

Always around Celeste's shifts.

He didn't want to fire her. But something in his brain kept whispering she wasn't right for the pack.

That phrase had landed in his mind like a moth. He didn't remember inventing it. But it fluttered there now—insistent, irrational. Something about her didn't belong. Or worse—she did, and that was the problem.

In the laundry hall, Celeste carried folded towels. Her skin carried tension.

She felt it. The pressure in the air.

Like someone had laid a hot coin at the base of her spine.

She passed a kennel. Three dogs turned away from her at the same time. Silent. Like they'd rehearsed.

The milagro on her apron felt heavier than it had that morning. She adjusted it without thinking.

The air around the intake room tightened—no smell, no temperature shift. Just density. A spiritual molasses.

Her ears rang briefly, as if something behind the drywall had hissed.

She whispered to herself—not a prayer, not panic—muscle memory.

Then she turned and walked the other way.

Rueben clicked again.

Celeste's face on the monitor: blank, calm. Dogs reacting. Never to her—but because of her.

He felt it again—that odd sensation he couldn't name. Like a warm breath just over his shoulder.

The screen flickered slightly. Just once. He stared, waiting to see if it did it again. It didn't.

Steph knocked and poked her head in. "Luna's in the intake room again. Just standing there."

Rueben waved her off. "I'll take care of it."

He rose, walked past the lockers, and turned the corner.

Luna sat in the middle of the room.

Facing the back wall. Still. Watching nothing.

Not the door. Not the kennels. Not him.

Just that spot—like she was waiting for something to come out of it.

Rueben didn't touch her. He couldn't.

By the time he reached his desk again, the decision had settled into him like sediment.

Celeste had to go.

* * *

The Pack Station's office had no right being as dim as it was. Fluorescent lights buzzed overhead, but half of them flickered like a nervous tick. The blinds were drawn crooked, casting long stripes across the cluttered desk like shadows from prison bars.

Celeste sat up straight in the guest chair—back not touching, hands resting on her thighs. The canvas pouch sat in her lap like a relic. The milagro pinned to her apron glinted each time the lights stuttered.

Rueben shifted behind his desk, rubbing his fingers together like he was trying to find the thread of a thought he'd lost in his sleep.

"I just think..." he started, then paused. "It's not... You haven't done anything serious."

He cleared his throat.

"There've been some small issues. Missed feedings. One of the gates was left unlatched. A couple of the dogs— uh—seemed stressed after your shifts."

Celeste didn't blink.

Rueben forced a smile, weak and uncertain. "Nobody's mad. But the vibe here—it matters. The dogs feel it when something's off."

Celeste tilted her head slightly, just enough to signal she was listening.

"And I'm off," she said, her voice calm. She wasn't offended. She was just repeating it for him, to get it out of the way.

Rueben's mouth opened, then closed again. He nodded. "Yeah."

He sounded relieved. Like she'd done him the favor of ending it for him.

Celeste stood with the grace of someone who knew how to leave without creating sound.

She reached into her pouch and unwrapped a small cloth bundle with the care of someone handling an offering. Inside, nestled against faded fabric, was another milagro—this one shaped like an eye. The silver had tarnished around the edges, dark like smoke, but the center gleamed.

Without asking, she walked past Rueben and knelt at the back wall, behind the adoption leash rack mounted above the tile baseboard.

"What are you doing?" Rueben asked, half-standing.

Celeste slid the charm between the bracket and the wall. Pressed it flat into the gap until it disappeared.

"You'll need it," she said. Not a warning. Not a threat. Just a fact.

Rueben stared at her. "For what?"

She didn't answer. Just straightened her back and stepped away.

Then, the temperature in the room dropped.

Luna stood in the doorway.

Not walking. Not panting. Not reacting.

Just present.

She filled the space with silence, a void where sound refused to live.

Rueben's heart kicked once against his ribs. He glanced at the spot behind the leashes where Celeste had placed the charm. He didn't move toward it.

Celeste passed Luna on her way out.

She didn't hesitate.

She didn't look at the dog.

And Luna didn't stop her.

She was already watching something else.

Something Rueben couldn't see.

CHAPTER FOURTEEN

Detective Nia Wallace sat at her desk, a cup of black coffee cooling untouched at her elbow. The printout lay in front of her, pale gray letters marching down the page with all the life of a morgue slab. She read it again, slowly this time, mouthing pieces of it under her breath.

Las Cruces Police Department – Homicide Division
Case No.: 2025-0814-0457
Date/Time of Response: 02:47 AM
Location: Residential property, Metro Verde neighborhood, Las Cruces, NM
Reporting Officers:
Det. Nia Wallace (Lead)
Ofc. James Ortega (Uniform Patrol – First on Scene)

Summary of Incident:
At approximately 02:21 hours, LCPD dispatch received a 911 call from an anonymous neighbor reporting loud disturbances and possible assault noises coming from a residence in the Metro Verde subdivision. Units were dispatched and arrived on scene at 02:34 hours.

The victim, later identified as Richard "Smash" Delmonte, a 44-year-old male resident, was discovered deceased in his front yard near the east side chain-link fence. No signs of forced entry were observed at the property.

Condition of Victim:

Male subject located supine, extensive craniofacial trauma noted.

Multiple depressed fractures to left zygomatic arch and orbital socket consistent with repeated blunt force impacts.

Dental trauma significant; several molars and incisors shattered.

Jagged lacerations and puncture wounds to oral cavity consistent with a glass bottleneck being forced into the mouth.

Mandibular dislocation with bilateral tearing of tendinous tissue; fracture lines observed along the temporomandibular joints.

Cervical strain with associated damage, but no complete cervical fracture. Cause of death attributed to blunt force trauma combined with mandibular dislocation and associated asphyxiation.

Scene Notes:

Broken beer bottle recovered near the victim with heavy blood saturation.

Length of rusted chain located approximately four feet from the body, bearing fresh blood and tissue transfer.

Front door of the residence was ajar upon arrival. Inside, kitchen sink basin contained traces of diluted blood; water was still running at low pressure.

No signs of robbery or ransacking. Electronics, cash, and other valuables were left untouched.

Additional Observations:

No witnesses located at scene.

Victim's dog, described by neighbors as a male pit bull named Axel, was not present at the time officers arrived. Chain anchor in the yard appeared recently detached. Area canvass yielded no sightings of the animal.

Neighbors reported hearing an argument and loud impacts, but could not identify additional voices beyond the victim.

Preliminary Conclusion:

Evidence suggests victim was attacked outside his residence by an unknown assailant utilizing both improvised weapons (chain and glass bottle) and manual force. Degree of overkill indicates possible personal motive, though lack of theft points away from burglary.

Investigation remains ongoing.

Nia laid the paper flat against the desk and rubbed the bridge of her nose. The words were clinical, the kind of language that boiled horror down to bones and scientific terms. But she could feel the brutality under it—the way the chain and the bottle weren't just weapons, they were statements. Whoever did it didn't just want Smash dead. They wanted him ruined.

She turned her notepad sideways, began sketching ideas in half-legible shorthand:

Personal vendetta? Overkill fits.

Gang-related? Smash's name carried small-time weight.

Debt? Drugs? Bottle in hand → drunk? Easy target.

Dogfight? Pit bull not on scene. Coincidence? Doubt it.

She circled *dogfight* twice, then stopped. Her wrist resisted the pen.

Her mind drifted back to the Tompkins interview. Ted, rigid and off-tempo, like a man on delay. And the wife—bright, grounded, but watching him too closely. Nia could read couples in minutes; this one set her teeth on edge.

But it was the pit bull. That animal. Sitting there, like it owned the room. When she'd met its eyes, something in her had staggered, the way you miss a step going down the stairs. She'd laughed it off at the time, blamed fatigue.

Now, without thinking, her pen wrote a single word under the "motives" list:

Luna.

She froze when she saw it. Drew a hard line through the name, then another, like that would erase the fact she'd written it at all. Her hand hovered, pen tip twitching.

"Get it together," she muttered, but her voice sounded thin, even to herself.

CHAPTER FIFTEEN

The house was quiet. But not the kind of quiet that felt earned.

It was the silence of something holding its breath.

Ted sat on the couch, laptop open in his lap, the soft glow of the screen painting his face in bluish light. He wasn't typing. Not really. Just touching the keys now and then, fingers tapping like they were trying to remember how language worked.

Luna lay across his feet. Her head was flat on her paws, eyes half-lidded. Not asleep. Just… watching.

She hadn't moved in an hour.

Gabriela stood in the hallway, leaning against the frame of the dining room arch, arms crossed. One slipper on. The other somewhere behind her in the kitchen. She didn't remember kicking it off.

"Celeste was fired," she said.

Ted didn't look up. "Who?"

"The new girl at The Pack Station. The one who gave you Luna's leash last time. Kinda shy."

"Oh. Yeah." He blinked. "Did she do something wrong?"

Gabriela stepped into the room, barefoot now, crossing the tile with slow, silent strides. "I'm not sure. Rueben didn't say."

Ted shrugged, eyes on the screen. "Probably just didn't fit."

Gabriela sat at the edge of the armchair across from him, hands resting on her thighs. Her gaze dropped to Luna.

"She told me Luna was testing me."

Ted's fingers stopped moving.

Gabriela leaned forward slightly. "Not you. Me. She said Luna tests people. Watches to see where the cracks are."

Still nothing from Ted.

Luna lifted her head.

Slowly. Deliberately.

Her eyes met Gabriela's with a calm that bordered on smug. Not aggressive. Not challenging. Just... present. Unyielding.

Gabriela didn't look away.

Not this time.

Her spine straightened. Her breathing slowed.

In the hallway, the light dimmed a fraction. Not a flicker—just a slight drop, like a hand cupped over a flame.

And then—just for a fraction of a second—Luna blinked.

Not a twitch.

A blink.

A cooling sensation touched Gabriela's temples. The kind of feeling you get when someone thinks about you from far away.

Gabriela exhaled, low and steady, like she'd just passed through a checkpoint she hadn't known she was approaching.

She stood and walked to the bookshelf near the window. Pulled down the tin that held her milagros—the old ones, the real ones. Some were bent. One was rusted. They clinked softly as she poured them into her palm and sifted through them with her fingers.

She chose four. The heart. The eye. The hand. The ear.

Protection. Sight. Action. Listening.

She placed them in a shallow ceramic dish on the windowsill, but whispered nothing over them. Not yet. Just an arrangement.

The air seemed to hum. Barely. Like a throat clearing in the walls.

Behind her, Ted made a noise—a small one. Almost a question. But when she turned, he was staring blankly at the screen again, eyes unfocused, hands still.

Luna hadn't moved.

Gabriela looked back at the charms.

No prayers tonight.

But she was thinking about it.

* * *

The Pack Station was closed.

Outside, the wind moved in low bursts across the parking lot, stirring mulch from planter beds and sending a forgotten tennis ball skittering under a car. The stars above Las Cruces were clear and sharp, like someone had etched them in glass.

Inside, the boarding wing held its breath.

No human voices. No barking. Just the soft, synchronized sound of sleeping dogs.

A red light blinked from the ceiling-mounted camera in the hallway—steady, mechanical, indifferent. The time-stamp ticked forward in the bottom corner of the frame.

01:14:07

01:14:08

01:14:09

Twelve kennels.

Twelve dogs.

No. Eleven dogs. One kennel stood empty.

Camera logs didn't note the absence. No barking had been reported. But the absence was real—visible. Empty space framed by shadows.

One by one, the dogs rose.

No signal. No alarm. Just motion—slow, controlled, eerie in its precision.

The first sat up, head cocked slightly to the left.

The second mirrored the movement exactly.

Then the third. Then all the rest, as if called not by sound, but by shared instinct.

None of them barked.

None moved toward their gates or paced their enclosures.

They simply sat, facing the same direction: the back wall of the hallway.

Not the cameras.

Not the doors.

The wall.

To any human observer, there was nothing there. Just tile and grout and the mounted bracket for the leash rack— empty now, waiting for morning.

But the dogs stared as if it mattered.

As if something had been buried there, or had emerged.

The camera's feed stuttered once—horizontal lines streaking across the screen. A flicker, then black.

01:15:00

01:15:01

01:15:02

The video resumed.

The dogs were lying down again.

No sound.

No motion.

But the wall behind the bracket was different now. The faint smudge of dust that had outlined Celeste's hidden milagro was gone. The charm itself had vanished.

No sign of it on the tile. No hint of disturbance.

But the air wasn't the same. Something had come through.

Not loud. Not fast. But real. Like the moment after a seal breaks on a jar—you don't hear it, but you feel the pressure change.

Only the subtle, invisible tension in the air. The feeling of a place where something small had been removed—something that had been holding a boundary without anyone knowing.

The camera's red light blinked twice, then steadied.

The recording rolled forward into morning.

As if nothing had happened.

CHAPTER SIXTEEN

"Accidents"

The ambulance lights spun slowly and soundlessly in the morning haze, casting red pulses across the stucco walls of David Clark's house. Gabriela stood at the edge of her own driveway, arms folded tight against the still-cool air, watching as the EMTs loaded David into the back.

He winced with every movement, cradling his right arm like it belonged to someone else.

"I swear to God, I tripped over something," he muttered. "I felt it. Big. Like a dog."

One of the paramedics nodded politely as they fastened another strap.

Gabriela glanced at the sidewalk. No blood, no fur, no leash. Just a broken length of picket fence from David's little white boundary line, splintered outward like something had pushed through from the inside. A rolled-up newspaper still sat in the grass—flattened, unopened.

Luna was sitting beside her, unnaturally still.

Not relaxed. Not tense. Just… poised.

Ted stood a few feet behind them, barefoot on the gravel, sipping his coffee like this was background noise. His robe hung open at the collar, exposing the white T-shirt beneath, spotless, pressed. He hadn't said a word since they'd stepped outside.

"He's okay," Gabriela offered, half to Ted, half to herself. "Just a fracture, they think."

Ted sipped again. Swallowed.

"It's a clean break," he said finally. "He'll heal."

Something in his tone brushed the edge of emotion and stopped short. Not cruelty. Not detachment. More like irrelevance.

Gabriela turned slightly. "He said he tripped over a dog."

Ted blinked. "Luna was inside."

"Not ours."

He didn't answer.

Luna looked up at him, and Ted's gaze flicked down—just briefly—before returning to the sidewalk where the fence had snapped. Gabriela saw the exchange. A non-verbal checksum. Like a script confirming itself.

She scanned the street. The cul-de-sac was still, save for Mrs. Mendez watering her roses across the way. A few curtains stirred with watching neighbors. The air smelled like dust and ozone—leftovers from a weak storm that hadn't delivered on its thunder.

And something else—something sour. Gabriela wrinkled her nose. It passed before she could name it, but it clung behind her teeth like iron and mildew.

Gabriela took a step forward and crouched near the break in the fence. There were gouges in the dirt—deep ones. More like claw marks than shoe prints. Parallel tracks, erratic, like whatever caused them had circled back and then vanished.

One of the pickets was wet near the base. Discolored. A splintered nub showed a smear—not blood, not sap. Something gray-brown and fibrous, like a sliver of old hide. She didn't touch it.

She stood. "If it wasn't a dog... it should've left footprints."

Ted shrugged. "Maybe it was a raccoon."

"In broad daylight?"

He said nothing. Just turned and walked back toward the house, coffee mug in hand. Luna followed. She didn't trot. She didn't wag.

She just walked behind him, like a shadow with muscle memory.

Gabriela stayed put for a few seconds longer, watching the ambulance roll away. David hadn't screamed when they adjusted his arm. He'd gone pale instead—eyes wide, breath shallow. He looked less like a man in pain and more like someone who'd seen something he couldn't name.

And for just a second—when they wheeled him past Luna—he had flinched.

Not from her teeth. From her eyes.

Gabriela turned slowly and followed her husband inside, locking the door behind her with a hand that suddenly felt cold.

* * *

The house felt colder than it should've.

Not in temperature—in presence. Like something had slipped in with them and shut the door quietly behind.

Gabriela moved to the kitchen without speaking. She needed rhythm. Tasks. Coffee, toast, clean surfaces. But when she reached for the kettle, Ted was already there—standing still, one hand on the handle, the other holding his half-empty mug like it was fused to his fingers.

He hadn't changed out of his robe. The sleeves hung like forgotten promises.

"I've got it," she said softly, brushing past him.

Ted didn't move at first, then stepped aside like a machine completing a programmed sequence. He set his mug down exactly in the center of a coaster—without looking—and walked to the refrigerator.

Luna was already sitting near the fridge.

She wasn't begging. She wasn't even looking at the refrigerator.

She was looking at Ted.

And Ted—without a word—opened the fridge, reached into the cheese drawer, and pulled out a slice. He unwrapped it like he wasn't even present, tore it in half, and set it gently on the floor beside Luna's paws.

She didn't lunge. She didn't even sniff. She waited five seconds before bending slowly, precisely, and eating it.

Gabriela watched the whole exchange from the other side of the island. She didn't speak, didn't interrupt. She just observed.

When Ted turned back toward the coffeepot, she finally said, "You didn't used to give her cheese in the morning."

Ted blinked. "She was hungry."

"She's always hungry."

"She's been good."

There it was. That strange, creeping justification. As if Luna were a coworker with performance metrics.

"She didn't even ask," Gabriela added. "Not really."

Ted didn't respond. He poured another cup, filled it only halfway, and took the first sip like it might rewire his brain.

"Did you sleep?" she asked, changing lanes.

"Sure."

"In the bed?"

He tilted his head slightly, considering. "Started there. Moved to the couch. Luna was restless."

"You were following her around last night," Gabriela said. "Every time she moved, you moved."

"That's not…"

"What?"

Ted blinked again. This time slower. "I just didn't want her to be alone."

Gabriela's hand tightened around the edge of the counter. "She's a dog, Ted."

Ted looked at her then—not sharply, not with anger—with a delay, like the statement had to buffer before it registered.

"I know that," he said.

But he didn't sound convinced.

Luna had finished her cheese. She was lying down now, head resting between her paws, eyes flicking between them like she was cataloging the tones of their voices.

Gabriela reached into a drawer and pulled out a folded piece of paper—her hidden map of the neighborhood. She didn't open it. Not yet. Just laid it flat on the counter between them, the creases showing how many times it had been unfolded and marked.

"I think something's happening on our street," she said.

Ted tilted his head.

"David's injury," she continued. "The car crash at the corner. The Peterson kid's cat that went missing last week. The ladder fall on Larkspur. All in the last two weeks."

"Coincidence," Ted said, sipping his coffee.

"You don't even know what I wrote down."

He shrugged.

Luna let out a single breath. Not a huff. Not a sigh. Just a measured exhale. Ted glanced at her. Like clockwork.

Gabriela watched him do it.

"What if she's doing something?" Gabriela said, her voice barely above a whisper.

Ted's shoulders went still. The coffee mug paused halfway to his mouth.

Gabriela pressed on. "Not just being clever. Not just training us. What if it's… something else?"

"She's a good dog," Ted said, setting the cup down carefully. "She hasn't done anything."

"You say that like she's your boss."

He didn't rise to the bait.

He just looked down at Luna, then back at Gabriela, and said, "She's part of this house."

And with that, he left the kitchen—mug in hand, feet padding silently on the tile. Luna stayed a beat longer before following, tail low, ears neutral.

Gabriela stood alone in the quiet, the folded paper between her hands now damp with sweat.

She looked down. Her hand had left a faint print on the counter, like she'd been leaning on a hot stove.

She unfolded the map. Red circles marked every accident.

And in the center, a small ink star:

Their house.

CHAPTER SEVENTEEN

The light was dying in long strips across the pavement when Nia Wallace stepped out of her car. She killed the engine but left the door open. The day's heat clung to the seats like sweat.

She crouched near the intersection of Larkspur and Cholla View, the soles of her boots flattening into dust. The blacktop here was gouged with two long, angular skid marks—jagged arcs that peeled off hard from the curve and ended in a slumped silver sedan kissing the base of a leaning lamppost.

The impact hadn't been fatal. A single occupant, mid-thirties, shaken but alive. Claimed a dog had darted out in front of him "like it wanted to die." Said it wasn't any breed he recognized. "Big. Low. Silent."

No sign of a dog. No hair. No prints.

Just the two stripes baked into the asphalt, and a busted fender sagging like a torn smile.

She pulled her phone out and snapped a photo of the angle, the distance from the corner, the stretch of broken curb. Every part of her mind said "accident"—except the part that counted.

Because this wasn't the first one. And it was too close to the others.

Too close to him.

She rose, brushing off her slacks with a hand that was slower than usual. Her hip ached. The low desert air carried a fatigue she couldn't name. Not tiredness. Not heat. Just a kind of… friction. Like her thoughts were rubbing raw against something they couldn't push through.

The sun had dropped behind the roofline now, casting the Tompkins' house in long shadow.

She didn't remember walking toward it, but there she was—shoes crunching over gravel, the smell of watered plants and distant dog food thick in her nose.

There was no reason to knock. It wasn't official. Not yet.

She just wanted to see.

The windows glowed faintly with interior lights, pale gold behind sheer curtains. And behind one of them— motionless, unmistakable—stood the dog.

White fur. Tan mark over one eye.

Eyes locked on her.

Luna.

Nia stopped in her tracks.

The dog didn't bark. Didn't pace. Didn't tilt her head like a curious mutt in a window.

She just stared. Still. Intent.

Something in Nia's spine twitched—reflexively straightening. Like her nervous system remembered something before her mind caught up.

"Jesus," she muttered under her breath.

She turned her head deliberately, pretending to scan the yard. Then she looked back.

Still there.

Unblinking.

Not just looking *at* her, but looking *through* her. Like Luna had already filed her away.

Nia's hand dropped to her side and unhooked her small notepad from her belt loop. She flipped to the back pages—the habitual space for odd notes.

There it was again.

Luna.

Already written.

Twice.

Once in block print, scratched out.

The second, in her usual handwriting. Undated. Circled. No context.

She didn't remember writing it either time.

She looked back at the window.

Empty.

No dog. No movement. Just the curtain.

She flipped the notebook shut, rehooked it, and told herself nothing was wrong.

She walked back toward her car with even steps. But as she opened the door and settled into the seat, her right hand hovered over the ignition for a few seconds too long.

Inside her skull, a thought whispered—not spoken, not rational:

What if this has nothing to do with Smash?

What if Smash was just the first one who deserved it?

She shook her head once—hard. Reaching into the glove box, she found a protein bar and bit it in half with more force than necessary.

"Get your head on straight," she whispered.

The last of the daylight drained out behind her as she pulled away from the curb, tires whispering over the road like something retreating.

Behind her, the curtain stirred once more.

No wind. Just movement.

CHAPTER EIGHTEEN

The house had fallen into a rhythm Gabriela didn't trust.

Ted moved in silent loops: garage to kitchen, fridge to couch, bedroom to Luna's bed, and back again. His footsteps didn't echo anymore—they just existed, like furniture that changed position overnight.

Luna rarely left his side during the day. At night, she wandered. Always came back. Always watched.

Gabriela waited until both of them had settled—the evening lull that wasn't quite peace. Ted had taken a lukewarm shower and fallen asleep with the TV on, a documentary about shipwrecks murmuring into static. Luna lay coiled at Ted's feet like she was guarding something. Not Ted. Not the house.

The silence.

Gabriela stepped lightly across the tile and closed herself in the study. She didn't lock the door. That would draw attention. But she clicked it closed and placed a folded towel at the base—just in case Luna had learned how to nudge with her nose.

She lit a candle first. Unscented, stubby. Just enough to push back the dark.

Then she pulled the map from the bookshelf—folded four times, worn soft along the edges. A street layout of

"

Metro Verde printed in faded black and white, given to them years ago by the HOA, along with a passive-aggressive letter about parking rules.

Gabriela flattened it on the desk, held the corners down with a cup of pens, a chunk of rose quartz, and the ceramic dish where she kept her keys and a few bent bobby pins.

She pulled the red pen from her pocket and began to mark.

X—David Clark's house. Broken arm, front yard, claimed he tripped over "something big." Nothing visible. Luna present.

X—Crash on Cholla View. Swerving to avoid a dog. No injuries. Luna unaccounted for that evening.

X—Petersons' missing cat. Gone three days now. Last seen near the alley behind the Tompkins' fence.

X—Ladder fall. Retired veteran on Larkspur. Slipped, broke his hip. Claimed he saw a dog pacing behind his fence—gray, scarred, silent.

She paused at that one. The description didn't match Luna.

It matched Axel.

She tapped the pen gently against her chin, then drew a small arrow next to the X.

Finally, she circled the center point of the map—their own house—and drew a thick, deliberate ring around it. A quarter-mile radius, roughly. Barking range. Visual range. Influence range?

She didn't know what to call it. But everything inside that ring felt warped.

Her pen hovered just past the boundary, near a block she hadn't circled. A house where the dogs never barked back. One of them—fluffy, indifferent, always watching but never joining.

Not Luna's. Not part of the rhythm.

She didn't mark it. Didn't even write a name. But her pen lingered, like her hand knew something her mind didn't want to admit.

She leaned back in the chair, arms crossed. The candlelight danced against the map's creases, casting shallow shadows like rivers. The house creaked behind her—the familiar sigh of settling, but now it sounded like a dog exhaling.

She stood and moved to the small bookshelf in the corner. Pulled down her old anthropology binder— *Symbols, Spirits, and Settlements*. Tucked inside were two milagros: one shaped like a heart, the other like a dog. She set both next to the candle and closed her eyes.

No prayer. Just focus.

"I see you," she whispered.

Behind her, the doorknob creaked. The door swung open on a whisper.

Gabriela turned slowly.

Luna stood in the hallway, half in shadow, half in candlelight.

Not moving. Tail not wagging.

Watching.

Gabriela didn't flinch. She stepped to the desk, picked up the dog-shaped milagro, and held it between her thumb and middle finger like a surgeon with a scalpel.

"This is my space," she said quietly. "You don't come in here."

Luna didn't move.

Didn't blink.

But something shifted behind the eyes. Not fear. Not submission. Calculation.

The milagro in Gabriela's fingers began to warm—just slightly. Enough to sting her skin like a penny held in the sun. She didn't drop it. But she felt it push back.

Then Luna stepped back into the darkness and vanished.

Gabriela exhaled slowly. Blew out the candle. Folded the map carefully and tucked it into a worn manila envelope labeled: *"Insurance – Old,"* something no one would check.

She opened the door. Listened.

Nothing but the hum of the fridge and the low wash of television static.

She walked past the living room. Ted hadn't moved. Remote still in his lap. His head tilted back against the cushion. One eye slightly open.

Luna was nowhere in sight.

Gabriela paused at the edge of the hallway and touched the frame of the family photo on the wall—her and Ted at

195

White Sands, back when things made sense. When dogs were just dogs.

She didn't believe that anymore.

And she didn't believe in accidents.

* * *

The clock read 2:13 a.m.

Gabriela sat upright in bed, still as a struck bell. She hadn't meant to wake, hadn't heard a sound—no bark, no footfall, no whisper of movement—but something had reached her. Not a noise, but a shift in pressure. Like the air itself had taken a breath.

Ted lay beside her, one arm draped uselessly across his ribs, mouth slightly open. The room smelled faintly of his sleep and Luna's fur—warmth, salt, something faintly metallic. Gabriela turned her head slowly.

Luna wasn't in the room.

The dog always returned by midnight. That was her rhythm. Always inside before the air turned cold enough to sting.

Gabriela swung her feet off the bed and padded out of the room, to the front window. She didn't turn on the porch light.

She didn't need to.

Axel was pacing the yard.

Not trotting. Not wandering.

Pacing.

Back and forth across the gravel strip near the front gate, shoulders rolling like a train engine left in idle. His head was down, not sniffing, but tracking. His eyes scanned the darkness like he expected it to spit something back.

He moved like a guard dog—but not for territory. For someone.

Gabriela pressed two fingers to the blinds, just enough to watch without being seen. The moon cast him in partial relief—slate gray, white chest patch, and scars that looked carved, not earned. He made no sound. No panting. No grunt of exertion. Just quiet muscle and method.

A junkyard sentinel, Gabriela thought.

Like something guarding a car lot of broken machines.

Or a man.

He turned abruptly and stopped, staring at the front door like he was listening through the wood.

Gabriela didn't breathe.

Behind her, the sound of claws on tile clicked softly. One-two. Pause. One-two. A pattern with intent.

She didn't turn around.

"Stay," she whispered—not as a command, but as a hope.

The clicking stopped.

Down in the yard, Axel lifted his head. His ears were cropped and stiff, torn at the edges like burnt paper. His breath steamed once, then vanished.

Then he looked up.

Straight at her.

Gabriela held his gaze. No fear. No challenge. Just presence.

Axel didn't flinch.

Behind her, claws clicked again—this time retreating.

She turned slowly. Luna stood at the far end of the hallway, just visible in the moonlight. Her posture was calm, but something in her angle was off. She wasn't watching Gabriela.

She was watching outside.

She knew Axel was there.

She always knew.

Luna sneezed once. Quick and soft. Like a system reset. Then resumed her stare.

Gabriela stepped back from the window and let the blinds fall. The plastic strips whispered closed. She pressed her hand to the sill—felt the pulse in her wrist pounding like footsteps trying to get out.

Luna was still there when she turned around. Not blocking the hallway. Not moving.

Just present.

Gabriela met her gaze.

"You're not the only one who watches," she said aloud.

Luna blinked.

It was the first time Gabriela had ever seen her do it in response to a statement. Not random. Not idle. Responsive.

Then Luna turned and walked away.

Not hurried. Not threatened.

Dismissive.

As she passed the living room, the TV crackled—one frame of static over the sleeping screen. Not enough to wake Ted. Just enough to be noticed.

Gabriela stood in place long after the hallway was empty, the house silent again. The weight of something not-quite-human pressed against the edges of the drywall and furniture like fog against glass.

Ted hadn't moved. She returned to the bedroom.

Outside, through a window that faced the side yard, Axel resumed his patrol.

One lap.

Two.

Then stillness.

He sat near the edge of the property line, square and silent. Facing the street. Facing the dark.

Like a soldier waiting for something to come that hadn't yet earned a name.

CHAPTER NINETEEN

Nia Wallace parked at the edge of a dark lot behind the precinct. She didn't need to be here. She wasn't on the clock. But the walls inside her apartment felt wrong tonight—too close, too quiet. The kind of quiet that made you miss mistakes.

She left the engine off and cracked the windows to let the night air bleed through. Las Cruces didn't have much of a skyline, but the glow still hovered over the city like a false dawn—neighborhood lights, porch bulbs, TVs flickering behind curtains. It all buzzed low in her ears, like insects.

Her notepad sat on the passenger seat, half-open and folded backward. She'd tried to close it. Twice. But it kept drawing her back.

She thumbed to the case notes on Ricky Delmonte—Smash.

Still no confirmed suspects. No weapon recovered. The official cause of death: blunt force trauma from a chain and a broken bottle. No signs of robbery. No forced entry. No clear motive.

Except that the guy was a piece of shit.

Plenty of people wanted him dead. But that kind of logic was emotional, not evidential.

And that didn't sit right with Nia.

She flipped a page. Then another. And then there it was.

Luna.

Written twice.

Once underlined. Once circled.

No context. No timestamp.

No explanation.

She stared at the word like it had been left by someone else. The loop of the 'L' wasn't hers. Or maybe it was, but from a different state of mind. She couldn't remember writing it. But she couldn't shake it either.

The dog.

The way it had looked at her.

Not aggressive. Not friendly. Just aware—like it had read her badge number before she got to the door.

She'd tried to file it away as instinct, paranoia, something that comes with homicide work after too many weird scenes and too little sleep.

But the feeling hadn't faded. It had grown roots.

Nia pulled out her voice recorder and hit record, letting the static fill the space for a moment.

"Case log, Wallace. Informal. Not for submission."

She paused. Looked out the window toward the empty street beyond the precinct fence.

"Delmonte case remains stalled. No new evidence. No witnesses willing to flip. Crime scene incongruent with known habits. Dog was missing. Anchor chain was damaged at the scene."

Another pause. She tapped the recorder against her knee, fast.

"I interviewed Ted Tompkins and his wife two weeks ago. On paper—clean. Professional. Suburban stability. But the man had dead eyes. Not vacant. Just… delayed. Like his thoughts were buffering."

Her voice got quieter.

"The wife was sharp. Watching everything. Holding something back. Not fear. Just calculation."

She stopped recording. Replayed it. Deleted it. Started again.

This time she didn't speak. She flipped back through her notepad and let her eyes land on the list she'd started unconsciously:

David Clark – Broken arm

Car crash – no injuries

Petersons' cat – still missing

Larkspur fall – fractured hip

Smash – murdered

Axel – missing

Luna – ??

All within two blocks.

All inside a radius.

Her pen hovered. She wanted to draw a circle. She wanted to draw a leash.

But that felt insane.

She exhaled hard and turned on the dome light. Bad idea. The sudden brightness made her flinch. She clicked it off and stared into the windshield, where her own reflection stared back—blurred by dust, broken by streetlight glare.

Behind her own eyes, for a split second—

A tan mark. A white face. A canine stare.

Then it was gone.

"I'm missing something," she whispered.

The words didn't echo. They just sat there.

Something moved outside.

A shape—gray, low, fast—crossed the far end of the parking lot and vanished between dumpsters.

Nia reached for her gun instinctively, but didn't draw. She opened her door slowly, stepped out, and stood in the desert breeze.

No sound. No footfalls. No panting.

But she could feel it.

Something had looked back.

She scanned the shadows again. Nothing.

She returned to the car and locked the doors, sat with her hand on the ignition switch, not turning it.

Instead, she reached for the notepad.

Wrote one word. Big. All caps.

AXEL

Then added a second underneath it.

LUNA

Then underlined both.

Her pen snapped in half with a sharp pop.

Ink bled across the page, black and chaotic.

The pattern it made—almost a circle, but broken at the edge—like something had tried to complete it and failed.

She stared at it for a long time, then ripped the page out and shoved it into the glove box.

No filing. No report. Kept close, just in case.

CHAPTER TWENTY

The house was too still.

Not quiet—still. Like the air had congealed. Like sound had been told not to enter.

Gabriela lay on her side, eyes open in the dark. The digital clock glowed red against the wall: 3:38 a.m.

She hadn't heard Ted come to bed. But he was beside her now—his breathing shallow, rhythmic, too even to be natural. Not snoring. Not dreaming.

Just on.

He lay like someone obeying sleep.

She turned her head and looked at him.

His face was soft, expressionless. One arm was bent awkwardly beneath the blanket, like it had been placed there instead of moved there. His eyes were closed, but his lids twitched every so often—not in REM, not in rest. Like flickers of light behind a locked door.

At the foot of the bed, Luna was curled in her usual position. Perfectly still. Not guarding. Not relaxed. More like occupying the space. Her head rested on her paws, but her eyes were open.

Watching the hallway.

Gabriela tried not to breathe too loudly. Not out of fear, but out of strategy. She felt like a spy in her own house, playing dead to avoid being noticed.

She slid one hand beneath her pillow and felt the edge of the folded map she'd hidden there. No symbols. No legends. Just red Xs and a ring that was getting larger every day.

Luna didn't move.

Not even when a breeze kicked through the slightly cracked window.

Gabriela turned onto her back and let her gaze drift upward. The ceiling fan was still. She hadn't touched the remote. Neither had Ted. The silence pressed down, heavy and deliberate, until she felt the weight of her own heartbeat in her ears.

A low sound cut through the dark.

Not inside. Outside.

A scuff of gravel. A short, deliberate step. Then another.

She sat up, slowly and silently, and looked out the window above the headboard.

Axel.

He was back.

Pacing again—same rhythm, same route. Gravel, grass, gravel, pause. Like he was measuring the perimeter of something no one else could see. His scarred shoulder caught the moonlight in bursts, revealing the torn edge of his ear, the tension in his spine. Not stalking. Not hunting.

Patrolling.

Gabriela turned to look at Luna.

Still watching the hallway. Still ignoring the window.

That was the strangest part.

She knew he was out there.

But she didn't stop him.

Didn't confront. Didn't challenge.

She simply allowed it.

As if she understood his purpose—and knew it wasn't her place to interfere.

Gabriela whispered into the dark, a prayer she didn't know the words to: "Let him stay."

Axel paused near the corner of the house, turned his head slowly toward the bedroom window, and blinked once.

Then resumed his route.

Back and forth.

Back and forth.

The sentry nobody summoned.

The protector nobody trusted.

Gabriela lay back down and pulled the blanket to her collarbone. She didn't close her eyes.

She couldn't.

Not with the map under her pillow.

Not with Ted twitching beside her.

Not with Luna guarding the hallway like the bed was a throne room.

Not with Axel drawing silent circles through the dirt.

Not with the sense that the house had already chosen its hierarchy—and Gabriela was still deciding whether to accept it.

She stayed awake until the sky turned lavender.

She never moved.

But before sunrise, with her heart still thudding, she whispered toward the ceiling: "You're not going to win, Luna."

She didn't care if the dog heard her.

In fact, she hoped she did.

CHAPTER TWENTY-ONE

The Pack Expands

The morning was cool in that deceptive way desert mornings are, with just a breath of chill left behind by the night, already surrendering to the sun. Ted clipped the leash to Luna's collar and stepped outside without thinking. It was routine. Or it had been.

She moved differently now. Not unruly or aggressively, just… ahead. A foot farther than usual. A pace that didn't match his. Like she was walking him.

They passed the usual houses, same hedges, same patches of burnt grass, same driveways with oil stains like old blood. A retriever behind one fence let out a single bark. Ted didn't flinch. Dogs bark. It's what they do.

But then a shepherd two houses down barked once, same pitch, same beat.

Then the pit mix on the corner. Then the chihuahua by the mailbox. All single barks. Same rhythm. One after another.

Ted scratched his ear absently, like there was something in the air. He glanced at Luna. She hadn't barked. She hadn't looked. She just walked.

His stride shifted half a beat to match hers without him noticing.

Another bark.

This one came from a backyard across the street, muffled by stucco walls. Then another. Like a code being passed—one bark at a time, like sonar pings from some hidden trench.

Ted paused for a moment. "Weird," he said aloud, trying to name it without caring to understand it.

Luna stopped. Not to sniff or pee, she just stopped, turning her head slightly toward the corner house with the boarded windows.

Inside, a dog howled. Not a bark. A low, rising wail.

Ted blinked, suddenly aware that his breath had synced with hers.

Luna's head snapped away. She kept walking.

Ted followed.

Behind them, in yards and windows and garages, dogs pressed noses to glass. Some stood on hind legs. One scratched at a door, as if knocking. Ted didn't see any of it. He kept his eyes on the sidewalk.

The leash stayed slack, but his shoulders leaned ever so slightly toward her—gravity behaving like allegiance.

Ahead, Luna's tail twitched once.

Behind them, the barking stopped all at once like a conductor had dropped the baton.

The next block was quieter—too quiet for mid-morning. No lawnmowers. No leaf blowers. Even the wind felt like it was holding its breath.

Luna's gait shifted.

Ted noticed just enough to glance down and say, "What is it, girl?" in that half-aware voice people use when they're not really expecting an answer.

She had already stopped.

Across the street, Ruby stood with her human. An older woman, fifties maybe. Her hair was in a braid that hung halfway down her back, with a wide-brimmed sun hat shading her face, and a heavy reusable grocery bag slung over one arm like a shield. Ruby stood beside her, tall and thick around the shoulders. Part chow, part mystery—built like a door that didn't budge unless you had the right key.

The woman didn't look over. Didn't acknowledge Ted. She didn't pause in her steps. She just walked.

Ruby didn't.

She stared at Luna with the focus of someone who had seen storms and wasn't afraid of wind.

Luna's hackles raised—not dramatically, not puffed— a ripple across her back like static under fur. Her lips stayed closed, but her body vibrated once.

Then came the bark.

One bark. Just one. Not loud, but surgical—cutting across the street like a crack through glass. It wasn't a "hello" or a "get back." It was a command. A signal.

Ruby didn't blink.

She didn't bark back either. Just stood her ground. Her ears twitched once. Her eyes narrowed.

Then came the growl.

Low. Subsonic. Like a diesel engine idling in a garage. It wasn't for Ted. It wasn't even for Luna, not exactly. It was for something else. Something deeper. The thing behind the eyes.

Ted squinted across the street. "That's Ruby, right?" he said to nobody. "The chow mix from over— What's wrong with her?"

Luna took a single step back. Almost unnoticeable. Her tail didn't tuck, but it didn't wag either. Her ears twitched sideways.

Ruby's human, still walking, gave the faintest nod— like she'd just heard a thought and dismissed it. Her hand flexed on the grocery bag, then relaxed.

She didn't look at the dogs. Didn't need to.

Ruby's human never broke stride. Didn't look at the stand-off, didn't pull the leash. Just kept walking as if she knew the growl would be enough.

And it was.

Luna turned her head first, then her whole body. They resumed the walk, but her pace was off now. Slower. Less assertive.

Ted reached into his pocket, found a cheese cube wrapped in plastic, and handed it to her without thinking. She took it gently, like she always did.

But she didn't look up at him.

She kept glancing back—once, twice—toward Ruby, now just a dot disappearing into the morning's heat haze.

Ruby didn't look back. She didn't need to. Her job was already done.

The street stayed quiet long after they'd passed.

*　*　*

It began as background noise.

The kind you filter out: the scrape of a leash clip, a bark three houses down, the low rattle of a screen door closing behind someone calling, "Just five more minutes."

But underneath the soundtrack of suburbia, something else had taken root. A new tempo.

And those who lived there—bored, tired, obedient themselves—never noticed the shift.

A woman in blue pajamas stood barefoot in her kitchen at 3:12 AM. Her eyes were puffy. The microwave clock glowed green behind her. Her Pekingese barked once— sharp, precise. She opened the fridge. Her fingers hovered, trembling, then settled on an unopened block of Gouda cheese. She unwrapped it with care, sliced it into perfect coins, and laid them on a porcelain saucer.

The dog watched from the hallway, eyes gleaming like wet buttons.

She knelt like she was lighting a candle in a cathedral.

She placed the saucer at his feet and whispered, "Only one slice at a time, baby."

She didn't go back to bed.

She sat on the floor and waited for his cue.

Mr. Wilkins, a retired postal worker and knee replacement veteran, spent twenty minutes folding an old moving blanket into a perfect triangle in the garage. He slid it across the concrete, aligning the edge with the freezer. His beagle, Hershey, trotted over, sniffed it once, then turned in a tight circle and curled up on it.

Wilkins watched for approval.

He got a tail twitch.

He smiled, whispered, "Good boy," and limped back into the house to get a fresh water bowl—just in case.

In a split-level on Arroyo Vista, a young couple installed blackout curtains over every window. It was a Monday. They both had work. But when their whippet refused to leave the guest bedroom, they took turns calling in sick.

By noon, the lights were off, the doors locked, and the dog lay on a velvet pillow in total silence.

The curtain-light painted them like worshippers at an altar.

The husband sat cross-legged on the carpet, drawing concentric circles on his arm with a black Sharpie. The wife braided old phone charger cords into a leash. Neither spoke.

A teenager in basketball shorts paused mid-skate-trick in his driveway. His golden retriever had barked once—high-pitched, clipped. Not a warning. A command.

The boy stepped off the board and walked it back to the garage. His friends across the street yelled, "Yo, come on!"

He didn't answer.

He opened the freezer, took out a popsicle, and held it until his dog took a bite.

The boy held it like communion.

Then he finished what the dog left.

Three backyards in a row, dogs had stood on picnic tables. A boxer, a mutt, and a corgi. They all stood like generals at war briefings, staring down at their owners from above.

No one noticed the oddity.

One man called up to his corgi like it was a toddler on a playground slide. "Careful now," he said, smiling. "You wanna jump to Daddy?"

The dog didn't move.

Inside a duplex with peeling paint, a woman who worked double shifts at the urgent care center stopped cooking dinner to place her forehead against her pit bull's. It had started as a quick nuzzle. Something familiar. But now she stood like a supplicant, eyes closed, whispering promises into his fur.

"I'll quit night shifts. I'll stay home more. I swear."

The pit bull blinked slowly, then walked away.

She stood there for a long time.

A man opens five cans of wet dog food, mixes them with peanut butter, and uses a silicone spatula to smear the mixture into the slats of a baby gate.

A woman loads her car with camping gear—blankets, jugs of water, dog toys, rawhide chews. She never loads a tent.

A teenage girl sews patches onto a denim vest for her chihuahua: "Leader of the Pack," "Stay Human," "He Barks, I Listen."

A barista holds up the line at a local coffee shop to walk outside and hand a whipped cream cup to a mutt sitting alone on the patio. "He looked patient," she says with a shrug, and no one objects.

At the dog park, the silence was the most unnatural thing of all.

Dogs usually ran. Barked. Snarled. Begged. But now they formed circles—one near the shade structure, one under the slide, one by the drinking fountain. Each circle faced inward, heads low, tails still.

Their owners sat on benches, phones forgotten in their laps, watching their dogs like cult members in pews.

Some mouthed silent words they couldn't remember learning.

A stranger might have walked in and thought it was a training session. But no leashes twitched. No commands were issued. No treats exchanged.

Just reverence.

Just alignment.

And above it all, in a neighborhood that used to run on clockwork and calendar apps and dinner bells, a new rhythm was rising. Not loudly. Not quickly. But steadily. Coordinated.

Barks were no longer just barks. They came in patterns —four short, one long; one long, three short. Some carried high like a clarinet. Others thudded low like timpani.

The neighborhood didn't hum anymore. It throbbed.

Like a signal sent from bone to bone, echoing down leashes that no longer needed hands.

* * *

The grocery store smelled like bleach and slow decay. Meat cases hummed under fluorescent light, everything too bright, too cold. Ted stood in front of the hot dog section like he'd forgotten what he'd come for. A mother wheeled a cart past, her toddler pointing at Luna and giggling. Ted didn't notice. His eyes were fixed on the meat.

Rows of sodium-packed tubes, identical in size, color, and promise. His hand moved before his brain did. Not the brand they usually bought. Something cheaper. More of them.

He picked up three packs. Then added a fourth. Five seconds later, he set one back, almost like he was embarrassed.

It felt like a decision, but it wasn't. It was remembering something she hadn't said yet.

He carried them to the self-checkout in a daze. He didn't get anything else. No buns. No mustard. Just meat in plastic.

In the parking lot, Luna jumped into the backseat of the Jeep like she already knew the routine. But there was no routine. Not today.

Ted opened one of the bags right there, the packaging snapping like sinew. A quiet hiss of escaping preservatives. He held out a single hot dog.

Luna sniffed it. Took it without ceremony. Didn't chew.

She had been waiting for it. Not impatient. Just... expectant.

Ted put the rest on the seat beside her, unwrapped. Meat sweating under the desert heat, shining like wet skin.

The passenger seat had become an altar.

He pulled out of the lot without turning on the radio.

Halfway home, he slowed to a crawl behind a garbage truck. Something about the rhythm of its compactor clunking felt hypnotic. He matched its pace for three blocks, not thinking, not rushing.

Luna stood on the seat now, front paws on the armrest, watching the truck, ears forward.

Ted reached over and scratched behind her ear, slowly, without looking.

"You like trucks now?" he asked softly, but it wasn't a real question. More like a verbal tic. A reflex left over from a different version of him.

Luna didn't move. Just stared forward like something important was about to happen.

Ted blinked, and for a second, saw something in the side mirror—a shape at the curb, watching. But when he looked again, it was gone.

When they got home, Ted forgot to close the garage. He left the groceries on the kitchen counter—if you could call them that. He didn't put the meat away. Didn't refrigerate it. Just... set it there, limp and sweating, like evidence.

Then he walked into the living room and sat down on the couch without removing his boots. The TV remote was in his hand, but he never turned it on.

Luna padded in behind him. Jumped up. Settled next to him, her warm flank pressed against his thigh.

Ted blinked slowly. His jaw was slack. Something inside him itched—not pain, but a presence. A tug at the back of the brain like he'd left the stove on in a house he no longer lived in.

He scratched at his temple. Nothing there. No words. Just the low pulse of breath beside him.

Then—

Outside, a dog barked three times in quick succession.

Then, from somewhere across the street, another replied —long, deep, and delayed.

Ted didn't notice. But Luna did.

Her eyes opened.

Her ears twitched.

And her tail, slowly and deliberately, curled once across the couch cushion, as if to say:

Good.

He's learning.

CHAPTER TWENTY-TWO

Detective Nia Wallace didn't know why she'd come back to the block. Officially, she told herself it was a follow-up—routine confirmation of a statement, checking camera angles, neighbor interviews. But she wasn't holding a clipboard. Wasn't even wearing her badge. Just jeans, a gray tee, and sneakers. Civilian. Watching.

The houses on Alta Monte looked the same as always. Cookie-cutter stucco and adobe, Xeriscape yards lined with gravel and bleached bone rock. Not much moved. A wasp circled a porch light. A palm frond rustled. A kid's bike leaned against a tree.

And then—

Barking.

First one dog, then another. Then three, four. Layers of sound folding over each other, close and distant. Not frantic. Not alert.

Rhythmic.

Short bursts. One bark. Then silence.

Another. Then silence.

Like call and response across streets, across fences.

Nia turned her head—not toward the noise, but away. An unconscious flinch. A gut-level avoidance, like her ears knew better than her eyes.

A woman across the street wrestled with a trash bin. Her Labrador stood beside her, leash loose, body still. Not looking at the woman. Looking straight across the street. Right at Nia.

She blinked. The woman cursed at the bin lid, oblivious. The Lab didn't move. Didn't pant. Just watched her.

Nia took two steps back and broke the gaze. She felt cold.

She crossed to the curb, forcing herself to study a storm drain, pretending to check street infrastructure. She was good at pretending. But the barking didn't stop.

Across the road, a Doberman sat in a fenced yard. No leash. No collar. Its head slowly turned as she passed, eyes tracking her like a turret.

Another bark. This one from behind her.

She whipped her head around—too fast, too sharp—and caught herself. Forced her hands to stay at her sides.

"No big deal," she muttered. "Dogs bark. That's what they do."

It was a sentence she'd said before. She just didn't remember when. Or why.

She didn't believe it.

At the end of the block, a woman in a bathrobe opened her front door and poured something into a dog bowl. It wasn't dog food. It was spaghetti. Steaming, fresh, red-sauced spaghetti.

The German shepherd at her feet wagged once, then sat.

The woman smiled like she'd just fed a child, then shut the door gently.

Nia's pulse picked up.

She started back toward her car, pretending again. Hands in her pockets, eyes low. But at the corner, a movement stopped her.

A man came out of his house, shirtless, cradling a small black dog like a baby. He walked barefoot down the driveway and sat cross-legged on the sidewalk, setting the dog in his lap.

Then he started humming. Wordless. Eyes closed. Dog motionless. Their bodies rocked together slightly, like a lullaby.

Nia took a step closer, and her phone buzzed.

She jumped, heart hammering.

Just a message:

LCPD CASE #087-11

REMINDER: Interview follow-up: Ted Tompkins.

She turned off the screen and looked up.

The man with the dog was gone. No sign. No sound.

But a new sound joined the air—a low rumble. Not a growl.

A car idling.

She looked down the street.

Ted Tompkins' Jeep was parked two houses down, crooked in the driveway. The rear window was open.

A dog's face appeared in the gap.

Nia froze.

Luna.

She didn't bark. Didn't move.

She just was—a presence, magnetic and absolute.

Nia couldn't see her eyes clearly from where she stood, but it didn't matter. Something passed between them anyway.

A sound behind Nia changed pitch—wind in a gutter, or breath through a throat. She turned halfway, instinct twitching, but the Jeep turned off. Just like that.

No sound. Just a sudden absence of it. The engine died. The window rolled up.

And Luna disappeared.

Nia backed up two steps. Then three.

She turned. Walked fast, but didn't run. Back to her car. Back to the normal world where dogs didn't stare you into forgetting your own name.

She got in. Locked the door. Started the engine.

Then sat there for a moment. Hands on the wheel. Breathing.

The barking had stopped.

She hadn't noticed when.

But she knew, deep in her molars, that when it started again…it would be speaking directly to her.

CHAPTER TWENTY-THREE

Rueben

Gabriela parked crooked in front of The Pack Station, two wheels kissing the painted line. She killed the engine, sat back, and stared through the windshield.

The place looked normal. Too normal.

No stray dog hair stuck to the windows. No muddy paw prints near the entrance. The sign—*THE PACK STATION: Dog Daycare & Training*—gleamed like it had been Windexed twice. Someone had even hosed down the walkway, judging by the faint rivulet trailing off into the gutter. It was the first time she'd ever seen the place not look… lived in. That bothered her.

She exhaled sharply and stepped out. Her boots tapped on damp concrete. Above the door, a small bell jingled as she pushed it open.

Inside, the familiar scent of dogs hit her, but it was subdued. Sanitized. As if bleach and air freshener were fighting to drown out the usual musk of fur and slobber. The front lobby was spotless. The couch near the window had been vacuumed to within an inch of its life, and the wall of dog portraits—usually filled with candid shots of tongues and muddy paws—now hung in rigid symmetry, all perfectly aligned.

Rueben was waiting.

He stood behind the front desk like a department store mannequin. Shirt pressed. Name tag straight. Hands folded. No coffee cup, no open jar of peanut butter for treat time, no half-chewed rope toy on the counter. Just him. Still. Watching.

"Gabriela," he said, voice flat as linoleum. "You're early."

She forced a smile. "Just wanted to check on Luna. I thought I might walk her home."

Rueben nodded slowly. "The quiet one. She's doing well."

That phrase stuck: *The quiet one.* Not *Luna*, not *your dog*, not even *she*. Gabriela's brow twitched.

"Mind if I go back and see her?"

A beat too long passed before Rueben responded. "Of course. I'll escort you."

He stepped out from behind the counter like a curtain being pulled back. His movements were precise, robotic, each footfall measured as if he were walking a tightrope. Gabriela followed him down the hall, past framed certificates and motivational pet posters. The usual din of barking and squeaky toys was absent. No rhythmic thuds of paws on vinyl. No whining. No trainer calling out *Sit! Stay! Good!*

Just silence.

And then—

Soft breaths.

They rounded the corner into the main room.

Dozens of dogs sat in organized rows. Not lying down, not playing. Sitting. Upright. Facing the door. Eyes locked on Rueben and Gabriela as if they'd been waiting. A Doberman near the front tilted its head. A husky yawned—slow, exaggerated, like a silent scream. Behind them, a pair of retrievers blinked in eerie synchrony.

Gabriela stopped cold.

"What… What is this?"

Rueben didn't answer. He stood beside her, arms at his sides, watching the dogs with something between reverence and calculation.

A mutt in the second row licked its lips, eyes unblinking.

"Where's Luna?" Gabriela asked, her voice tighter now.

Rueben turned his head—mechanically, slowly—and gestured toward the kennel hallway.

"She's resting," he said. "She prefers the quiet."

There it was again. *Quiet.* Like a code word.

Gabriela took a tentative step forward. The dogs didn't move, didn't growl, didn't even wag their tails. Only their eyes watched. Heavy, pulsing stares. Rueben shadowed her, too close now. She could smell antiseptic on his clothes.

"I've never seen them like this," she said. "Where's— Where's Stephanie?"

"She had a nosebleed," Rueben said, still staring at the dogs. "She's resting too."

Gabriela turned. "What? Is she okay?"

"No one is injured." He said it like a fact, not a comfort.

She moved past him, toward the side hall that led to the kennels. One of the dogs—a brindle boxer—stood up and blocked her path. Not aggressively, just there. Tall enough to make her hesitate.

Rueben took a step closer. "Perhaps I should walk Luna to your home later," he offered. "She's very calm today."

"No," Gabriela said. "I'll take her now."

She brushed past the boxer, who didn't resist, but didn't move either. Its head swiveled as she passed, tracking her. A row of smaller dogs behind it stood in unison, eyes on her like searchlights.

She pushed forward, pulse rising.

The kennel hall was dimmer than usual. The overheads were off—only the sun through the side windows lit the path. Shadows cut long stripes across the floor. As she moved, she felt them like tripwires.

Then, there she was.

Luna.

She was in the fourth kennel down, lying on her belly, chin resting on her front paws. Her eyes met Gabriela's. No tail wag. No bark. Just watching.

"Hey girl," Gabriela whispered.

Luna's ears perked slightly. That was it.

She knelt, fingers wrapping around the gate latch—but stopped short.

Something was wrong with her hand. Not numb, but... reluctant. Like her own body wasn't convinced it should move forward. She shook it off and unlatched the gate.

Luna didn't move.

Gabriela reached forward, stroking behind her ears. The fur was warm, soft, real. But the dog didn't lean in. She didn't lift her head. She just accepted the touch like a statue receiving weather.

Behind her, Rueben stood at the entrance to the hallway, motionless.

"You alright, girl?" Gabriela whispered. "Wanna go home?"

Luna blinked, then slowly—*slowly*—pushed herself up and walked forward.

Not toward Gabriela.

Past her.

Toward Rueben.

Just before reaching him, Luna stopped, turned, and sat. Facing Gabriela again. Watching.

The spell—whatever it was—tightened.

Gabriela rose slowly, pulse now an audible thud in her ears. She didn't know whether she was sweating or freezing. She couldn't tell if she'd walked into something sinister or if her own mind was unraveling.

"Rueben," she said, steady as she could manage, "what the hell is going on here?"

He didn't blink.

"She's very calm today," he repeated.

And then he smiled.

Not warmly. Not politely. Just a slow curve of lips that didn't reach his eyes.

The dogs in the main room were still sitting.

Still watching.

Still waiting.

* * *

Gabriela didn't realize she was backing up until she felt the wall against her shoulder blades.

Luna had walked into the kennel on her own—silent, composed, like she belonged there. Gabriela reached out and latched the door without thinking. No sound. No resistance. No joy. Luna simply lay down, folded her paws, and stared forward, regal and still.

Rueben hadn't moved either, but something about him had changed. His hands were still at his sides, but his fingers twitched, almost imperceptibly—thumb brushing the edge of his palm, over and over. A nervous tic, or maybe a rhythm. A metronome. A signal.

Gabriela stepped past him, not making eye contact. She felt a sudden spike of self-awareness, like she was being recorded, like every move was being judged, weighed. She moved down the hallway and back into the main room.

The dogs were no longer seated.

They were standing now.

Lined up. Still silent. Still watching. But closer.

The air in the room had thickened. Gabriela blinked twice, unsure if the lighting had shifted or if her vision was tunneling. It felt like the ceiling was sinking. Or maybe the walls were growing.

Then she noticed it.

There were more people in the room.

Not just Rueben.

Three staff members had materialized while she was in the kennel hallway. She recognized them vaguely—faces she'd seen at the front desk before. A tall woman with dyed red hair. A stocky man with a fading sleeve tattoo. A young guy with sleepy eyes and a broken wristwatch.

None of them spoke.

They weren't standing together. They were dispersed, casual but strategic—near the doors, the exits, the corners.

The redhead was wiping down the counter with no cloth in her hand.

The tattooed man stood by the supply closet with a leash in each fist, just holding them.

The sleepy-eyed guy was crouched near the pack, one hand resting on a mutt's shoulder like a priest giving confession.

And still, no barking. No tail wags. No excited panting. Just… silence. Controlled breathing. Synchronized presence.

Gabriela swallowed.

"Is… uh… is Stephanie okay?" she asked the room.

No answer.

She moved slowly toward the lobby, retracing her path, but something felt off in her steps. The floor seemed tacky under her soles, like every step was being second-guessed by the linoleum. Or by something beneath it.

The dogs parted just enough to let her pass, but didn't break formation. It was like walking through a crowd that *wanted* you to know it was a crowd.

Gabriela reached the front desk.

Rueben had followed silently. He now stood behind the counter again, as if nothing had changed.

The smile was gone.

"You know," she said, trying to inject normalcy into the air like a defibrillator, "I think I'll just come back later. Maybe when Stephanie's here. I—I didn't mean to interrupt anything."

Rueben tilted his head slightly.

"You didn't interrupt," he said. "She's watching."

Gabriela froze. "Who?"

He blinked. Once.

"Luna."

The room contracted.

Gabriela could feel it—not just tension, but *convergence.* Every eye in the room, human and canine, seemed to narrow, just slightly, like aperture rings around a target.

"She's in her kennel," Gabriela said, too sharply. "I just saw her."

Rueben didn't respond. He looked past her toward the main room. So did the redhead. So did the tattooed man. So did the sleepy-eyed kid with the dog.

Gabriela turned.

The dogs were closer.

No longer standing in rows. They'd moved in. Spread out. Angles and vectors. Blocking paths without touching them. One was perched on the front couch. Another sat at the front door, nose an inch from the glass, like it was waiting for a ride that hadn't come.

She turned back to Rueben.

"This isn't okay," she said, her voice flat now. "I don't know what's going on, but I'm leaving. You can keep Luna for the afternoon. Ted will pick her up."

Rueben nodded once. "That's wise."

The way he said it was not comforting. It was dismissive. Like a chess player agreeing to let you forfeit.

Gabriela moved toward the front door. The mutt guarding it didn't move.

She stopped two feet from it. Looked at it.

Its eyes were cloudy—not sick, not old—just… distant. Like it wasn't fully here. Like something else was watching through it.

"Hey, buddy," she whispered, trying her best not to tremble. "Can I get through?"

The dog didn't growl. Didn't move. Didn't blink.

She reached for the handle.

"Gabriela," Rueben said from behind her.

She turned her head slightly.

"You shouldn't leave just yet."

She faced him.

"Is that a threat?"

Rueben actually seemed to consider the question.

"No," he said. "It's an observation."

The dogs took a collective half-step forward.

It was so slight, so quiet, it might not have registered to someone else. But Gabriela felt it. Like the air pressure shifted around her body. Like the pack was ready to close in, but hadn't been given the signal yet.

She turned slowly, eyes scanning.

There were at least thirty dogs in the main room. All ages, all sizes. And they were positioned in a way that left no clear path. Every exit was flanked by both dogs and humans.

The redhead was at the rear door, standing in a pose too stiff to be casual.

The tattooed man was now near the kennel hallway, his leashes draped in front of him like garrotes.

The sleepy-eyed kid was standing fully now, one hand behind his back.

Gabriela took a deep breath, centered herself.

"Let me out," she said, voice low and sharp as cut wire.

Nobody moved.

Then a dog—an old yellow lab near the back—let out a single *huff* of air. Not a bark. Not a growl. Just a breath. Loud enough to be heard. Measured.

The room shifted again. The pressure went from suggestion to intent.

And yet— Gabriela noticed something strange.

There was *one* dog near the corner.

Not looking at her.

Not looking at Luna.

It was looking at the front door.

Head cocked. Ears stiff. As if it expected something.

Not from inside.

From *outside*.

The tension around Gabriela froze for a moment, like the pack had noticed the same thing but couldn't act on it yet.

She didn't know why, but she felt it in her chest.

Something's coming.

Rueben spoke again, voice suddenly softer.

"You'll understand soon," he said. "She's helping us all."

Gabriela's voice was a whisper now.

"She's not helping me."

Rueben smiled again. This time, smaller. More like a private joke he didn't plan to share.

"You're resisting," he said. "That's unfortunate."

The old yellow lab huffed again.

Another half-step forward from the pack.

Gabriela braced herself, feet planted, every nerve screaming—but not in fear. In *defiance*.

Then—

The front door's bell jingled.

The air snapped like a rubber band.

And everything broke loose.

* * *

The jingle of the front door wasn't loud, but in the suffocating silence of the room, it might as well have been a gunshot.

Every head turned.

Except one.

That dog—the one near the corner, the one Gabriela had clocked just moments earlier—didn't move. Didn't flinch. While the rest of the pack shifted in eerie synchrony, it stayed locked in its posture, focused on the door like it had been waiting for the sound. Like it had *known*.

The air in the room fractured.

Gabriela didn't know how to describe it any other way. One moment, she was the target in a noose of mutts and muted handlers. The next, that noose had slackened—not released, not gone—just… loosened.

The dogs froze in awkward mid-pose, as if their instructions had just been garbled. The redhead near the rear door blinked hard, her grip twitching on the knob. The tattooed man turned toward the sound but didn't complete the motion, like his muscles had run out of script.

And Rueben—

He stepped backward.

It wasn't much. A half-inch shuffle. But Gabriela saw it. A break in his center of gravity. A moment of *hesitation*.

That's when Gabriela turned fully and looked.

Through the open front door stepped a middle-aged woman in dark jeans and a loose-fitting hoodie, keys jangling in her hand. She wore wraparound sunglasses and walked with the slow, casual posture of someone who had nothing to prove.

At her side trotted a dog.

Thick coat. Sturdy build. Curled tail.

Chow mix.

Ruby.

Gabriela didn't know the woman's name. She had seen her only once or twice across the street, walking her dog before dusk, but she recognized Ruby instantly.

And so did the room.

The yellow lab near the back *whimpered.*

Not a growl. Not a command.

Fear.

The dog closest to the door, the one that had blocked Gabriela earlier, backed away half a step—an almost comical break in formation.

Ruby didn't snarl. Didn't bark. She didn't even growl. She *walked.*

That was all.

She crossed the threshold and entered the room as though it belonged to her.

The woman with her—Ruby's owner—glanced up, smiled at Rueben, then froze mid-greeting.

Her smile faded. Confusion slid across her face like a film of oil.

"What… What's going on?" she asked, voice trailing off.

Rueben didn't answer. He didn't even look at her. His eyes were locked on Ruby.

Ruby had stopped six feet into the room. She hadn't looked at Gabriela, hadn't looked at the other dogs.

She was staring at Rueben.

No emotion.

No aggression.

Just calm, ancient judgment.

Like she had seen this before.

Gabriela stepped sideways, positioning herself just behind Ruby, body taut. Her hands were trembling now, but not from fear. From recognition.

She didn't know what Ruby was. She didn't know what was happening.

But she knew—*knew*—that Ruby wasn't under whatever influence had infected the others.

The energy shifted again.

Not dramatically. Not with violence.

With tension.

The kind of pressure that comes before thunder.

Rueben blinked once, slowly and deliberately.

"She shouldn't be here," he said.

Gabriela looked down at Ruby. The dog's ears were tilted forward, tail slightly raised but not wagging. Her stance wasn't aggressive—it was *assertive*.

Like she was holding the line.

The other dogs were no longer advancing. Some had backed up. A cluster near the couch was visibly shaking. One whimpered again, low and guttural, then turned and padded away toward the kennel hallway.

Rueben's voice dropped to a whisper, just loud enough to reach Gabriela.

"You brought a fracture," he said. "She's not one of ours."

Gabriela didn't respond.

Ruby took another step forward.

That's when the howling began—not from Ruby, not from Gabriela, not even from the front row of dogs.

It came from *the back*.

Deep in the building.

From the hallway behind the kennels.

One long, broken, wounded *howl*.

Gabriela's stomach turned.

She recognized the sound.

It was Stephanie.

Somewhere in the building.

Screaming like her skull was splitting in half.

Gabriela lunged, but Ruby blocked her, body turning sideways to cut off the path like a guardian intercepting danger.

She wasn't stopping Gabriela from helping.

She was positioning herself for what was coming.

And something *was* coming.

Gabriela turned and looked again at the single dog that hadn't joined the pack.

It was now *standing* at the edge of the couch, eyes locked not on Rueben, not on Gabriela, but on Ruby.

Like it had *known*.

Ruby looked back at it.

And Gabriela saw something pass between them.

Not a growl. Not a nod. Not anything she could describe.

Just *acknowledgment*.

And in that moment, the room held its breath.

Everything was about to snap.

* * *

It started without a sound.

No bark. No shout. No warning.

Just motion.

Ruby lunged—not violently, not recklessly, but *decisively*. Her body cut between Gabriela and Rueben like a blade made of fur and muscle, and every other body in the room flinched.

Every.

Single.

One.

Rueben staggered back, his hands flying up—not in defense, but as if shielding his mind from a sudden burst of light. His expression collapsed into something unrecognizable. Not fear. Not pain.

Disruption.

The redhead by the rear door screamed—short, sharp, and utterly human. She dropped to her knees as if someone had cut her strings. The tattooed man's eyes rolled back. He stumbled sideways into the wall and slid down it, leaving a wet streak of sweat or tears or both on the drywall. The sleepy-eyed kid gasped and doubled over, clutching his skull as if it had just cracked open from the inside.

The dogs?

They collapsed.

Some whimpered. Some bolted to the farthest corner of the room and curled together in a pile—whining, yelping, trembling like they'd just stepped out of a thunderstorm that only they could hear. The Labrador that had earlier controlled the room now crawled across the floor, tail tucked so tight it might've been fused to its ribs. One of the retrievers vomited quietly near the water station.

Gabriela couldn't move. Not out of fear, not from any hold—just awe.

Ruby wasn't snarling. She hadn't bared her teeth. She wasn't even looking at the dogs anymore.

She was locked onto Rueben.

And Rueben was *losing*.

He pressed his palms to his temples, his jaw flexing with unnatural tension, as though trying to hold in a scream that couldn't decide if it belonged to him.

"She's not… supposed to…" he muttered, then grunted—a noise like something slipping out of his throat that wasn't his own voice.

He dropped.

Straight to the ground.

Hard.

No hands to catch him. No grace in the fall.

His face hit the tile with a thud Gabriela would remember forever.

Behind him, the lights flickered.

The kennel hallway lit up in a stuttering pattern—*click-click-click*—as though every bulb were recalibrating to something it no longer understood. From the back, Gabriela heard footsteps—unsteady, uneven.

Stephanie stumbled out into the main room.

Her hair was matted with sweat. One of her nostrils was streaked with blood, dried like rust. Her eyes were wide and unfocused, pupils dilated to the size of dimes. She looked like someone who had just survived a bomb detonation at point-blank range.

She saw Gabriela.

Her lips moved.

No sound came out.

She tried again. This time her voice cracked like torn paper: "Get... out..."

Ruby was already moving. She brushed past Gabriela again, gentler this time, her body curved slightly as if directing Gabriela like a sheepdog with a stray.

Gabriela followed.

The moment she stepped over Rueben's crumpled form, she felt it—the air was *clearer*. The static had lifted. Her joints didn't feel frozen anymore. Her mind no longer buzzed like it was on the wrong frequency.

Ruby was at the front door now.

The mutt that had once blocked Gabriela's path was now lying on its side, belly up, paws twitching in residual spasms like a nightmare was being drained from its core.

Gabriela reached the door, grabbed the handle, and paused.

She turned.

The room was chaos, but silent.

The humans weren't uttering a sound, except one.

Rueben was moaning softly, a sick, wet sound from where he lay on the floor. The other staff members were down or dazed. Stephanie leaned against the hallway entrance like her bones were temporary. The dogs were crumpled together in a shivering, whimpering knot.

Except Luna.

Gabriela spotted her.

Still in her kennel.

Sitting up now.

Head tilted.

Watching.

Just watching.

Her tail thumped once against the plastic kennel floor. A slow, measured beat.

Gabriela stared at her. Something in her chest twisted. Grief and guilt and horror mixing into something unnameable. Her breath hitched.

Luna didn't blink.

She didn't look afraid.

She looked *curious*.

As if this scene wasn't a tragedy.

As if it were an experiment.

And Gabriela had just become the control group.

Ruby nudged her leg gently.

Gabriela turned and opened the door.

Cool air slapped her in the face like a baptism.

They stepped outside.

The sun had shifted overhead, hot now, harsh. The air smelled of cut grass and someone grilling down the street. Normalcy trying to assert itself like nothing had happened.

Ruby's owner stood just outside, still frozen.

Gabriela grabbed her by the elbow.

"You okay?" the woman asked finally.

Gabriela blinked. Her throat felt like sandpaper.

"No," she said. "But I'm better than they are."

The woman looked past her into the daycare, then quickly back to Ruby.

Ruby had turned around, facing the door now. Standing guard.

The bell jangled as the door swung shut behind them.

Gabriela didn't look back.

CHAPTER TWENTY-FOUR

The kitchen smelled like toast and garlic salt—Ted's idea of dinner when left to his own devices. Gabriela sat at the table, hands wrapped around a lukewarm glass of water she hadn't touched. Her knuckles were white. Her knee bounced beneath the table. No part of her had stopped moving since she had walked in the door.

Ted stood by the stove, flipping something in a pan with way too much wrist. He hadn't really looked at her since she'd come home. Just offered a casual, "You alright?" and moved on when she said, "No."

That had been twenty minutes ago.

He scraped something crispy and unidentifiable onto a plate and walked it over.

"You should eat," he said, setting it in front of her like that solved anything. "You're pale."

She didn't look at the food. She didn't look at him. She stared at the grain in the wooden table like it might spell out a warning if she concentrated hard enough.

"Something's wrong with that place."

Ted sighed as he sat down across from her.

"Gabriela—"

"I'm serious." Her voice cracked like a windshield spidering under pressure. "The dogs… They weren't acting like dogs. They were coordinated. They blocked the exits. The staff—Rueben—he wasn't right. None of them were. They were all under—"

"Under what?" Ted interrupted, calm but firm. "Hypnosis? A spell? Come on."

"I'm not joking, Ted. I'm not exaggerating. I *felt* it. Like pressure, like static in my teeth. They weren't barking. They weren't even moving unless they were supposed to. Like someone was directing the whole thing."

Ted folded his arms and leaned back in his chair, lips pressed into a patient smile he'd probably picked up during some company leadership seminar. The kind that says, *I've heard your concern, and now I'm going to gently disregard it.*

"You're emotional," he said. "You had a bad experience. Maybe it triggered some—"

"Don't do that." Her voice sharpened instantly.

He raised his eyebrows.

"Don't reduce it to that. Don't give me the therapist voice. You're not that good at it."

Ted exhaled slowly, rubbed his eyes with the heels of his palms, and finally looked at her. Really looked.

"Okay. Let's pretend I believe you. Let's say Rueben and his staff are possessed by dog spirits or whatever you're implying. What do you want me to do? Call the cops? Tell them the daycare gave you *psychic vertigo*?"

Gabriela didn't answer.

Because she didn't know.

Because it *sounded* insane.

But it *wasn't*.

She could still feel the pressure in her bones, like radio static burned into her spine. She could still see Rueben's face as it collapsed and hear Stephanie's voice cracking as she whispered, "Get out."

"I'm not asking you to believe every word," she said. "I'm asking you to stop pretending everything's fine."

Ted gave her a long, measured look. Then he reached down.

Luna was lying under the table, chin on her paws.

He scratched the top of her head gently.

She made a soft huff, then thumped her tail once against the hardwood floor.

Gabriela flinched.

Ted smiled down at her. "See? This one's not evil."

Gabriela stood abruptly. Her chair scraped back with a screech.

"I'm not doing this," she muttered. "I'm not going to sit here and pretend our dog doesn't have *something* to do with what's happening over there."

"She's a dog, Gabby."

"No. She's not."

Ted's expression stiffened. Not anger, but something worse.

Dismissal.

"You've been on edge since the Smash thing," he said quietly. "I think you're connecting dots that don't exist. Maybe you need—"

"Stop." Gabriela's voice had turned cold. "Don't you dare tell me I need help. Don't turn this into that."

Ted stood, palms open in a peace-offering. "Okay. Okay. I'm sorry. I'm not trying to upset you."

"You're not listening to me."

"I am," he insisted, taking a step closer. "But you have to admit, it *sounds…*"

He didn't finish the sentence.

Because Luna had stood up.

She padded over to Gabriela slowly, softly, not like a dog but like a ripple in fabric. She stopped by Gabriela's feet and looked up.

And smiled.

That canine smile—closed mouth, ears tilted just enough, eyes wide with adoration.

Then her tail thumped once.

Slow.

Measured.

Not excitement.

Not affection.

Acknowledgment.

Gabriela stared down at her.

"Don't pick her up," she said suddenly, her voice barely a whisper.

Ted blinked. "What?"

"Don't pick her up."

He looked confused.

But the moment hung.

Long.

Sharp.

Luna sat back down. Tail still. Head tilted.

Ted's phone buzzed on the counter.

He walked over, checked the screen, and sighed.

"That's my pickup reminder. I've gotta go get her from The Pack Station."

For a beat, neither of them acknowledged the obvious—Luna was right there in the room.

On the floor. Watching. Listening.

Gabriela didn't say a word.

She sat back down, placed her palms flat on the table, and stared at nothing.

Ted grabbed his keys. "I'll be right back."

Luna padded after him.

At the door, he stopped and looked down. "You wanna ride along, girl?"

Her tail wagged.

Twice.

The door clicked shut.

Gabriela stared at the place Luna had been.

The air still felt cold there.

CHAPTER TWENTY-FIVE

Gabriela's Doubt

The house had a new silence, the kind that pressed against the ears until you heard your own blood. Not peace. Not rest. A silence that closed the door and turned the lock from the inside.

Gabriela laid the cloth out on the dresser. Indigo, frayed, folded more times than she could count. She smoothed it flat with both hands like a nurse making a bed. The old ritual came without thought—glass of water to the back left, a white candle in the center, the Virgen de Guadalupe on her printed glass to the right.

She tipped the milagro box until its contents spilled like silver bones: a heart, a hand, an eye, and a pair of tin feet no bigger than seeds. She arranged them the way her grandmother had, the way Alma had taught her again after she'd forgotten. Heart above the flame. Hand at the edge. Eye facing the hallway. Feet angled toward the door.

"Así," she whispered. *Like this.*

The rosary hung on the bedpost. She lifted it free, let it slip into her palm in a pool of small cold beads. A red thread wrapped twice around her wrist, knotted hard, the knot pressed exactly where her pulse lived.

She began in Spanish, voice so low it was barely audible. "Dios mío, guíame. Dame claridad. No milagros —claridad."

Her lips trembled at the word clarity. She wanted proof, not visions. Proof that she wasn't inventing shadows. Proof that Ted wasn't himself. Proof that the dog was not simply a dog.

The candle burned steadily for a moment. Then the glass of water quivered—just enough to make the reflection of the Virgin's eyes swim.

Gabriela froze.

From the hallway came the single sound of a tail tapping the floor.

She turned her head slowly. Luna lay in the doorway, paws crossed, chest rising and falling in the rhythm of a creature who knew no hurry. Her eyes were half-lidded, golden in the light, watching as though the prayer were a television show she'd grown bored with, but refused to leave.

"Quédate," Gabriela whispered. *Stay.*

The tail stilled.

She tried again. "Saint Michael, defend us in—"

The prayer faltered. Her tongue felt thick. She could still say words, but they came out like shapes that no longer fit her mouth.

Not now, she thought. *Don't let her win now.*

She switched to the older phrases, the ones from the kitchens and porches, not the church: "Bendice la casa, que la puerta cierre al mal, que el agua se lleve lo que no es mío." *Bless the house, close the door to what is bad, let the water take what isn't mine.*

The candle flickered. The flame leaned hard, as though a breath had leaned close. The Virgin's printed face bent with it, her eyes shifting away from Gabriela in refusal.

Gabriela pressed the milagro eye flat against the base of the candle. "Mírame," she hissed, throat dry. *Look at me.*

From the doorway came the smallest huff of dog-breath. Not a growl. Not friendly. A sound of acknowledgment.

The silence afterward was worse.

When she finally blew out the candle, the smoke rose in a long gray rope and bent toward Luna. The dog's tail tapped once more. The sound was louder than a gunshot.

* * *

She told herself she was going to Alma's for coffee. She didn't mention the bag she'd packed that morning and shoved under the bed.

Alma opened the door before Gabriela knocked. Her hug was long and smelled of sage smoke.

"You look pale," Alma said.

"I'm fine," Gabriela lied.

Alma's casita was crowded with saints and light. Tin milagros hung from a wire strung across a painted retablo.

Candles dripped wax onto saucers. A dish of herbs lay beside a half-burned stick of copal. The air was thick with smoke and patience.

"Tell me," Alma said.

And Gabriela did—halting, broken pieces, the parts she could bear to say. The silence in the house that wasn't silence. The rhythm in Ted's voice that she didn't recognize. The way the dog seemed to hear prayers better than God.

Alma listened, chin down, eyes locked steady on Gabriela's. When Gabriela faltered, Alma filled the space with a small sound, a nod, a "qué más."

Finally, Alma reached across the table and pressed her hand over Gabriela's. "There's something with you," she said. "I can feel it. Not demon. Something else. Dark, yes. Old. But not demon."

Gabriela closed her eyes, relief and terror in the same breath. "Then what?"

"I don't know yet. But you're not wrong."

The candle flame snapped, leaned sideways, then straightened. No draft moved the air.

Alma stood and gathered what she needed: a sprig of ruda tied with red thread, an egg, and a dish of salt. She lit the copal in a small clay burner shaped like a bird with too-wide black eyes. Smoke filled the room, thick and sweet.

"Feet together. Hands loose," Alma said.

Gabriela obeyed.

The herb brushed her hair, circled her temples, traced the bones of her shoulders. The egg rolled in slow spirals across her scalp, her throat, her chest. Alma murmured—not Latin, not always Spanish, but something in between. The cadence carried more weight than the words.

When the egg passed her throat, it dragged heavy, like iron at the end of a rope. Alma paused, frowned.

"There," she said softly. "It likes to sit there."

"It?"

Alma didn't answer. She cracked the egg into water. The yolk sank, white strands rising in twisting shapes. Some curled like smoke, others like fingers.

Alma studied it without speaking. The silence grew heavier than the smoke.

"It isn't envy. It isn't a curse bought cheap at a market. It's something that learned to live in a house by watching us do it."

"Luna," Gabriela said.

Alma covered the copal bowl with a lid, then uncovered it again as though the smoke itself had objected.

"Wear your red," Alma said. "Salt at the doors, but only a whisper—don't draw lines, just suggestions. Pin the milagro where you sleep. And if it looks at you, don't speak to it. Speak only to your husband. The thing feeds on the attention."

Gabriela nodded. Her throat was tight.

"Do this too," Alma said, handing her a small tin eye from her milagro jar. "Put this where it can watch the hallway. And if you must leave, pack the bag. Don't threaten with it. Just know you can go."

Gabriela almost laughed. "I thought about it this morning."

"Then don't think. Do. A bag doesn't mean you'll leave. It means you're not owned."

The egg in the glass of water sat there, yolk intact, white climbing like heat ripples. Gabriela stared until the shapes seemed to move on their own.

"See?" Alma said.

Gabriela looked away. She didn't want to see.

* * *

The next morning, Ted made breakfast.

It was nothing—eggs, tortillas, coffee—but the act struck Gabriela like lightning. He moved through the kitchen whistling, the way he used to. Not a hollow sound, but careless, alive.

"Morning," he said, and kissed her cheek.

Hope bloomed in her chest like a cruel joke. Maybe the storm had passed. Maybe the prayers had worked.

They ate together. He asked about her classes. He asked about her mother's knee surgery. He smiled when she told him the story about her student who tried to hand in homework written on the back of a grocery receipt. The words came easily.

Luna lay on the rug, eyes half-shut. Her ears twitched in rhythm with every exchange, as though she were marking a score.

When Ted reached for the coffeepot, Gabriela whispered a thank-you to God under her breath. The tension in her chest eased.

"More coffee?" he asked, already pouring.

"Yes, please."

He set the mug in front of her and smiled. A smile so real it hurt.

Then he said, "Drink up, cariño."

The cadence was wrong. Too even. Too perfect.

Gabriela froze. She had heard this voice before, but not from Ted. From the dog.

Her eyes lifted. In the reflection of the sliding glass door, Luna stared back, gaze sharp, as if waiting to see if Gabriela would notice the ventriloquism.

She gripped the mug with both hands. The coffee smelled like home. But the words hung between them like a hook on a wire.

CHAPTER TWENTY-SIX
Scalpel and Suture

The room was glass on three sides, silence on the fourth. A long conference table dominated the space—dark composite with sharp corners and a built-in array of unblinking microphones. At precisely 8:59 AM, the door clicked open and the Kestrel team entered like ordnance.

Colin Narvez, Kestrel's lead systems integrator, walked point.

No handshake. No smile. Just a nod. He wore a charcoal suit, no tie, and a flag pin on the lapel like it had jurisdiction. Behind him, Dr. Mariah Voss, Kestrel's lead analyst, carried a trifold packet of charts tucked under one arm, expression already set to unimpressed. Behind her came Dwight Chen—the program manager—binder in hand, closing the door with the kind of finality that makes your stomach remember other things it's forgotten.

Emi Takahashi was already seated. Her posture was pure architecture—grace in tension, one palm resting lightly on a closed Moleskine. Renee Calderón sat two chairs down, eyes scanning her tablet like she was reading prayers. Marc Shevlin occupied a low-drain emotional state near the end of the table, quietly powering on a laptop that didn't need him. Arjun Mehta fidgeted with a stylus and was halfway through a nervous blink when the door opened.

Ted arrived three minutes late.

He didn't rush. Just slid into the seat beside Emi, shirt collar askew, eyes glassy like a man trying to remember what the meeting was for, not about. He offered no apology. Didn't meet her eyes. Just exhaled through his nose and turned toward the screen at the end of the room.

It was off.

Emi didn't speak. Just gave him a long, slow look—a kind of diagnostic silence.

Colin cleared his throat. "Let's begin."

Mariah cut in with the cold edge of facts.

"The integration milestone was missed by six weeks. Hardware delivered late, firmware non-functional. No executable prototype, no backend coherence. You cited 'AI-adaptive filtering conflicts' in your last update. That's not a blocker—it's an admission."

She flipped open her folder, paper crackling like frost underfoot.

"Your own words, Mr. Tompkins. 'The AI mesh will allow seamless interpolation between non-linear data arrays.' That was from your February brief."

Ted blinked. Something in his brain began walking in a circle, looking for a door.

Mariah continued, her tone clinical. "There is no interpolation. There is no mesh. There's a loop-back artifact cascading through every channel."

Ted reached for his laptop, opened it. The screen stayed black. He stared at it like it might boot from willpower alone.

Dwight Chen hadn't spoken yet. When he did, the lights didn't dim—but it felt like they had.

"The Phase 2 payment gate is frozen," he said, tone flat. "1.2 million on hold, pending remediation."

His voice was like a clause in a mortgage agreement.

"You can't bill for forward momentum if you're skating in place."

He laid a hand on the binder in front of him. Thick. Red-tagged. Numbered sections visible even when closed. "Liquidated damages clause kicks in at thirty days. Ninety-three hundred per calendar day after that."

Arjun leaned forward, lips parting, but Colin shut him down with a glance. Not a glare. Not even a frown. Just the subtle clearance of a man who'd sunk programs bigger than this one with nothing but a pause and a breath.

Ted straightened slightly, forcing a sound that passed for composure.

"We're, uh… testing signal stability through loop-back pairs—temporary, not systemic."

He blinked again. "The AI layer… needs time to parse non-causal triggers in signal domain…"

His voice drifted off. His hands hovered over the keyboard, unsure what to type. Still no power.

The laptop wasn't turned on.

Renee jumped in. "We're updating the rollout Gantt to reflect parallel threading for QA and debug cycles. We believe with focused triage, we can—"

Mariah didn't raise her voice. She didn't need to.

"We've seen your timeline, Renee."

Renee sat back like she'd been slapped by a ghost.

Emi stood.

No one else did. That was the point.

Her voice was smooth—not cold, not angry. Just measured. Like water flowing into the exact shape of the problem.

"Ted will be stepping back from operational leadership during recalibration. Effective immediately, Marc Shevlin will assume day-to-day ownership of the prototype sprint. Triage will be complete in ten working days. You'll have results on your desk by then."

She paused, eyes sweeping the Kestrel side like an MRI.

"We don't dismiss the severity of your concerns. But we don't accept failure as a narrative."

A longer beat.

"You brought a scalpel to this meeting, Mr. Narvez."

She leaned forward, just slightly. "Let me assure you— we brought the sutures."

Colin closed his folio. The sound was exact.

"Ten days. Working prototype. Or we escalate."

He didn't shake hands. Just stood, nodded once, and walked out. Mariah and Dwight followed without a word.

The silence left behind wasn't awkward. It was institutional.

The room emptied in fragments.

Marc murmured something about syncing dev branches and left. Arjun stayed behind for an awkward second before Emi nodded toward the door. Renee lingered longest, hands shaking slightly as she tried to re-pack her tablet bag like a person performing surgery on a zipper.

Then it was just Ted and Emi.

He hadn't moved. Still staring at the blank screen.

"You're going home," Emi said.

Ted didn't react.

"Starting today. You'll call it leave. Rest. Reset. What-ever word makes it feel like your choice."

He turned toward her. His eyes weren't angry. Just tired.

"Does it matter what word I use?"

Emi blinked. Something flickered. Compassion, maybe. Pity. Then it was gone.

"No. It matters what you do with it."

She left him sitting there.

Ted didn't remember walking to the elevator. Didn't remember pushing the button. He stood inside as it closed, the metal door sliding shut like a lid.

Back at his desk, he'd left his mug. Half full. Cold.

Some part of him noted that.

But the rest was already drifting. Thinking about the hallway. The door. The couch.

And whether she'd be sitting there.

Waiting.

Not angry.

Just patient.

* * *

Ted came home before noon. The garage door groaned open and shut again too quickly, like he didn't want the neighbors to notice. Gabriela was at the dining table, papers spread in careful rows, her reading glasses perched halfway down her nose.

He stood in the doorway longer than he should have, keys still in hand.

"I'm taking some time off," he said finally. His voice had the wrong cadence—too measured, like he was quoting someone.

She looked up. "Time off?"

"Couple of weeks. Maybe more. Just… stepping back. Getting things sorted."

No explanation. No context. The vagueness hung in the room like a fog.

Gabriela studied him. She'd been collecting these moments the way you collect warning lights on a dashboard—one by itself means nothing, but together they start to feel like prophecy. The silences. The blank looks. The way his words sometimes seemed borrowed.

Still, she nodded slowly. "Maybe that's good. You've been stretched thin."

Ted smiled, but it wasn't tethered to any emotion. "Yeah. Good idea."

He didn't sit down. Didn't ask about her work. He just crossed the room, bent to scratch Luna behind the ears, and walked to the refrigerator. The door opened with a suction-pop, light spilling across his face. He pulled out an unopened pack of cheese and tucked it under his arm like it was part of the leash.

"Whole pack?" she asked.

He shrugged. "She likes it."

There was nothing else to say. He was already out the door, Luna trotting close at his side, nails clicking proudly.

Gabriela sat back in her chair, the silence closing in around her again. *Time off. Getting things sorted.* The words should have comforted her, but they felt hollow, preloaded, like a voicemail left on loop.

She reached for the phone. Her fingers hovered only a second before dialing Alma. The line rang once, twice— then, softly, "Hola…"

Ted drove with the windows down, desert air pouring through the cabin. The package of cheese rode shotgun, unopened and sweating through its plastic. Luna stood in the back seat, paws on the center console, nose thrust into the wind. Her ears flattened into the slipstream, eyes locked forward like a navigator charting invisible terrain.

The dog park waited.

And for the first time all morning, Ted felt certain of something.

Not work. Not home. Just this: a ride, a dog, and a gift of cheese.

* * *

That evening, Gabriela tried to believe.

Ted sat with her on the couch, her feet in his lap. He rubbed her arches like he used to when she came home tired from long days at the university. A sitcom laughed from the TV, the kind of canned laughter that used to irritate her but now sounded like safety. His thumb found the spot that always hurt, pressed, and the pain made her body jolt in recognition.

"This good?" he asked, eyes on her.

"Yes," she said, and let herself smile. For a moment, she believed again.

During the next commercial, Ted turned to her, his warm hand still resting on her ankle. His voice softened. "Don't leave me."

Her breath caught. It should have sounded desperate, human. Instead, it sounded staged—like an actor feeding his line at the perfect pause.

She pulled her hand back slowly. "Ted…"

He looked at her with a softness that wasn't his. Flat. Empty. Waiting for her to complete the scene.

Then, at the doorway, Luna entered. She padded across the floor, curled herself into a tight circle, and placed her muzzle across her paws with the exact timing of an exclamation point.

Gabriela's chest went tight.

The smile on Ted's face didn't falter. It was warm. It was wrong. It was rehearsed.

She stood. "I need air."

On the porch, the desert evening pressed close— cicadas screaming, sky burning down behind the mountains. Gabriela gripped the porch post and lowered her forehead to the wood. She whispered, "Alma was right."

Inside, the laughter track rolled again. A second later, Luna's tail hit the floor once. The sound reached her through the wall.

CHAPTER TWENTY-SEVEN

Detective Nia Wallace sat in her car three houses down, notebook open on her thigh.

She had told herself she was done with this case for tonight. Told herself she had other reports waiting, other files stacked like bricks on her desk. But she had parked here anyway, engine off, windows down, watching the Tompkins' house.

The notebook was a mess of false starts. *Ted—flat affect. Gabriela—protective. Dog—* She had written the word *Luna* twice. The first time she'd gouged the page deep enough to leave marks on the sheet below, then slashed it out hard. The second time, she'd boxed it in, as if geometry made it rational.

Her hand hovered. She forced herself to keep writing. *Unknown variable. Interference?*

Her vision blurred. She blinked hard. The fog came again—the same dulling of urgency she'd felt the last time she'd stood in front of that dog. Not fear, exactly. Not even distraction. Just... the ease of forgetting why she cared.

Nia ground her teeth. "Count," she whispered.

Back from 200 by sevens. 193, 186. She tapped the steering wheel with each number, letting the pain in her jaw and the tap of her fingers anchor her.

Curtains in the Tompkins' front room shifted slightly. No silhouette. Just a shift, like someone had touched the fabric with two fingers and let go.

Nia's stomach tightened. She wrote: *Observation: curtains moved. No visible figure.*

She paused. Then wrote, underlined twice: *Dog unseen.*

Headlights approached from behind. A pickup passed, bed empty, driver hunched low. Its taillights disappeared around the corner, and the night settled back into its old shape.

Movement caught her eye near the Tompkins' yard. Not Luna. Bigger. Broader. A slate-gray pit bull pacing along the fence line, muscles rippling under the sodium glow of the streetlamp. It turned, paced, turned again, silent as a sentry.

Nia froze. She recognized the dog as Axle, the scars along the shoulder were visible even from her car. The dog paused, sat, then stared at the house as though guarding it.

She reached for her phone, then stopped. Her instincts screamed not to call it in, not yet. Saying it out loud would give it a weight she couldn't take back.

She wrote in her notebook: *Unidentified dog presence. Guarding?*

Her pen hovered, then scratched the word out. Wrote it again. Scratched it out again.

The fog pressed harder at the back of her skull. She shook her head, rolled her shoulders until the muscles burned. "Stay sharp," she whispered.

When she looked up again, the gray dog was gone.

She slammed the notebook shut. Her hand shook once before she gripped the wheel tight.

She told herself she would leave in five minutes. She told herself that twice more. Then she started the car and drove away without ever looking back at the house.

CHAPTER TWENTY-EIGHT

The first one was built like a doorframe in a sleeveless vest—long arms, red tattoos baked deep into the leather of his skin. His cut bore the same MC patch Smash had worn: a burning wheel over crossed pistons. His name, according to the patch on his vest, was Buckshot.

The second one was leaner, meaner-looking, and kept his sunglasses on even though the sun had dipped. Crawler, they called him. Eyes twitchy.

They rolled up just after midnight, riding in a staggered formation. No mufflers, exhausts popping like rifle cracks, tearing the stillness of the neighborhood apart.

Ted had just turned off the porch light.

The bikes stopped in front of the house—one in the street, the other half-angled up onto the curb. Engines idled a moment, then choked off.

Crawler dismounted first. Buckshot stayed straddled on the saddle, one boot down.

Ted opened the door before they could knock. He didn't know why.

He just did.

"Evenin'," Crawler said. The word slithered. "You Ted Tompkins?"

Ted didn't answer. He could feel his pulse behind his eyes.

Buckshot stood now, all bulk and silence, arms loose at his sides. His hands weren't fists yet, but they were warming up to the idea.

"You knew Smash," Crawler said, smiling with half his mouth. "Didn't ya?"

Ted looked past them. No cars on the street. No neighbors peeking out. Even the crickets had gone quiet.

"I knew him," Ted said. "He was a neighbor."

"Was," Buckshot echoed. The word thudded out like a dropped hammer.

From the side yard came the faintest shift of gravel.

Nobody noticed.

Yet.

"You know he's dead, right?" Crawler asked, voice still greasy. "Got himself all smashed up. Funny name for it."

Ted's mouth tasted like copper. "I heard."

"You hear how?"

Ted shook his head. "Didn't say."

"Oh, they said," Crawler replied. He took a step forward. "They said you were the last one to see him alive."

Buckshot cracked his knuckles, and it sounded like a threat.

"You think you can stomp out one of ours and just hide behind your porch light and your lawnmower?"

Ted's jaw clenched. He didn't even own a lawnmower.

The air changed.

Not cooled. Not warmed. Just tensed.

From the shadows between the Jeep and the trash bins, Axel emerged.

No sound. No growl. No bark. Just mass.

He moved like gravity with a heartbeat—shoulders wide, head low, eyes unreadable.

Crawler didn't see him yet.

Buckshot did.

"What the hell—"

Axel lunged.

The sound was wet.

Buckshot went down like a side of beef, screaming as the dog hit him full in the chest. They crashed onto the grass, then rolled. Buckshot's voice cut off in a choke as Axel sank his teeth into his shoulder, shaking hard enough to make bones pop.

Crawler turned—too slow, too stunned—just as Buckshot's blood sprayed across the curb.

"Shit! Shit!"

He ran for the bikes.

He didn't make it.

Axel released Buckshot and pivoted mid-run, pure torque in motion. His paws hammered pavement as he closed the distance. Crawler had just gripped the handlebars when the weight hit him.

Axel didn't maul—he slashed. A clean arc across the calf.

Crawler screamed and fell sideways into the gravel, clutching his leg. His shades flew off, cracking against the curb.

"Help me! Somebody help me!"

But the street was dead. No porch lights. No eyes in windows.

Just the sound of blood dripping on asphalt.

Ted didn't move.

Didn't run.

Didn't scream.

He just stood there. Hands by his side. Watching.

Luna padded up beside him, slow and silent. She didn't look at him.

Didn't need to.

Crawler crawled—true to his name—across the street, panting, sobbing, dragging one leg like a rag. Axel didn't follow.

He stood between Ted and the rest of the world. Chest heaving. Muzzle wet.

Buckshot was still groaning on the lawn. One arm spasmed. The other bent wrong.

Ted finally breathed.

Behind him, Gabriela's voice cracked through the door. "Ted?! What the hell is happening?!"

He didn't answer.

He was watching Axel now. The way the dog stood there—still coiled, still ready.

But not for him.

Never for him.

Luna turned away first. Her tail brushed his leg like the sweep of a curtain closing.

She walked into the darkness.

Axel followed.

No leash. No command. No hesitation.

Just order.

Ted stood alone on the porch, blood spattered across his jeans.

From somewhere down the block, a single dog barked once—short and flat.

Then silence returned.

* * *

The blood was still on the sidewalk.

Dried into the concrete, dark and clotted like a memory that wouldn't scab. A small section of the grass was torn up where one of them had thrashed.

Detective Nia Wallace stood over the spot, notebook closed in one hand, eyes scanning the front yard with surgical silence.

Ted stood ten feet away, arms crossed, trying to look present.

Luna sat between them.

Not watching. Not blinking. Just *there*.

Like a statue with a pulse.

"So," Nia said, voice flat as sunbaked asphalt, "you're telling me these two guys showed up around midnight?"

Ted nodded. "Something like that."

"And what time did you call it in?"

"I didn't. Someone else must've… Neighbor, maybe."

She looked at him. That long, quiet stare meant to push people into rambling. Ted didn't flinch.

Not because he was calm.

Because he wasn't sure what had happened.

"You knew the victim," Nia said, flipping open the notebook but not writing. "Smash Delmonte."

Ted nodded again. "Neighbor. Didn't talk much."

"You had any run-ins before?"

"No."

"Fights?"

"No."

"You sure?"

"I'm sure."

She scratched at the page without looking down. Just a line.

"What about the dog?" she asked. "The one that did the damage."

Ted shifted. "It wasn't mine."

"But it was here?"

He hesitated. "Yeah."

"Is it still here?"

He looked toward the side yard. Empty. The gate was ajar, swinging gently in the breeze.

"No."

She noted that. Real this time.

Gabriela stepped outside, arms crossed over her chest, not speaking. She stood on the porch, halfway between support and suspicion.

Nia looked at her. Looked back at Ted.

"You're not bleeding," she said.

"No."

"Scratches?"

"No."

She raised her eyebrows. "That's interesting."

Ted's jaw flexed. "Why?"

"Because two men were nearly torn apart on your lawn," Nia said, voice cooling even further. "And somehow you don't have a mark on you."

Luna blinked once.

It was the first movement since Nia arrived.

The detective's sentence stalled.

Just a hiccup of thought.

Then she looked down at her own hands.

Why had she said that last part?

Why did it matter that Ted wasn't bleeding?

Luna tilted her head slightly.

Nia cleared her throat.

Her next question slipped. "Did they… Did they say anything? The bikers?"

Ted shrugged. "Accused me of killing Smash. I told them I didn't."

"And then what?"

"Then the dog showed up."

Nia blinked again. Her pen hovered over the page, but her hand didn't move.

"You said it wasn't your dog."

"It's not."

"But it showed up."

Ted nodded. "Outta nowhere."

"Like it was protecting you?"

He paused too long. "I don't know."

Luna stood.

Slowly.

Nia took an involuntary half-step back. It didn't register in her conscious mind, her feet moving before her brain did.

Luna walked to the bloodstain. Sat down.

Directly on it.

Nia watched her.

A stray memory surfaced: her own dog, gone six years now. A golden mutt named Mako, who used to sit on her boots when she was upset. She hadn't thought of him in ages.

She blinked hard.

"What kind of dog is she?"

Ted looked surprised by the question. "I don't know. Mutt."

"I'm gonna have to talk to those two bikers once they're out of surgery," she said. "But for now…"

She looked back at Luna. The dog was staring at her.

Not blinking.

Not breathing, for just a moment.

Nia's mouth opened. Nothing came out.

Then she smiled. Just a flicker.

"I'm blaming them."

Ted looked up. "You are?"

"Yeah," Nia said, voice lighter. Almost dazed. "They came onto your property. They were known associates of a dead man. Could've been retaliation. Could've been drunken grief."

She closed the notebook.

Gabriela frowned. "You don't want to investigate further?"

Nia shook her head. "I already know what happened."

She didn't.

Not really.

But she believed herself.

She turned to leave. Took three steps down the walk. Then paused.

Luna was beside her.

Nia looked down.

And reached out.

Hand on the crown of the dog's head.

"Good girl," she said.

The words tasted wrong in her mouth. Like she was repeating something she hadn't meant to say.

She withdrew her hand quickly.

Walked to the cruiser.

Didn't look back.

Ted stood still, feeling the porch wood under his feet like it might crack open.

Gabriela didn't move either.

Luna returned to them. Calm. Centered.

As if the interview had never happened.

From her cruiser, Nia stared through the windshield.

Her hand hovered near the ignition.

But she didn't turn the key.

Just sat there.

Her notepad open on the seat beside her.

On the top page: the word *Luna* crossed out in pen.

Written again underneath.

Then crossed out again.

CHAPTER TWENTY-NINE

The night pressed thick.

Ted slept beside her, breathing in his familiar rhythm —two short, one long, pause. The sound was the same as always. And yet not.

Gabriela lay on her side, eyes open, watching shadows stretch across the ceiling. The milagro heart she'd pinned high above the bed caught the faintest edge of streetlight, its tiny flame gleaming like it was burning in another world.

The glass of water sat fresh on the dresser. The candle stood unlit, the Virgin's face turned outward.

Luna lay at the threshold of the bedroom, her body stretched along the line where someone would have to step if they tried to leave. Eyes open. Reflective in the faint light, not glowing like fire but like cold metal.

"What are you?" Gabriela whispered.

Luna's tail lifted an inch and tapped once against the floor.

The sound filled the room.

Don't speak to it when it looks at you. Speak to your husband.

Gabriela turned her head toward Ted's sleeping form. Her lips barely moved. "I love you. Even if I have to leave. Even if I stay."

Ted murmured in his sleep, a small sound. Then, clear enough to hear but soft enough to pretend otherwise. "Good girl."

Gabriela's blood turned to ice. She gripped the red thread on her wrist until the knot dug into her skin. She pressed hard, made the pain sharp, clung to it.

God of the church. God of the kitchen table. God of my grandmother's backyard. God of thread and water and tin. If You can't take it away, then keep me from feeding it.

The dresser creaked softly, wood swelling. The water in the glass trembled once, then stilled.

Luna blinked. Slowly.

Gabriela closed her eyes, but the dog's presence didn't leave. She could feel it—the weight of waiting, the patience of something that had already won but wanted her to admit it.

She fell asleep with her hand clenched around the thread, pulse hammering beneath it, and the last sound she knew was not Ted's breathing, not the hum of the fridge, not the settling beams of the house.

It was the faint tick of a tail against wood. Steady. Certain. Like a metronome counting down to something she didn't yet understand.

CHAPTER THIRTY

The Kill Command

He didn't know how he got here.

The Jeep sat crooked in the driveway, engine off, one door still ajar like it had been interrupted mid-thought. Ted stood just inside the garage, barefoot on the concrete, T-shirt clinging to his back with sleep sweat. The fluorescent bulb overhead flickered once, then steadied. Somewhere inside the house, a clock ticked without urgency.

Luna sat near the side door, eyes on him. Her posture was regal—still as a carved idol, ears raised but not alert. Waiting, but not eager.

Ted walked past the workbench, fingers brushing over a socket set without registering the numbers. His hand moved with memory, not intention. Second drawer down. Nestled in the rag pile. The key was already warm in his hand before he remembered what it opened.

He didn't put on shoes. Didn't grab a flashlight.

Just walked.

The Corleys' house looked like a real estate listing left on overnight display. The iron gate clicked shut behind him without protest. White stucco walls glowed faintly in the moonlight, and the graveled yard was still raked into geometric order like nothing could ever disturb it.

Except tonight, it had.

He moved past the side yard, where trimmed agave cast long spiny shadows across the walkway, and reached the rear fence. A gate sealed the back—simple, utilitarian, and locked.

Except it wasn't.

The latch lifted.

The chain-link pens stretched before him, just as he remembered. Eight clean rectangles laid out in surgical precision, each concrete pad scrubbed, each stainless steel bowl catching the moonlight like chrome. The air smelled like disinfectant and desert dust.

And the dogs—silent.

One male. Three females. Four adolescent pups. All standing.

They didn't bark.

They didn't whine.

They didn't move.

Ted's hand found the first latch. Slid it open. Moved to the next. And the next.

The metal clinks were soft, intentional. He wasn't sneaking. He wasn't rushing. He was completing something.

One by one, the dogs stepped forward. No growling, no tail-wagging, no hesitation. The adult male turned first, padding toward the fence with a gait so smooth it didn't disturb the gravel. The females followed in tight formation. The pups brought up the rear, clumsy but mimicking the rhythm.

None of them looked at Ted.

Not until they reached the fence line.

They didn't jump immediately. They waited. Held formation. Eight bodies poised in a line like black glass—holding a shape no human had taught them.

Luna watched from the Corleys' rear patio, seated on the concrete lip like she'd been there the whole time. She hadn't barked. She hadn't led.

But she was the reason they waited.

The adult male turned and locked eyes with her.

Still, she sat.

Still, she watched.

And then—nothing. No nod. No tail flick. Just the moment passing like a shadow.

The male leapt. The others followed in perfect silence, over the chain-link and into the darkness beyond the groomed property. They hit the gravel beyond like water hitting sand. Gone before the sound caught up.

Ted stared at the open pens. At the quiet order of it.

His heart wasn't racing. His breath wasn't short. He felt nothing at all.

Luna stepped down from the patio and moved to his side. She didn't touch him. Just stood close enough that her presence pressed against the edge of his awareness like a radio signal—stronger than sound, more binding than words.

Ted turned without a word.

Walked home through moonlit streets.

And behind them, the Corleys' back gate hung open like a question someone had forgotten to ask.

* * *

The Corley house was silent. Not the kind of silence that soothed—but the kind that pinned you in place. No music. No television hum. Just the tick of the thermostat and the even breath of artificial sleep.

In the master bedroom, the air conditioner sighed through a wall vent, pushing lavender-scented air over the taut white comforter where Lissette Corley slept on her back, arms folded neatly across her stomach. Brian lay beside her, one ankle crossed over the other, snoring through his mouth like a man too efficient for dreams.

Somewhere beyond the iron fence and raked gravel, the breeze shifted. A dry sound, like skin peeling off polished tile.

Lissette's eyes opened.

She didn't sit up. Didn't blink. Just stared at the ceiling, a frown already forming—not fear, not yet, but the precursor to it. Something felt... off. The kind of feeling that usually meant one of the pups had gotten loose and triggered the yard camera. She turned her head to check the digital clock.

3:13 AM.

The number unsettled her. Prime. Irregular.

She sat up and reached for her phone. But the screen was blank. Dead. No glow. No buzz.

That's when she noticed it—the dogs hadn't barked. Not a whimper. Not a click of claws on concrete.

The silence felt preloaded.

She was halfway to the hallway when she saw the shadow.

At the far end of the room, framed in moonlight, something sat at the foot of the bed. Motionless. Its eyes shimmered—not glowing, just… reflecting more than they should.

Lissette opened her mouth.

The shape launched.

Brian woke to his wife screaming.

He rolled instinctively toward the nightstand, hand reaching for the pepper spray they kept clipped to the drawer. But something latched onto his forearm—tight, sharp, fast. The pain was white-hot. He didn't scream; he gurgled. Blood hit the wall in an arc. Another form slammed into his ribs, knocking the air out of him. He heard something tear—a ligament, maybe, or part of his own scream folding in on itself.

Lissette's voice disappeared mid-note.

Brian struggled, limbs flailing. He tried to roll, but something heavier than instinct pressed him flat. Claws raked down his side. Hot blood soaked the comforter, pooled in the bed's center seam. A snarl exploded near his ear—low, guttural, but still too quiet.

He managed to look left.

The sleek adult male stood on the bed, front paws planted on Lissette's chest, holding her down with casual force. Her eyes bulged wide, mouth open, silent. Her hands scrabbled at the dog's flanks, leaving shallow claw marks that the animal didn't flinch from.

Another shadow moved past the open bedroom door.

Pup? No. Too smooth. Too fast.

Brian twisted again, trying to crawl. His ankle snapped under his own weight. He collapsed, dragging himself across the floor.

Then a new pressure—teeth on his calf. Not ripping. Holding.

Waiting.

In the hallway, a framed family photo tipped forward and fell—*crack*—the sound absurdly loud in the otherwise cushioned deathscape.

The pups were in the kitchen now. He heard the brief sound of claws tapping on tile, then nothing. Cabinets opening. A clatter of metal bowls being knocked down.

The air smelled like steel and lavender.

By the time it ended, both Corleys were still. The dogs were not frantic. There was no blood frenzy. No torn flesh hanging from their mouths.

They moved like chess pieces sliding off the board.

The front door opened.

No paw pressed the latch.

But it opened.

One by one, the dogs filed out.

No one spoke. No one watched.

Except, Luna—somewhere blocks away—who lifted her head and stared into the night as if hearing the final step land.

CHAPTER THIRTY-ONE

The files wouldn't stay in order.

Detective Nia Wallace sat at the kitchen table in a tank top and sweats, hair pulled back, screen glow washing her face in pale blue. The case notes had been reviewed a dozen times. She'd read her own handwriting so many times it looked foreign. And still—no pattern, no motive, no suspects....

Except the one she kept crossing out.

Her notepad lay open beside the tablet. She stared at the words.

~~*LUNA*~~ written in block caps, then angrily struck through.

Beneath it:

Ted?

Then, scribbled like a child's angry repetition: *Biker brothers? Gang tie? Wrong place? Wrong time?*

Her pen hovered above the page like it was waiting for permission.

Then it happened again.

Not a sound.

A presence.

A shift in pressure across the air, like the barometric drop before a storm. She straightened in her chair and turned toward the open kitchen window. The curtains didn't move, but her spine did, posture tightening like she was being watched.

Then she heard it.

Not barking exactly—something *like* barking. But warped. Reversed. The hiss of a tape spooling backward through an old cassette.

She stepped barefoot onto the tile and moved to the front door, unlatched it out of reflex, and opened it onto the Mesilla night.

Warm air met her face. Desert stillness. A streetlamp buzzed down the block. Sprinklers ticked on somewhere.

Then she saw them.

Far off—past the cul-de-sac, just beyond the last row of adobe duplexes—a low ridge cut against the moonlit sky like a scar. And on it… eight figures.

Dogs.

No movement. No barking. Just silhouettes holding a line.

Nia squinted.

One of them turned its head. Not quickly. Not startled. Just… *aware.* The eyes reflected amber for a moment— just one moment—like coals catching wind.

Then the pack moved as one, shadows peeling off the ridge, melting into the creosote and scrub. Gone.

Nia stepped forward, bare feet on concrete, not noticing the sharp grain of it until the cold crept into her toes.

Coyotes, her mind said.

Coyotes don't move like that, said something deeper.

She rubbed her arms, skin rising with gooseflesh. She stepped back inside, closed the door, locked the deadbolt. Then locked it again.

She sat down hard at the table, staring at her notepad.

Luna had been crossed out once.

Now there were two lines through it.

She didn't remember drawing the second one.

She circled the word anyway.

Seven times.

CHAPTER THIRTY-TWO

Ted didn't remember walking there.

Didn't know the street. Couldn't name the block. The house didn't belong to anyone he recognized. It sagged near the corner of a cul-de-sac, its yellow stucco faded to gray, a busted satellite dish drooping off the roof. One porch light flickered, giving the whole yard a fevered look.

A chain-link fence ran around the front. Behind it, a dog barked—raspy, high-pitched, panicked. Not at Luna. At Ted.

Ted stood motionless on the sidewalk, unsure what had drawn him here. His hands hung at his sides. One fist clenched. The other open, fingers twitching like a reset hadn't finished.

The barking didn't stop.

It got closer.

A man stepped out of the house barefoot, wearing a torn A&W T-shirt and jeans slicked with mechanic's grime. His beard was patchy, his walk drunk or pissed off—probably both.

"Goddamn it, shut up!" he snapped, voice rough with sleep and nicotine. He reached the dog, grabbed its collar, and yanked hard enough to lift its front paws off the ground. The dog yelped. Not dramatic—just a sharp intake of pained breath. The man raised his hand.

Ted moved.

He didn't mean to.

He was through the gate before he realized it, the latch swinging wide behind him. Gravel crunched under his feet. The man turned, confused. His mouth opened.

Ted spoke, but the words didn't feel like his. They came out even, measured. He didn't remember deciding what to say.

The man stepped forward. "What the hell are you—?"

Ted's right arm snapped forward. Not a punch. A strike. Fast and flat and cold.

The man's nose collapsed with a wet crack. He stumbled backward into a ceramic pot, fell, and caught himself on the edge of the porch step. Blood ran freely—fast, no clotting. A hand went to his face; the other flailed for balance.

Ted stepped over the fallen pot, lifting something off the ground without thinking.

A red leash.

It had been lying beside the fence, half-buried under a broken lawn chair. No collar attached.

The man tried to stand.

Ted brought the metal clasp down onto his wrist.

Once. Twice.

The man screamed, loud and sharp, not unlike the dog a minute earlier. He kicked out, missed. His heel scraped concrete.

Ted wrapped the leash around his own fist. Looked down at the man's face. Saw the color shifting—rage into fear, fear into confusion.

He didn't hate him.

That was the worst part. He felt nothing.

The man's dog sat frozen near the edge of the yard, half-hidden behind a tipped recycling bin. Its body was low, tail tucked, but its eyes stayed locked on Ted. It didn't run.

It didn't whimper.

It just *watched.*

Ted blinked.

The man was gone. Inside? Fled? He didn't know. Couldn't tell.

He stood alone in the yard, blood on his knuckles, leash still looped in his hand. His breath was calm. His mouth dry.

He looked down at the leash. Red nylon, frayed near the clasp, the handle loop stiff from sun and old sweat.

He didn't own a red leash.

He looked toward the street.

Luna stood ten yards away, at the edge of the sidewalk. Watching.

Not judging.

Not waiting.

Just *there.*

He stepped past her, leash still in hand, and they walked into the dark together.

* * *

Ted woke with his mouth open.

No breath came at first. Just air stuck behind his tongue, as though he'd been shouting in a dream and the scream had scabbed over. His eyes blinked twice—dry, raw, like they'd been open all night.

Luna lay at the foot of the bed, curled in a crescent moon, spine touching the arch of his soles.

She was asleep.

Or pretending.

Ted sat up slowly. The room was cool, shaded from the sunrise by drawn blinds and quiet denial. His shirt clung to him. Damp. His right hand throbbed—two fingers swollen, knuckles scraped pink.

He didn't remember hitting anything.

But he remembered the *dream.*

If it was a dream.

A house he didn't recognize. A man shouting. A barking dog that wasn't Luna. His own hands wrapped around something. Pulling. Snapping.

He stood up too fast. The room listed.

He steadied himself against the nightstand and went to the bathroom, but didn't turn on the light.

In the mirror, his reflection was a smear of early shadow. His face looked normal. But his pupils were too wide. A sliver of red along the right sclera. Stress, he told himself. Nightmares. Nothing more.

He flicked the light on.

The lie peeled back in layers.

Dried blood along the inside of his wrist. A smear on the hem of his shirt. Not much—but not nothing.

He opened the medicine cabinet, stared at the antiseptic like he didn't recognize the label.

Then closed it again.

He crossed to the closet. Hesitated.

Opened the door.

Inside, his shoes were neatly aligned. A folded box of winter clothes. A backpack.

And hanging from the low rack: a red nylon leash.

It wasn't his.

The clasp was scratched, like it had been dragged against concrete. A hair—not Luna's—was stuck in the stitching. Thinner. Lighter. Curled at the end.

Ted reached for it.

Stopped himself.

He backed away, closed the door with a soft click, and turned off the bathroom light.

When he returned to the bedroom, Luna was awake.

Not moving.

Just watching him in the dark.

Her eyes were sharp but unreadable. The kind of gaze that didn't ask questions because it already knew the answers.

Ted didn't speak.

He lay back down, pulling the sheet over his chest.

Luna didn't come to him. Didn't nose at his hand or lean that heavy head into his knee.

She lay down slowly, curling back into position.

But her eyes stayed open.

Watching.

As if he were the one who needed minding now.

* * *

The yard was still.

No footsteps.

No bark.

Just the whisper of disturbed gravel where paws used to pace—a silence more noticeable for what it no longer held.

Axel was already gone.

He hadn't barked or whined or scratched at the door like a normal dog with an itch. He had simply stood up from his place near Ted's porch, looked east, and started walking. His movements weren't rushed. They were deliberate, unbroken by hesitation. Each paw pressed into the dirt like it knew exactly where to land.

Behind him, the house slouched in shadow. Ted hadn't stirred. Neither had Luna. The whole neighborhood seemed drugged beneath the stars, but Axel walked with clarity—as though he were following a signal no one else could hear.

He slipped between fences. Crossed driveways where security lights didn't blink. Past Samson's yard, past Vera's empty dog bowl. Past the houses with motion lights, where blinds twitched and curiosity stirred—but no one opened a door. Not for him.

By the time he reached the arroyo, the air had thinned. No barking. No cars. Just the crush of gravel under pads and claws.

Up the ridgeline he climbed, legs built like pistons, chest low to the dirt. He didn't pause until he saw them.

Eight of them.

Waiting.

They stood in silhouette—slim black dogs, sculpted by smoke and shadow. They didn't move. Didn't blink. Just stared with those deep golden eyes, their outlines flickering against the stars like oil flame.

The alpha was unmistakable. Taller, heavier in the shoulders, a muzzle scarred with age and fire. He stepped forward, lowering his snout until it nearly touched Axel's.

The others didn't growl.

They didn't need to.

Axel didn't flinch. He stood still, body quiet, breath slow. Not submissive—just certain.

The alpha sniffed once. Then again. Something passed between them—something deeper than scent—a wordless accord.

And then, the line parted.

No ceremony. No howls. Just silence and welcome.

Axel stepped forward and took his place. Not at the head. Not at the rear. Just *with* them.

A low wind stirred. The brush rustled behind them. The ridge swallowed them whole.

By the time the sun threatened the edge of the horizon, there were no prints. No sound. No witnesses.

Just an old chain swaying from a post and a ghost pack slipping into the dust.

CHAPTER THIRTY-THREE

She had been sitting in the cruiser for fifteen minutes.

The engine was off. Windows cracked an inch. Morning heat already creeping in, crawling up her neck. The coffee in the cupholder was going cold, untouched.

Detective Nia Wallace had parked two houses down from the Tompkins place under the pretense of a routine neighborhood check. But the paperwork on her lap hadn't moved. Her pen hadn't twitched.

She watched.

Ted stepped out of his front door right on cue. Clean shirt, neutral expression. A man you wouldn't remember in a lineup. Luna padded out beside him, leash clipped, posture relaxed. She paused to sniff the concrete, then looked up at him like any other dog. It would've been a perfect scene.

But it was too perfect.

Too framed.

Ted crouched briefly to adjust her collar. Luna's tail wagged once—a slow, pendulum motion. Then they walked to the end of the driveway and turned left.

Nia's hand hovered over her notebook, ready to note something. Anything.

Instead, she looked down at her pad.

The page was filled.

Luna.

Written over and over.

Block caps. Circles. Diagonal slashes. Her own handwriting—dozens of times. But she didn't remember writing them.

She flipped to the previous page. Smash's timeline. Witness statements. The word "Luna" appeared there too, in the margin, then crossed out. Then circled. Then struck again.

She closed the pad.

Hard.

"No," she muttered.

Because she *wanted* it to be Ted. Wanted it to be the dog. Not out of bias—out of instinct. The evidence hadn't ruled them out. But her mind had. Her own thoughts had been pushing her away from that angle for days. Gently. Persuasively. Like a bad friend offering advice that you wish made less sense.

The biker brothers. The broken chain. The bottle wound. The missing pit bull.

It all screamed gang beef.

But the scream felt… piped in. Like ambient music in a store you didn't choose to walk into.

She looked back up.

Ted was gone from view, around the corner. But Luna—

Luna turned her head at the last second.

Looked straight at the cruiser.

Then blinked. A slow, deliberate blink. Like she was saying goodbye. Or hello.

Nia didn't breathe.

A shape moved on the ridge.

Far behind the houses—along the horizon—a single dog walked the crest. Sleek. Long-legged. Silhouetted by the rising sun. No collar. No leash. Not running. Just… pacing.

Watching.

By the time Nia looked back at the driveway, Luna was gone too.

She opened her pad again. Drew a square. Wrote "Smash" inside it.

Then added four arrows pointing out:

Dog missing

Chain ripped

No robbery

No defensive wounds

In the corner, she wrote: *Witness: Ted?*

But the word didn't land right.

She scratched it out.

Below that, she wrote *Luna* again.

Then again.

And again.

CHAPTER THIRTY-FOUR

Beneath the Bed

Gabriela didn't mean to snoop.

She was looking for socks.

That was the excuse she'd rehearsed for if Ted walked in. If she caught herself. If God was watching.

She stood barefoot on the cold bedroom floor, one dresser drawer cracked open, another half-shut, hands still. The house around her had that strange quiet it got when Luna wasn't in the room, but was *somewhere*. You couldn't hear her, but you felt her. Like a storm building behind drywall.

Gabriela crouched beside the bed and lifted the dust ruffle. There, shoved against the wall, was one of Ted's journals.

Not hidden. Not quite. But tucked away like something not *meant* to be found, unless you were looking for it.

She pulled it out slowly. The spine cracked like an ankle joint. Inside: torn pages, entries that stopped mid-thought, and margins filled with what looked like practice sentences.

It wasn't me.

She's never loud.

Not Smash. Not Smash. (crossed out once, then again)

The air grew heavier the longer she stared. The kind of weight you feel in your teeth before a migraine. She flipped toward the back.

No dates. Just one line on the last page, scrawled diagonally across the paper like a broken command:

Bury it beneath the bed.

A soft creak behind her made her flinch.

She turned.

Nothing. Just her own reflection in the mirror. And behind her, barely visible in the glass—movement. A dog-shape, lingering in the hall.

Gabriela closed the journal. Not slowly. Not reverently. Just closed it, like ending a conversation with something that had gotten too close to the truth.

She slid open the drawer on the bedside table. Beneath an old TV remote and a tangle of charging cables sat a small USB drive. Black plastic. No brand. A single initial written in faded Sharpie:

L

She turned it over in her hand. It was warm.

In the study, the laptop on Ted's desk was already on, left there in sleep mode, as if waiting. She plugged in the drive, the cursor blinking with that patient emptiness that says *someone knew you were coming.*

One file. No title. Just a time code: 00:01:17.

She double-clicked it.

No video. Just audio. A hiss, then—

Barking.

Not normal barking. Not even angry barking.

It sounded like barking inside metal. Barking echoing through bone. Barking slowed down, then sped up again—layered, reversed, doubled, like a throat mimicking itself in a cold tunnel.

Gabriela grabbed the desk with one hand. Her gut clenched like it was trying to turn inside out.

She reached for the trackpad, but her fingers wouldn't respond. Her ears rang. Her left eye twitched. She tasted iron in her mouth and thought for a moment she was bleeding.

She slammed the laptop shut.

The silence didn't feel like silence anymore. It felt like something had been *paused*.

From the hallway, Luna stood watching. Her posture was neutral. Her face unreadable. No tail wag, no threat display. Just there.

Just *present*.

Gabriela backed away from the desk. She whispered a prayer, not even realizing she was doing it, and felt her tongue trip over old Spanish that hadn't surfaced since childhood.

She picked up the journal again and shoved it into the drawer, buried beneath a pile of random receipts and folded-up coupons, like they could somehow neutralize it.

Then she went into the bathroom. She sat on the toilet lid, head in her hands, and cried without sobbing. Silent, shallow tears, like something leaking from a damaged pipe.

Outside, a car door shut in the distance. Ted, probably. She wiped her face. Brushed her hair behind her ears.

When she stepped back into the hallway, Luna was gone.

But the USB drive was no longer in the laptop.

* * *

The knock came softly, then softer again, like someone reconsidering.

Gabriela stood at the door with her hand on the knob for a moment too long.

Outside, the wind pulled gently at the mesquite, dry leaves whispering against the stucco like something trying to scratch its way inside. No birds. No dogs.

Just the knock again—three soft taps. Then nothing.

She opened it.

Alma stood there with a woven satchel slung over one shoulder, a soft breeze tugging her silver-streaked hair toward the porch light. She didn't speak, just stepped forward and wrapped Gabriela in a hug so complete it felt like stepping into another time.

Gabriela didn't cry this time. She just closed her eyes and let herself be held.

Behind Alma stood a woman—shorter, thinner, head lowered—her shape half-swallowed by the porch's shadow. Gabriela didn't focus on her, not yet. She couldn't.

Alma pulled back and looked Gabriela in the eye. Her voice was sandpaper over calm water. "I brought what I could."

She stepped inside.

From the satchel came odd shapes—bundles wrapped in muslin, bone-colored sticks bound in red thread, an obsidian disk covered in smudged fingerprints. Alma moved slowly through the house, placing each item in deliberate corners: behind the couch, near the window, at the base of the hallway lamp. Each time she paused, she muttered something under her breath in a blend of Spanish and Nahuatl. The air felt thicker after each placement. Charged. Like someone holding in a scream.

Gabriela sat on the edge of the couch, hands in her lap. She watched Alma move like a priest preparing an altar.

"She's growing teeth," Alma said without looking up.

Gabriela blinked. "Who?"

Alma turned toward the dark hallway—the one that led to the guest room, the laundry, the back door.

"She knows we're talking about her."

Gabriela felt the shiver climb her back before she could stop it.

From down the hallway came the faint sound of paws on tile—unhurried, deliberate.

The guest room door creaked open, just a little.

Luna stepped into view.

She didn't bark. Didn't snarl. Just watched. Her eyes were too dark, like light had given up trying to reflect in them.

She sat halfway down the hallway. Her tail swished once, then stilled.

Alma didn't acknowledge her. Not directly. She lit a stick of copal and blew the flame out gently, fanning the smoke with her palm. Gabriela caught the scent and almost cried again—not from sadness, but from something older than that. The way the church used to smell when she believed God was paying attention.

"I brought someone," Alma said, lowering the satchel to the floor. "Someone who remembers."

The woman on the porch stepped into the doorway.

Gabriela turned and felt the air drop five degrees.

Celeste. From The Pack Station, but not anymore.

She looked… broken.

Pale, withdrawn, her smile twitching like a shorting wire. Her hands clutched her purse like it held her spine together. Her hair was clean, but she wore it too loose, as if she'd forgotten how she used to wear it.

She stepped in slowly. Luna stood to meet her.

The dog moved like royalty receiving a subject—soft paws, head low, posture warm. But her eyes never blinked.

Celeste's smile held just long enough to tremble.

Gabriela rose instinctively, unsure whether to hug her or shield her.

Alma placed one hand on Gabriela's arm and whispered, "Watch."

Gabriela froze.

Luna moved forward.

* * *

Celeste stepped into the living room like she didn't remember how feet worked.

They knew each other from Alma's spiritual gatherings—circles of prayer, energy work, protective rites. Alma had once called Celeste a sensitive, the kind who doesn't seek visions but gets them anyway. She'd gone quiet lately, missing calls, skipping sessions. Alma hadn't pressed. But that morning, Celeste had shown up pale and shaking, eyes red like she hadn't slept in days. Her milagro—her offering—was gone from The Pack Station wall. She hadn't seen it taken. No one told her. But sometime around 3:00 a.m that night., she woke up gasping, hand clutching her chest like something had been ripped from it. "The dog," she'd whispered. "It touched it. It took it." And then she wept—not like she was scared, but like something sacred had been defiled.

She glanced once at Gabriela, then looked away, as if eye contact might expose her to something contagious. Her voice came out quiet, trained, automatic: "Hi, Gabby. You look good."

She didn't mean it.

Gabriela tried to smile but couldn't complete the gesture. The floor between them felt uneven, like some unseen force was warping gravity.

Luna padded forward slowly.

Tail low. Ears soft. Eyes bright.

Celeste crouched on instinct.

Not a fearful crouch—more like someone greeting a toddler or a saint. Her knees popped audibly, but she stayed down, arms open, voice lilting with a kind of syrupy awe.

"Oh my sweet girl… You remember me, don't you? You do…"

Luna leaned into her. Placed one paw delicately on Celeste's thigh.

Celeste froze.

Luna didn't move. Her tail wagged once, lazily, as if bored with the act.

Celeste's expression shifted—not suddenly, but like wet paint under a heat lamp. Her smile began to twitch. Her pupils dilated. Her voice—still high and sweet—began to distort.

"I always loved her. You know that. I loved her *first*— I—*I never wanted to leave*—"

Her breathing stuttered, and one hand scratched at her collarbone like something was crawling under her skin.

Alma didn't move. She just placed a wrapped object onto the coffee table—cloth-bound, knotted with red twine. The air thickened, like the room was being vacuum-sealed.

Luna's ears flicked.

Celeste gasped. Like a drowning woman breaking the surface. Her head jerked up, eyes wide, and she tried to stand. Failed.

Then scrambled on hands and knees toward the door.

"Don't let her in—don't let her in—don't let—"

She flung the door open so hard it cracked against the wall and bolted out barefoot into the dusk.

A heartbeat later, the barking started.

One dog. Then two. Then a pack.

Gabriela stood in place, pulse roaring in her ears, staring at the door Celeste had just disappeared through.

Luna turned toward her.

Her tail swished once.

She walked over calmly, like none of it had happened, and pressed her head gently against Gabriela's thigh. A soft lean. Familiar weight. Warm fur.

Gabriela's hand moved—*without thought*—to stroke behind Luna's ear.

Then she stopped.

Her fingers hovered, trembling.

Luna leaned harder.

Gabriela's knees bent slightly. She felt her body giving. Not willfully. Like an arm under anesthetic—still hers, but no longer under her command.

Alma spoke.

One word. Sharp and low.

"No."

It sliced through the air like a drawn blade.

Luna froze.

Not visibly. Not dramatically. But Gabriela *felt* the pause in her pressure. The momentary withdrawal.

Then Luna turned.

No threat. No display. Just… a turn. A quiet exit. She walked calmly into the hallway, back toward the guest room, and vanished from view.

Gabriela stepped backward, her legs suddenly untrustworthy. She caught herself on the arm of the couch and dropped into it like someone who had just barely avoided fainting.

Alma knelt beside her. Didn't speak. Just placed a cool, flat stone in her hand—smooth and black. Obsidian.

Gabriela didn't ask what it was for.

Outside, the barking grew more distant.

Then stopped.

The house held its breath.

No barking outside. No movement in the hall. Just that *loaded quiet*— the kind of quiet you only hear in hospice rooms after the last breath.

Gabriela gripped the obsidian stone like it might bite her if she let go.

Alma moved without urgency. She pulled a deep green cloth from her satchel and laid it flat on the coffee table. Her hands moved with ceremonial calm—unwrapping, sorting. A bone-handled knife. A vial of what looked like ash. A red wax candle.

She didn't explain anything. She didn't ask for permission.

She just *began*.

The candle flared as if it had been waiting to be lit.

Alma dipped her fingers into the ash and touched Gabriela's forehead with one soft mark.

Gabriela flinched.

The ash was cold.

In the hallway, the sound of claws on tile. Slow. Testing. Not footsteps—*assertions*. Luna wasn't charging or pacing. She was reminding them: *This is still mine.*

Alma closed her eyes and began to chant.

Not loud. Not rhythmic. But dense with purpose. The words weren't all Spanish—some of them were older, curved and brittle. Language with teeth.

The air changed.

Not temperature. Not humidity.

Pressure.

Gabriela felt it first in her sinuses, then down her spine. A pulling inward, like the walls had begun to lean.

Then came the growl.

Not loud. Not meant for intimidation.

It was *disappointment*.

Luna stepped out of the hallway shadows like a queen forced to attend a meeting beneath her station. Head low. Posture coiled. Not submissive—calculating.

Alma didn't look at her. She held up a small square of mirror—obsidian, the size of a compact. The reflection didn't catch Luna's eyes.

It caught her *shadow*.

And that shadow recoiled. Just for a blink.

But Gabriela saw it. A twist in geometry, like Luna's shape had tried to stay in the room while her body stepped backward.

Alma's voice dropped into a near-whisper, a phrase repeated over and over—each time sharper, more pointed.

Luna didn't bark.

She didn't show teeth.

But she backed up. One paw at a time. Like the hallway had become a slope and gravity had changed sides.

She stepped into the guest room. The door didn't shut.

She simply disappeared into the dark.

Gabriela stared at the space she'd vanished into.

She said nothing.

But in her chest, something tightened. Not fear. Not exactly.

Doubt.

Alma exhaled—long, slow. Her eyes still closed. Her hand trembling slightly.

She whispered, "Not gone. Just waiting."

Gabriela nodded.

She didn't know what else to do.

The house slowly began to breathe again.

CHAPTER THIRTY-FIVE

Detective Nia Wallace sat at her desk long after the building had gone quiet.

The overhead lights had flickered off twice—motion sensors assuming she'd left—but she'd waved her arm absently each time, keeping herself cocooned in fluorescent hum. The stack of evidence photos hadn't moved in hours. She'd flipped through them so many times she could tell them apart by thumb-feel.

Photo one: Smash lying face-down, the bottle's neck embedded in his jaw.

Photo two: chain anchor ripped from the fence, dirt torn into a spiral.

Photo three: the Xolo house. Glass shattered inward, not out. Cages open. Blood in the kitchen.

Nia picked up a pen.

Legal pad. Fresh page. Top margin still sharp.

She wrote:

Retaliation.

Loyalty.

Biker crew escalating violence.

Then stopped.

She stared at the words. Not with suspicion, but with regret. Like looking at a counterfeit bill she'd printed herself.

She flipped back three pages.

No evidence of forced entry.

No eyewitnesses.

No motive.

And yet—she kept circling back to the bikers Smash used to ride with.

Something about their silence. The way one of them wouldn't look her in the eye.

But none of that *meant* anything.

She *knew* that.

Still, her pen moved.

Establish circumstantial pattern"

Interview neighbor with pit bull (Tompkins).

Eliminate Luna as suspect—not possible.

not possible

not possible

not—

She stared at the word until it blurred.

Then she wrote a name.

LUNA

Big block letters. Middle of the page.

Then slowly—carefully—she drew a line through it.

Not a scribble. A clean strike-through. Neat. Intentional. Like deleting a virus from a medical chart.

Her hand trembled.

She flipped to a new page.

Started again.

Biker MC had motive.

Biker MC had opportunity.

Pattern of escalation.

Her handwriting wasn't hers anymore.

It was neater.

Smaller.

Obedient.

The room felt colder. Not like the AC had kicked on—but like her own body had started to evacuate heat. She leaned back in the chair, looking at the ceiling tiles.

She whispered, "I know this isn't right."

And then she wrote:

Probable cause: biker feud.

CHAPTER THIRTY-SIX

Gabriela couldn't sleep.

Not just because of the day, though that would have been reason enough.

Ted was already out. Shirtless, breathing through his mouth, one arm crooked behind his head like a man on vacation.

She lay beside him like a guest in someone else's bed.

Luna wasn't there.

That was worse than if she had been.

Gabriela sat up, careful not to shift the mattress too hard. She stepped onto the floor like she were stepping onto ice.

The hallway light was off. The whole house carried the texture of a held breath. But her hand moved anyway, reaching for something she didn't know she'd been searching for all along.

She crouched beside the bed and lifted the dust ruffle again.

The journal wasn't there. She'd moved it earlier. She knew that. But she checked anyway.

And found something else.

A red leash.

Old and worn. Not Luna's. Not any dog she remembered. Nylon frayed, stiff and weathered. There was a metal tag on it—blank. No name. No address. Just a polished circle where a name should have been, like someone had scrubbed the identity out of it.

Her breath caught.

She didn't touch it.

The light in the hallway flickered once.

She stood slowly, and backed out of the bedroom. Her bare feet moved silently across the tile, the obsidian stone still warm in her pocket.

From the back room came a sound.

Not barking.

Not growling.

Scratching.

But not from a dog.

It was higher-pitched. Deliberate. Like nails. Human nails. Raking softly against wood.

Gabriela turned toward the sound, heart skidding inside her chest.

At the end of the hallway, the guest room door was open a few inches. Just enough to see the edge of the darkness inside.

And in the doorway—perfectly still—stood Luna.

She wasn't growling. She wasn't staring.

She was *watching.*

Her posture calm. Her eyes locked.

Not accusing. Not threatening.

But aware.

Gabriela's hand moved to the wall, fingers brushing the light switch, but she didn't flip it.

She whispered, barely audible, "I see you."

Luna didn't react.

But Gabriela had the strangest sense she'd said the wrong thing.

CHAPTER THIRTY-SEVEN

Pack Mentality

It started with silence.

Not peace, not quiet—silence. That unnatural hush that creeps in right before something breaks. Across Las Cruces, in alleys and on sidewalks and sunbaked lawns, the dogs had stopped barking. One by one, without cue or command.

In the Mesquite Historic District a black mutt and a brindle shepherd sat shoulder to shoulder on the stoop of a low adobe duplex. They didn't sniff each other. Didn't jostle or play. Just sat. Staring down a crosswalk like they were guarding it.

On the edge of the North Valley, a pair of Labs, once separated by fences, now lay curled together in the same yard—no holes dug, no gates opened. The owner had no memory of letting them in.

At a Shell station on Solano, a clerk named Frankie Montoya crouched on the hot pavement outside the automatic door, feeding boiled chicken to a droopy-eyed basset hound from a Tupperware container. The dog sat motionless, tail still. Frankie's apron was soaked with sweat, his register left unattended. When a customer knocked on the glass, he didn't flinch.

"She gets anxious when I'm not with her," he murmured, eyes unfocused. "Gotta make sure she eats."

The basset didn't blink. She just stared at him.

Ruby stood on the porch of her human's house. She didn't sit, didn't pant. Just stood, all four legs locked, ears flat. Her gaze was fixed on something miles away—on a pulse she could feel but not trace. The air tasted wrong.

Her human called from the kitchen. Ruby didn't move.

Back on the east side, in the cracked heart of Luna's neighborhood, it was worse.

Gabriela watched from the front window as three neighborhood dogs—Baxter the pit mix, Suki the collie, and an unknown mutt with no tags—walked past in a tight line. Not a leash in sight. They stopped at the corner, turned in sync, then continued west.

"Are those dogs running together now?" Gabriela said out loud.

No one answered.

Ted was in the garage. The Jeep was parked half-in, half-out, like he'd meant to finish something but forgot what.

Luna stood in the driveway. Still.

She wasn't following the trio, wasn't leading either. Just... observing.

Baxter looked back at Luna. He held her gaze for a breath too long. Then he tucked his head slightly and turned away, tail low, posture subdued.

The submission was unmistakable.

Up the block, Mrs. Cantu's cocker spaniel had taken to sleeping outside, refusing to come in even when offered treats. She'd tried dragging him inside once—he'd growled. Not snapped. Just a single warning sound that had made her freeze like he'd pointed a gun at her instead of a bark.

She let him stay out now.

In a different cul-de-sac, a small boy with autism who'd never spoken a full sentence was caught on a Ring camera kneeling in his yard beside his dachshund, whispering something repeatedly into its ear. The words were indecipherable, a murmur caught in static.

She didn't want to know.

In the middle of all of it, Luna walked.

Not with purpose. Not in haste. She moved like royalty strolling through a garden. Calm. Balanced. Her presence seemed to rearrange things. A wind chime went still when she passed under it.

She paused in front of a chain-link fence where a malamute once barked at anything with wheels. The dog stood silent, tail limp, body low.

Luna gave it a long look. No sound. No gesture. The malamute sat down.

She walked on.

Gabriela stepped onto the porch as Luna passed by the old sycamore near the sidewalk.

"She's not just changing people," she whispered. "She's changing *them*."

She meant the dogs.

Behind her, Ted rummaged for something on the workbench, muttering about a wrench he hadn't lost.

"Hey, Ted?" Gabriela called without turning.

"Yeah?"

"Do you remember when the neighborhood was noisy?"

He didn't answer.

She didn't ask again.

* * *

Luna walked the neighborhood like it belonged to her.

Not with swagger. Not with teeth.

With gravity.

Her paws hit the sidewalk in perfect rhythm. Each step was deliberate. Soft. She didn't sniff fences. Didn't chase squirrels. She moved like she had somewhere to be, but was in no rush to get there like time itself was adjusting to her pace.

Across the street, a shepherd mix watched from a second-story window. It didn't bark. Didn't wag. Its ears flattened and its head lowered until only its eyes remained above the sill.

On the east corner, a mutt named Theo—always nervous, always yapping—lay belly-down behind a gate, tail tucked tight. His owner had once joked he'd bark at a thunderclap three States away.

He was silent now.

Ted leaned against the open garage door, rag in one hand, socket wrench in the other. The Jeep sat idle, hood open, but he wasn't looking at it. He was watching Luna.

Not directly. Not openly. Just through glances. Like staring too long might draw her gaze.

She was passing the Morales' house now, where two shih tzus used to go ballistic anytime a leaf dared cross the yard.

They didn't make a sound.

Instead, both dogs—fluffed, pampered, always wearing bows—stood pressed against the wrought-iron gate, eyes locked on Luna. Their heads dipped as she passed. Not all the way to the ground, but low enough.

Submission again. Unmistakable.

Ted wiped his hands on the rag, even though they weren't dirty.

Inside the house, Gabriela stood in the doorway arms folded.

"She's doing it again," she said, half to herself.

Ted didn't respond.

Gabriela stepped out, her slippers whispering on the concrete. "That's the third time this week."

"I know," Ted said. Voice low. Mechanical.

"She's not just walking."

"I know."

They watched together as Luna turned down the next street, slow and steady. She didn't look back. She didn't need to.

Somewhere beyond the rooftops, a distant dog barked—high-pitched, frantic.

It stopped mid-yelp.

A subtle hum clung to the air. It wasn't sound. Not exactly. It was more like a presence, like the way a room feels before a storm or right before someone says something they can't take back.

Gabriela shivered.

Ted didn't seem to notice.

"She's not a pet," Gabriela whispered.

Ted wiped his hands again. "I think we both knew that."

Gabriela nodded once, then looked at him.

"You still love her, don't you?"

Ted didn't answer right away. He just stared at the corner where Luna had disappeared.

When he finally spoke, it came out like static.

"She needs me."

A car door slammed somewhere nearby. A dog across the street howled once—long and low—and then stopped.

Gabriela stepped back inside. "So did I," she said under her breath.

Ted didn't hear. Or pretended not to.

In the distance, Luna walked alone.

But she wasn't alone.

Not really.

Behind fences. Beneath porches. From living room couches and back alley shadows—they were watching.

One by one, they were beginning to understand.

And Luna—calm, still, unspeaking—was teaching without words.

* * *

Officer Miguel Rendon pulled into his driveway at 1:17 a.m. His patrol cruiser's reds-and-blues flickered. The engine rumbled down into idle.

He sat with the car running, staring straight ahead through the windshield, hands fixed at ten and two like he was still on shift.

Except his shift had ended almost an hour ago.

And he didn't remember the drive home.

The radio crackled softly. Dispatch asked something about a noise complaint—dogs fighting near Calle de Nubes.

Rendon didn't respond.

He reached out and switched the radio off.

Not muted. Off.

He stepped out onto the driveway. Slowly. Carefully. Like the air had changed its weight while he was inside the car.

The porch light was still on. The door was unlocked.

Inside the kitchen, he set his utility belt—gun, baton, radio, keys—on the tile counter one item at a time. Laid them out with the reverence of ritual.

He paused over his badge.

Thumbed it once.

Then set it down too.

In the hallway, his dog waited.

A red heeler named Pinto, old enough to have cataracts but still sharp. Ears perked, tail twitching low.

Rendon looked at him and blinked. Something inside him bent.

He dropped to his knees without a word.

Then to his elbows.

Then rolled slowly onto his side until he was lying flat on the tile, cheek pressed to Pinto's ribs.

The dog didn't flinch.

Didn't sniff or lick.

He just adjusted slightly, enough to let Rendon tuck closer.

"Good boy," Rendon whispered. "Tell me what you need." His voice cracked halfway through.

Pinto didn't respond. But his breathing deepened. His eyes closed.

Rendon placed a hand across the dog's spine like a man touching the Rosary.

He stayed there.

Minutes passed.

Through the kitchen window, the neighborhood shimmered in streetlamp amber. Motionless. Too quiet.

Rendon's cruiser lights were still strobing faint red against the fence—he'd never turned them off.

Like a heartbeat.

Somewhere else in the city, another badge was being laid down. Another uniform folded neatly.

The dogs were teaching.

And the people were listening.

CHAPTER THIRTY-EIGHT

Gabriela Acts

The living room had been stripped of its ordinary shape. No couch, no coffee table, no framed desert prints on the wall. Just open floor, candles, and a circle drawn in ash and honey.

Gabriela knelt at the edge of it, palms flat on the hardwood. Her hands trembled, not from fear, but from the pressure of what they were doing—of what it might invite.

Across from her, Alma sat with her legs folded, a gourd bowl in her lap and a cigarette clinging to her lip like an afterthought. The bowl steamed with sage and something sharper. Copal resin or crushed bone, Gabriela didn't ask.

Between them, at the center of the circle, lay one of Ted's old shirts. Soft from washing. Faded green with a bit of Luna's fur still stuck to the collar. Alma had asked for it without explanation. Said it had to be something he wore during "a moment of truth."

Gabriela had picked this one from the back of the closet. It was the shirt Ted wore the night he fixed the shower head, soaking wet and laughing, trying to keep Luna from licking his neck while he held a wrench in his teeth. That night, he had seemed human again.

331

The candles swayed toward the center as if pulled by breath.

A pulse, Gabriela thought. Like a second heartbeat.

Alma pulled the cigarette from her mouth, ground it out with two fingers, and leaned forward.

"Don't speak unless I tell you. And whatever you do— don't lie."

Gabriela nodded.

Alma dipped her index finger into the gourd bowl and painted the ash mixture over the shirt. Circles. Lines. A spiral that hooked inward like a leash pulling from the other side.

She whispered. The words weren't Spanish, weren't English—something older. Náhuatl, maybe. Or something not made for mouths at all. Her voice rasped at first, then deepened, like the language was being spoken *through* her.

Gabriela closed her eyes and followed with breath. In through her nose. Out through her teeth.

From the bedroom, a creak.

Ted shifted in bed.

Gabriela didn't open her eyes, but she felt it. Felt the stir, the tension in the air snapping tight like wire. The room contracted around her. Not smaller… sharper.

One of the candles went out. Not from wind. From something else.

Gabriela opened her eyes just in time to see Alma slice the pad of her thumb with a bone-handled blade and let a drop fall onto the spiral.

The honey hissed where the blood landed.

Alma whispered something more, then nodded at Gabriela.

"Say his name. The name you used when you loved him."

Gabriela hesitated. Then, quietly, "Teodoro."

The second candle blew out. Then the third. The fourth collapsed into smoke.

A sound came from the garage.

Not a bark. Not a whine. Just the hollow thud of claws scraping the interior door. Slow. Repetitive. Mechanical, like a hand drumming without rhythm.

Gabriela turned toward it. So did Alma.

Luna was behind that door.

Alma didn't flinch.

"She feels it. But she can't reach him now."

The thumping stopped. Silence reclaimed the house.

Then, from the bedroom, the faint sound of Ted's voice: "Mmm… cheese…"

Gabriela let out a quiet, stunned laugh—half sob, half relief.

"He's dreaming," she said.

"Good," Alma replied. "Let him sleep while he still can."

They didn't speak again. The ritual was finished.

But neither of them stepped outside the circle until dawn threatened the windows.

* * *

The kitchen was quiet, too quiet for a house that had once held laughter. Gabriela stood barefoot on the tile, back to the sink, trying not to look at the bowl on the counter. It was ceramic—white with little blue flowers. One of the ones Ted liked because it reminded him of his abuela's dishes.

Inside: scrambled eggs, cheddar cubes, and half a hot dog sliced thin. All things Luna loved. Nestled in the folds was something new—a mild veterinary sedative, ground to dust and hidden like a secret between bites.

Gabriela had measured it carefully. Not enough to hurt her. Just enough to slow her down. Long enough to get her in the crate. Maybe get her to the vet. Maybe get help.

Maybe.

She carried the bowl to the floor and set it near the threshold between the kitchen and hallway. She knelt beside it like she used to when Luna was smaller—back when this all still felt like a rescue story.

"Luna," she called softly. "Baby, come here."

Nothing.

She waited. The silence throbbed. The fridge hummed like a throat clearing.

Then, the click of claws on wood.

Luna appeared at the end of the hall.

She didn't come forward.

She didn't wag.

She just stood there, back legs braced, head low, eyes locked on the bowl—and then on Gabriela. Watching both as if they were decoys.

Gabriela forced a smile. Tilted her head, hand out.

"It's okay, sweetheart. It's just breakfast."

Luna took one step forward.

Then stopped.

And tilted her head.

It was so slight. So calculated. A gesture Gabriela had seen a thousand times—but never like this. This wasn't confusion or curiosity.

It was scrutiny.

Gabriela's stomach turned. The air thickened. The dog wasn't sniffing the food. She was sniffing *intent*.

Seconds passed.

Luna's nose twitched.

She blinked once, turned, and walked away. Quiet as smoke.

Gabriela's breath broke like glass.

She didn't move for a long time. When she finally did, she picked up the bowl, dumped it in the sink, and ran the garbage disposal until the sound drowned her thoughts.

Then she slid down the cabinet and sat on the floor with her knees to her chest.

Somewhere down the hall, Ted murmured again in his sleep. Not words. Just a soft sound of confusion. He would come down soon. Ask what's for breakfast. Maybe pet Luna like nothing had changed.

But it had.

The sedative hadn't failed.

Luna had *rejected* it.

She knew.

And Gabriela had no doubt that Luna would never eat from her hand again.

* * *

The house felt hollowed out—gutted of its rhythm. The floorboards didn't creak like they used to. The fridge didn't hum. Even the ceiling fan, always off-kilter, had stopped making that little ticking sound Gabriela used to hear when falling asleep.

Ted hadn't come out of the bedroom all day. He'd stirred, muttered, shuffled once to the bathroom. But he hadn't touched Luna. Hadn't spoken to her. Hadn't reached for the leash or called her name.

Something inside him had been unplugged. Gabriela could feel it.

And so could Luna.

She had been pacing the hall for an hour. Back and forth, back and forth—pausing every few minutes to nose at the bottom of the bedroom door. But there was no pull on the line. No signal. Nothing.

And the silence—it wasn't rest.

It was *rejection*.

Gabriela watched from the living room doorway, barefoot and still, one hand clutching the corner of the wall like it might keep her steady.

Luna turned her head slowly. She had heard the shift in breath. Not a sound, not a step. Just the flick of air as Gabriela's lungs adjusted.

Their eyes met.

Something ancient and bright flared behind Luna's pupils. Not recognition. Not affection. Just raw calculation.

Gabriela didn't speak.

The dog turned and walked toward her—no hesitation, no wag. Each step was too soft for a dog her size. Her movements had grown *quieter* over the last week, as though the noise of her body had been absorbed by something else.

Luna stopped just short of the hallway threshold.

A line between worlds.

Gabriela raised her hand slowly, palm out.

"Luna—"

The lunge was silent.

No snarl, no warning.

Just sudden impact.

Gabriela went down hard, the air punched from her lungs. She hit the floor on her back, shoulder smacking the wood with a crack that would bruise. Luna's front paws landed on her chest, claws pressing into skin—not tearing, just *holding*. Her teeth closed around Gabriela's forearm like a set of pliers. Firm. Unforgiving.

But still no blood.

Gabriela's heart pounded in her ears. She froze. Every muscle screaming for her to move, but she didn't dare fight.

Not yet. Not like this. Don't give her what she wants.

Luna stared down at her.

The eyes weren't mad.

They weren't confused.

They were panicked.

Not wide, not wild—but *betrayed*. As if Gabriela had ripped something away from her. As if *she* had broken Luna's connection with Ted.

Gabriela whispered, her voice steady even as her fingers trembled, "He's not yours."

That broke it.

Luna released her arm, spun, and sprinted for the front door.

It was cracked open. Gabriela had left it that way. Just in case. Maybe part of her knew this was coming.

Luna slammed through it and out into the night. No hesitation. No backward glance.

She stopped just past the porch light, back legs crouched, breath fogging in the night air. She didn't turn her head all the way. Just pivoted her snout. One eye, burning amber in the light, met Gabriela's across the distance.

Not a stare.

A *marking*.

That moment, wordless and thick, stretched across the open space like a cord. Taut. Violent. Grieving.

Then Luna broke it.

She turned and vanished into the dark.

Gabriela lay there for a long time.

The pain in her arm was already blooming—deep purpling, not punctured but battered. Her breath came in short, ragged loops. The front door swung gently in the wind. Ted didn't stir.

And in the distance—too far to be sure—somewhere out past the houses, a low, coordinated howl began to rise.

CHAPTER THIRTY-NINE

Alma's house sat at the end of a cul-de-sac, the kind where porches stayed empty after seven p.m. and the neighborhood watch didn't bother with door-to-door flyers anymore. The porch light was still on, but most of the windows were dark. Late summer heat had pressed everyone into their air-conditioned silos.

Her old Camry purred into the driveway, headlights casting long angles across the gravel border and empty flower beds. She parked under the creaking basketball hoop and shut the engine off. A moment passed before she opened the door.

Alma stepped out slowly, bones creaking in rhythm with the chassis. She stood for a second with her hand on the roof of the car, eyes tilted toward the stars. The sky was open and clean above her, windless. No barking. No insects. Just a silence so pure it bordered on vacuum.

She felt it immediately.

The absence.

The unnatural stillness in a place that had always been alive with little noises—the neighbor's Chihuahuas, the wind chime two doors down, the hum of a porch fan—now *nothing*.

She exhaled through her nose.

"No good spirits walk with silence," she muttered.

Her hand drifted toward her purse, not for her keys, but for the small cloth satchel she kept there—red cord, a sprig of rue, a cracked milagro charm worn soft from thumb-rubbing. She didn't clutch it tight. She just held it.

Then came the first sound.

A single pawstep, soft on gravel. Too soft.

Alma turned her head slowly toward the side yard, where the shadows were deepest.

A dog emerged.

Not wild. Not foaming or rabid. Just… present.

A mutt. Brown, medium-sized, short coat. She recognized him. He belonged to the family on the corner, the ones who left the gate open when the kids got home from school. He had a limp.

He wasn't limping now.

His head was low, not submissive—*intentional*. His eyes locked on her, and behind them: nothing. Not fear. Not excitement. Not recognition.

Another dog appeared.

Then another.

From behind the car. From under the bushes. From across the street.

No barks. No growls.

Just silence, teeth, and coordination.

Alma didn't run.

She didn't scream.

She simply stepped back slowly, toward the car. Her foot hit the concrete pad with a slap that seemed far too loud.

The lead dog advanced.

Then another flanked him. This one older. Black patches on its face like a mask. One ear torn.

They were moving as a unit now.

Alma raised the red-corded pouch.

"This is not your place," she whispered. "You are not spirits. You are echoes. Sentinels of something that forgets it was once loved."

One of the dogs stopped.

Only for a breath.

Then the others moved forward.

She didn't pray. Not aloud. She didn't beg. Alma had seen too much to believe in bargains when blood was already on the tongue.

Instead, she tucked the pouch into her shirt, squared her stance, and whispered something that was not English, not Spanish. A language older than the dogs. Older than the leash.

It didn't stop them.

But it made them pause.

For one breath.

One beat.

And in that pause, she met their eyes—not as prey, but as a witness.

The first strike came from the side. Fast. Hard. Surgical.

Then the others followed.

She didn't scream.

CHAPTER FORTY

The strobe of the crime scene lights cast the whole street in an unnatural rhythm—blue, white, red, repeat. It made the neighborhood look like it was breathing wrong. Like it had slipped out of sync with the rest of Las Cruces.

Detective Nia Wallace stood at the edge of Alma's driveway, arms crossed, expression flat. The coroner's van idled beside her. A stretcher with a zipped black bag clicked into its final position. No one spoke.

Alma's front door was open, but untouched. No signs of forced entry. Nothing stolen. No one saw anything. No one *heard* anything.

And yet—torn flesh. Bite marks. Multiple dogs, coordinated. Local mutts, they said.

"Neighborhood dogs."

Right.

Nia looked down at the blood. Still drying in the cracks of the concrete, like it had settled there for a reason.

"What are we calling this?" asked a uniformed officer beside her. Young. Nervous. The kind who filled silence with questions.

"Animal attack," she said flatly. "That's what the reports will say."

"Jesus. Dogs don't *do* that."

Nia didn't answer. Her eyes were still scanning. Not for clues. For *sense*.

This made none.

It was the third time this week that something unexplainable had touched down in her jurisdiction.

First Smash.

Then the dog attack on the bikers.

Now Alma.

She turned and walked back to her cruiser. Inside, the heat was stifling. She left the door open and flipped her notebook to the page she'd been building since Smash's death.

It looked like a conspiracy theorist's scratchpad.

- *Smash Delmonte — bludgeoned in front yard, dog chain snapped*
- *Ted Tompkins — no alibi, conflicting boot treads at scene*
- *Luna — present at both homes*
- *Second leash program?*
- *Who trained that dog?*

She had written Luna's name four separate times.

Each time, she had tried to cross it out.

Each time, she couldn't.

There was no proof. Just a fog around everything. Witnesses forgetting things. Surveillance cameras not working. Phones losing time stamps.

And then there were the dreams.

That part wasn't in the notebook. That was *hers*.

Since her first interview with Ted and Gabriela, Nia had been waking up in the middle of the night, heart racing, unsure why. No dreams she could remember. Just the feeling of *being watched*.

Last night, she woke to find her notebook open on the kitchen counter.

She lived alone.

Now, as she stared at the word *Luna* underlined three times, she noticed her hand trembling.

"No," she muttered, closing the book too fast.

She rubbed her temples, fingers lingering near her eyes as if trying to block something out. She looked across the street, where a news crew had started setting up. Cops kept them back, but they were hungry. The scent of something ugly was in the air.

She rolled down her window and breathed in the night.

Across the driveway, a dog sat at the edge of someone's lawn. Unleashed. Upright. Watching her.

Not growling. Not pacing.

Just *watching*.

It was gone when she blinked.

A glitch in the eye, maybe.

Or something worse.

Back inside the cruiser, Nia flipped to a blank page. Wrote two words at the top.

Possible vector.

Then circled it.

Below that, she started a fresh list:

Behavioral contagion

Canine psychotropic?

Experimental conditioning?

Spiritual interference?

She hesitated on the last one.

Then crossed it out.

No she didn't. She *tried* to.

Her pen stopped an inch before the word, then veered sideways and underlined it instead.

She dropped the pen.

"No," she said again. Firmer. "I'm not crazy."

But her hand moved to close the book, and instead… turned another page.

And there, at the center of a fresh sheet, in faint pencil:

Luna

Scrawled in her own handwriting.

She didn't remember writing it.

She didn't remember carrying a pencil.

Her stomach tightened.

The lights outside continued their unnatural rhythm.

Blue.

White.

Red.

Repeat.

CHAPTER FORTY-ONE

The Leash Breaks

Ted woke on the cold garage floor, one side of his face pressed into concrete slick with drool and sweat. Something wet ticked near his ear. Blood. Not much, but enough to know something had broken.

The fluorescent light overhead was off, but the fridge's electric hum buzzed like a tuning fork buried in his teeth. Everything pulsed—not pain exactly, but distortion, as if his head were an overexposed photo and someone kept flicking the aperture. He rolled halfway onto his back. His arms didn't want to move.

Something was watching.

Luna sat five feet away, framed in the dark between his toolbox and the base of the fridge. Eyes wide. Tail still. She wasn't panting.

She had returned sometime in the night—unannounced, unashamed, as if the attack had been a glitch in the code, not a betrayal. Not the hidden pill in the cheese, not the shove toward sedation. Whatever Gabriela had done, Luna had overwritten it—walked back in like the house still belonged to her.

And somehow, Gabriela felt guilty. Not logical guilt—not the kind rooted in cruelty or regret—but something stranger, murkier. Like she'd violated a pact she hadn't agreed to but still somehow owed. The pill had been small, the intent humane, the outcome necessary. But now, with Luna back—silent, composed, unbothered—it felt like she'd tried to lie to a god and been forgiven without being understood. That forgiveness weighed heavier than blame.

Ted opened his mouth but couldn't find a name, just a vague pressure in his chest that used to be language.

She didn't move.

Not toward him.

Not away.

Just… waiting.

His hand twitched, instinctively reaching toward her. That old signal: *Come here, girl. Good girl.* But she didn't respond—not with a wag, not with a blink.

She watched him as if he were prey that was trying to remember how legs worked.

Then the door from the kitchen burst open.

Gabriela stepped into the garage like a breaking wave—carrying a worn journal in one hand, a cloth grocery bag in the other. Her breath was ragged. She looked ten years older in the light that wasn't quite light.

"Don't move," she said to Luna, without looking at her. "Just don't."

Luna turned her head slightly but didn't leave.

Gabriela dropped the bag near Ted and crouched beside him. "Ted? Can you hear me?"

He nodded, or thought he did. His neck made the motion, but the message didn't land anywhere.

She took his face in both hands, gently at first, then firmer when he didn't respond. "Your pupils are shot," she whispered. "Jesus, what did she do to you?"

He blinked slowly.

Gabriela glanced over her shoulder. Luna was gone.

She hadn't walked away. She'd disappeared.

Just space now, humming faintly.

Gabriela didn't comment. She pulled a small bottle of rubbing alcohol from the bag, along with gauze, a lighter, and a handful of white candles. She dropped the rest on the garage floor and helped Ted sit upright.

His head lolled. He smelled copper and oil and something older, like burnt dust and torn cotton.

She said, "I found something in notes Alma left me. A ritual. I don't know if it's real."

Ted groaned.

"I'm doing it anyway," she said. "Tonight."

His lips moved, but only a wet croak came out. Gabriela leaned closer.

"I don't care what you think it is," she said. "It's in her handwriting, and she said it worked once before."

He blinked.

"Can you stand?"

Ted didn't answer. His legs shook when she tried to pull him up, so she let him sink back down and sat beside him. The concrete was freezing.

"I think she's afraid," Gabriela whispered.

Ted turned his head toward her. "Luna?"

She nodded. "The leash is fraying."

He breathed through his nose, a rattle like gravel in a pipe. "How do you know?"

Gabriela glanced at the empty corner where Luna had been. "Because she's not fighting. She's waiting for something."

Ted tried to speak again, but this time, all that came out was a single word:

"Run."

Gabriela took his hand and squeezed hard enough to crack something. "Not tonight."

She stood and grabbed the grocery bag. A dog barked somewhere down the block—high-pitched, erratic. Another bark followed. Then another. But none of them matched. They weren't barking at something.

They were barking *apart*.

Gabriela reached into the bag and pulled out the book again—Alma's journal, cracked and brittle along the spine. She looked at Ted one more time and said, without fear, "We do this now. While she's still confused."

Ted said nothing. He just stared at the open doorway, where Luna had stood a moment ago.

Where something darker still lingered.

* * *

Gabriela cleared the table with one arm, scattering unopened mail and half a dog treat Luna had once rejected. Ted sat on a stool nearby, wrapped in a beach towel that smelled faintly of mildew and car wax. His skin was clammy. It was the look of someone wearing calm like borrowed clothing—creased in all the wrong places, stitched together by something that didn't understand human skin.

She opened Alma's journal with trembling hands.

The handwriting was uneven—part cursive, part printed letters, all of it underlined and rewritten and circled in overlapping red ink. There were instructions in Spanish, Náhuatl, even one line in Greek. Gabriela couldn't make sense of half of it. It was like Alma had written it while in a fugue, trying to transcribe something she'd once whispered in a church basement during a prayer that hadn't ended.

"Salt," Gabriela said out loud. "She wrote, 'use boundary salt.'"

She looked around the kitchen. No boundary salt. No black salt. No iron shavings. No powdered obsidian. What she had was a Morton canister with a smiling girl holding an umbrella.

"Fuck it."

She tore a paper plate in half and shook salt in a ragged line along the kitchen floor. Ted blinked slowly as she worked. His pupils were no longer blown wide, but they didn't match—one slightly larger than the other. A sign of damage. A sign of interference.

Outside, a low chorus of dog whimpers wailed like wind through reeds. Not quite barking. Not quite howling. Just… tremble-voiced confusion.

Gabriela tried to ignore it. She flipped through the journal again, muttering. "Candle at the threshold. Water in a bowl. Object of devotion in the center."

She pulled a chipped blue dog dish from the floor and filled it halfway with tap water. Set it in the middle of the salt circle. Then placed a candle at each corner of the room, anchoring the square.

Luna's leash lay near the refrigerator. Gabriela hesitated, then picked it up with two fingers, as if it might bite.

She placed it at Ted's feet, coiled like a serpent.

Ted didn't look down. His eyes tracked her, but his thoughts were somewhere deeper than the kitchen.

Gabriela said, "Do you remember what happened?"

He tried to answer. Failed.

She knelt beside him and whispered, "If she comes in… you can't look at her. You can't think of her."

Ted's brow twitched. "Hard… not to."

Gabriela nodded. "That's how it works."

A car passed outside, slow and hesitant. No music. No voices. Just tires on asphalt and the sound of dogs snuffling at fence lines.

She lit the candles.

The flames wobbled and bent slightly toward Ted.

Alma had drawn spirals in the margin of the ritual— clockwise, always clockwise. Gabriela mimicked the shape with her fingertip on the tile, whispering the first prayer. It was a half-remembered Catholic plea, slurred through years of disuse and dread.

She whispered again.

Nothing changed.

No shift in air pressure. No flicker in the flame. No static charge in the fingertips.

Ted exhaled heavily.

Gabriela flipped the page. The next line was scratched out completely. She squinted, holding the book near the candle, trying to read the indentations beneath.

Luna's toenails tapped once in the hallway.

Then stopped.

Gabriela froze. The air shifted. Not colder. Not warmer. Just… less.

Ted's eyes fluttered.

She skipped the line, moved to the next. "Protect the vessel with cleansing smoke."

Gabriela reached into the grocery bag and pulled out a half-burned bundle of sage. She lit it from the candle, but the smoke came out thin and watery, like it didn't want to be part of this.

She walked in a circle around Ted, muttering prayers, improvised phrases, and one line she remembered Alma saying during a vigil at a hospice months ago: *Come not for him, come not for now.*

Luna's claws tapped again, one-two, and stopped. Closer.

Gabriela hissed between her teeth. "You can't be here."

No sound answered. But the candle nearest the doorway trembled, and the salt line cracked like dried paint.

Ted swayed.

Gabriela clenched the sage tighter and whispered, "Please God. If any of this is real—make it work."

The candle at the doorway hissed once, and went out.

* * *

The candle at the threshold guttered out with a pop, and the remaining flames twisted inward like they were leaning away from something unseen.

Gabriela didn't move.

She stood inside the imperfect salt circle, clutching the still-burning sage bundle like a relic, her breath hitching in uneven intervals. Ted sat in the center, eyes drifting, lips parted. He looked like a man waiting to drown. Like a man who already had.

From outside—another thud. Wood creaked. Glass somewhere *flexed*. A growl echoed off the front door like a warning from something that used to be a pet and forgot how.

Gabriela glanced toward the living room, where light from the porch window flickered—bodies moving back and forth, too many shapes, too fast, too loud. The barking was no longer chaotic. It had become *orchestrated*. Snarls in unison. Paws hammering the stucco in pulses.

Luna stepped into the kitchen.

Not like a pet. Not like a dog. Like an idea that had figured out how to walk.

Her fur was dry but shone like it had been rained on. Her eyes were low—almost hooded—but fixed on Ted with unsettling stillness. No panting. No curiosity. Just focus.

Gabriela held up the sage and whispered something hoarse and mispronounced from the journal.

A crash against the front window—*crack*—splintered but not shattered. Gabriela's breath hitched.

Luna stopped at the edge of the circle.

The salt line had broken in one spot—where the plate edge had curled too shallow. Gabriela tried not to look at it, but she saw Luna's paw slide forward—over that rupture, pressing into the circle like it belonged there.

Ted's body flinched.

"No," Gabriela said, louder now. She reached for the salt shaker, dumped a line across the broken spot, and tried to smear it shut with her palm. It wasn't clean, but it was something.

Luna didn't move further in. But her stare deepened.

The growling outside *intensified.* Something scraped along the stucco near the kitchen window—tall, like a shepherd or Dane jumping full height. A second later, claws *raked* the front door. No howling now—just rage. Channeled. Hungry.

Ted twitched again. Then harder.

His arms stiffened at his sides, and his back arched. A noise escaped his throat—not a gasp, not a growl. A *glitch*.

Gabriela rushed to him, grabbing his face. "Stay with me, Ted—look at me, *me!*" Her voice cracked.

His eyes opened wide—but they were *wrong*. Not rolled back. Not vacant. Just… vacant of *him*.

She slapped him, hard.

Nothing.

Gabriela stood, kicked the dog bowl aside—it splashed across the floor like a baptism—and grabbed the closest candle, holding it like a weapon.

"You don't get to take him," she said to Luna. "He's not yours."

Another body slammed into the front door. The *hinges groaned*.

Luna didn't snarl. She didn't growl. She sat.

Just sat. Right there. Inside the line now, where it had cracked again.

Ted seized—his limbs jerking hard enough to slam one foot into the overturned dog dish. Water spilled toward the fridge, soaking the leash.

Gabriela dropped to her knees, trying to hold him still, but his body bucked like a live wire.

"*Damn it, Alma, what do I do?!*" she shouted at no one.

The book was useless now, its pages fluttering near the candle like they wanted to burn.

The window *bowed inward* once, visibly.

A high-pitched whine came from outside, as if the pack had *felt something shift*.

Gabriela saw the leash—coiled like a sleeping snake, half in the water—and something snapped in her chest. Not logic. Not memory.

Instinct.

She grabbed the leash and *threw* it at Luna.

It struck her muzzle.

Luna blinked once.

Then stood.

Ted gasped.

His body went limp.

Gabriela fumbled for another candle and scrawled a circle around him with melted wax, muttering a prayer her grandmother used when the power went out.

Luna didn't approach.

She didn't retreat.

She watched.

Watched as Ted rolled onto his side, blood in his teeth, eyelids fluttering.

Gabriela wiped his mouth and whispered, "Don't look at her. Don't let her in."

Ted blinked slowly. His hand curled around hers.

From the hallway, something shattered. A mirror? A lamp? Maybe a vase. Gabriela didn't know.

Outside—a yelp. A hard, sudden break in the barking rhythm. One of the dogs had cried out, and others joined.

Luna turned her head toward the sound. Her ears flicked back.

Then she looked at Gabriela.

Not with animal confusion. With resentment. And something colder.

Gabriela whispered, "Go. Just go."

Luna took a single step backward. Then another.

She never turned her back—just eased into the hallway like smoke leaving a lung.

Gabriela dropped the sage bundle. It had gone cold.

Ted lay still, breathing now, but shallow. Like something in him had been squeezed through a narrow place and wasn't all the way back.

Outside, a German shepherd barked.

Then a mutt.

Then… *nothing.*

Not silence.

Withdrawal.

The house hummed with silence, brittle and charged.

Gabriela closed her eyes and let out a breath she hadn't known she was holding.

It shook on the way out.

* * *

Ted was fading again.

His body had gone limp, but not peacefully. He looked like something spilled—his limbs folded awkwardly, his face slack and wet. His breath rasped, low and arrhythmic. One lung sounded like it wasn't even trying.

Gabriela knelt beside him in the ruin of her makeshift circle, salt scattered like beach sand across the floor. One of the candles had cracked in half. Wax puddled and hardened in strange, asymmetric shapes, like a warning in a language she didn't speak.

Windows rattled with the sound of hellbent barking, as if the house had been dropped into the center of a riot made entirely of teeth.

She grabbed the journal again, flipping pages with trembling fingers. The ink was smeared. The corner was singed. She could barely read Alma's handwriting.

"Protect the vessel."

"Do not speak her name after the seal breaks."

"Fire will betray you. Use water."

"Okay," Gabriela whispered, more to herself than anything else. "Okay, okay, okay."

She took the empty dog bowl and refilled it from the sink, splashing a good amount on the counter. The water came out too fast, knocking a fork to the floor. It clanged like a dropped blade.

The front door shook under a barrage of bodies—claws raking wood, jaws snapping at shadows, the whole pack sounding like it wanted to chew its way into the walls.

She dragged the bowl to Ted's side, set it near his chest, and dunked her fingers into the cold surface.

She didn't know the words.

Didn't remember the prayer.

Didn't trust the page.

So she made one up.

"En el nombre del alma, en el nombre del cuerpo," she whispered, circling her wet fingers above his heart. "Vuelve."

No flicker. No sound.

Just the drip of water from her hand and the soft whistle of Ted's half-functioning lungs.

She tried again. This time louder.

"En el nombre del alma. En el nombre del cuerpo. *Vuelve.*"

The last word cracked like a bone under pressure.

And something answered.

From *everywhere.*

A sound—not a bark, not a growl, but an inversion of both—howled through the walls. Not outside. Not around. It came through the structure. Through the vents. Through the wires. Through the part of the house that remembered being a home and now smelled like wet fur and rot.

Ted's eyes flew open. His back arched again.

The dog bowl flipped on its side, water splashing into the wax pools, sending smoke spiraling into the air.

Gabriela screamed—but kept going.

"*Vuelve!*"

Luna appeared in the kitchen doorway.

She hadn't walked in. She hadn't slinked.

She was just there, like a cutout laid over the frame of reality. Her eyes were wide now—glowing faintly. She opened her mouth, and a sound tried to come out.

It didn't.

Instead, every dog in the neighborhood screamed.

Windows cracked—not shattered, but cracked—like metal under heat stress.

The porch boards groaned. Something thudded against the wall, then something else—

And then it stopped.

A ripple passed outside the house.

Gabriela didn't know why at first—she was focused on Ted, on the ritual, but some instinct made her lift her eyes.

Somewhere outside, the barking faltered—one dog whined, another whimpered, and then the rhythm broke.

The porch light flickered.

And beyond the front window—visible only in silhouette —stood Ruby.

No leash. No human.

Just her.

Ears perked.

Mane bristling.

Eyes glowing a low gold-orange.

Built like a question no one wanted to answer.

She took a step forward.

The pit bull closest to the porch snarled and lunged.

Ruby didn't flinch.

And the pit bull folded.

Right there.

Dropped like it had been unplugged. Legs twitching. A wheeze escaping its throat.

Another dog backed away, whimpering.

A third tried to jump the fence—missed—and landed screaming in the bushes.

The rest began to panic.

Some ran. Some circled blindly. Some rolled onto their backs, whining like puppies that had just woken from a bad dream.

Gabriela didn't see all of this. Not clearly.

But she *felt* it.

Ruby walked among the chaos of dogs like a ghost cutting through smoke—untouched, unhurried, and impossibly still at the center of a storm. Where others foamed and lunged, she moved with silent certainty, not barking, not growling, just *being*—and that was enough. The pack reacted like cells recognizing a foreign presence: some convulsed, some collapsed, some fled in a blind panic, as if her very existence short-circuited the signal that had bound them. She wasn't fighting them. She was *rewriting* them.

Like a storm was being sucked inward and inverted.

The growling—gone.

The pressure—gone.

Only the weight of the spell remained.

Gabriela clapped her wet hand to Ted's chest. "*Vuelve! Ahora!*"

Ted gasped like a man waking underwater—shoulders jolting upward, spine jerking. He screamed—not from pain, but from re-entry.

Luna staggered.

Her head dropped half an inch. Her legs wobbled.

And then—

She turned and ran.

Click-clack-click—the sound of claws on tile. She didn't stop. Didn't glance sideways. A sharp gust of cold air knifed through the kitchen, and the back door unlatched with a soft metallic click—then drifted open, slow and deliberate, as if the house itself was exhaling.

Gabriela barely saw her go.

But the sound of retreat felt like the cork pulled from something long bottled.

The air in the kitchen tasted like metal and ozone, as if lightning had cracked reality open and stitched it closed again.

Ted coughed, hard. Blood came up. His eyes blinked in rapid succession like he was rebooting.

Gabriela held his face. "You're okay. You're *okay.*"

He didn't speak. Just looked at her.

Behind them, through the open door, the night outside looked somehow sharper, like something had been peeled back.

Luna's pawprints in the kitchen were wet with water, but thankfully not blood.

Gabriela stood.

She walked to the back door and looked out.

Luna was standing in the yard, just at the edge of shadow.

She wasn't shaking. She wasn't panting.

She was staring.

Directly at Gabriela.

Their eyes locked.

And for the first time since this began, Luna looked afraid.

No.

Not just afraid.

Wounded. And she hated it.

She held Gabriela's gaze for three long seconds.

Then turned and vanished into the dark—not into the neighbor's yard, not toward the street.

Into the wind.

Gabriela stood in the doorway, feeling every hair on her arms rise. Her heart still stuttered. Her hands shook.

Ted groaned behind her, shifting to his elbows.

She whispered—not a prayer this time, not a chant.

Just a truth.

"She's not done."

* * *

Ted was out again.

Not seized this time—just quiet. Unplugged. His body lay across the kitchen floor in a loose sprawl, one hand draped in the puddle where the dog bowl had spilled. The water was cold now. The wax had hardened. Gabriela watched him for a long time before moving.

His chest rose. Fell. Uneven, but steady.

She stood.

The back door still hung open, and the breeze that filtered in felt wrong—not sinister, not soothing. Just… *disoriented.* Like the wind didn't know what direction to blow.

Gabriela stepped to the threshold and looked out into the yard. Luna was gone. Not a sound, not a shape, not even a print in the dirt. As if she'd evaporated into nothingness.

Then the barking started.

Not nearby.

Everywhere.

One dog barked down the block—sharp, clipped. Another answered with a confused half-woof. Then came the chorus: dozens of dogs, all calling out in uncoordinated spurts, like a symphony that had lost its sheet music mid-performance.

Gabriela walked barefoot out onto the concrete patio. The neighborhood glowed in soft porch lights, silhouettes moving behind curtains. One yard over, a retriever stood motionless, staring at its own reflection in a rain barrel.

Across the street, a pit bull trotted in circles around a garden hose, tail wagging slowly, as though trying to remember what joy was supposed to feel like.

A little white mutt—some kind of Pomeranian-terrier mix—sat in the middle of the road, licking the asphalt in steady, mindless repetition. Gabriela watched it for thirty seconds before it stopped, tilted its head, and lay down with its chin on the warm tarmac.

They had all stopped barking.

Now they were *waiting.*

Not for commands.

Not for owners.

Just… waiting.

Gabriela shivered and backed into the doorway again. The house felt worse than the street—because it had held something, and now it didn't. The walls echoed.

She grabbed a dish towel and knelt beside Ted.

He'd rolled onto his back, breathing shallowly, eyes closed. She wiped his face—gently, carefully—like rinsing dust from an artifact. His lip was split. A dark bruise bloomed beneath one ear. He mumbled something under his breath, but the words were scrambled.

Gabriela sat cross-legged beside him and took his hand.

For a while, neither of them moved.

Then something heavy thudded across the roof.

Gabriela tensed—but no growl followed. No bark. Just the sound of claws dragging across shingles. Slow. Measured.

Not Luna.

Not a neighbor's dog.

Something else.

She waited until the noise passed, holding Ted's wrist with two fingers, counting the beats.

Steady.

Alive.

But not *back*.

Not yet.

She looked around the kitchen. Wax, water, blood, salt, a cracked journal. It looked like an autopsy of a haunting.

A wind chime rattled from somewhere down the street. One sharp ding, then silence.

Gabriela whispered, "What did we wake up?"

She wasn't expecting an answer.

And didn't get one.

But out in the street, a German shepherd lifted its head and began to pace—not toward anything.

Just pacing.

Like it couldn't stand still without instruction.

CHAPTER FORTY-TWO

Detective Nia Wallace sat motionless at her desk, the blue light of the monitor turning her skin the color of ash. Her fingers hovered over the keyboard, unmoving, as if the thought had stalled between neurons.

The cursor blinked.

She blinked back.

After a moment, she resumed typing.

Subject: Delmonte, Ricky – Case #1128-A
Summary Conclusion: Evidence supports fatal assault by known affiliates. No sign of robbery or forced entry. Scene suggests confrontation escalated due to prior criminal association. Probable cause to close case with suspects deceased or unavailable. Final recommendation: administratively closed.

She read it once.

Then again.

Then scrolled back to the top.

Her eyes were glassy. Focused, but unmoored. Like she was reading a script she didn't recognize but had agreed to perform.

On her lap, a small brown pug snored lightly, its chin resting on her thigh. It twitched once but didn't wake. Nia didn't seem to notice the weight. Or the wet spot the dog had left from its nose.

She reached for the mouse and clicked SUBMIT.

The monitor dimmed slightly.

That was it.

Case closed.

A small voice in the back of her mind tried to speak up—some part of her trained for patterns, for motive, for *gut instinct*—but it was drowned beneath a fog of quiet obedience.

The pug snorted, waking briefly, and began to lick her hand.

She let it.

Her other hand drifted to the side drawer and opened it.

Inside, a small photo of Luna.

Nothing official. Just a snapshot.

Nia stared at it for a beat too long.

Then turned it over and slid it deeper into the drawer.

Footsteps passed the frosted glass of her office.

She didn't look up.

Outside her door, the hallway was quiet—midnight-shift quiet. A single desk lamp illuminated the narrow corridor like a nightlight in a nursery.

And in that light stood a yellow Labrador. Service harness. Blue vest with faded lettering: ASSISTANCE ANIMAL – DO NOT PET.

It didn't move.

Just watched.

Its eyes were perfectly still, fixed on the frosted glass of Nia's door. Not threatening. Not curious.

Just… present.

A second passed.

Then another.

Then it turned and walked away, its nails clicking in soft rhythm on the waxed linoleum.

Nia wiped her hand on her slacks.

The pug turned in her lap and settled again, its warm body pulsing in sync with hers.

Nia leaned back in her chair.

And smiled.

Not with joy.

Not even with peace.

Just… stillness.

Like a command had been followed, and the mind had powered down.

CHAPTER FORTY-THREE

Legacy

Luna didn't run.

She moved like smoke through the dark, as if the night opened slightly wider for her and then closed behind her like it had never split. The porch lights of Metro Verde flickered as she passed. Some blinked out entirely. Others stuttered like dying stars.

She didn't look back.

A wind kicked up behind her, but never touched her coat. Dust moved around her paws in swirling hesitation, spirals that never quite settled. The dogs in the surrounding streets—those that hadn't yet followed her, those too old or too far or too stubborn—watched from driveways, porches, garages with half-latched doors. None barked. Not one tail moved.

Luna passed a yard where a child's ball rested in the grass. A black Lab lay next to it like a sentinel, gaze fixed straight ahead. The ball rolled slightly as she passed, as if nudged by a breeze that had no direction.

She crossed out of the paved streets and onto cracked earth. Streetlights surrendered to sky.

There the silence was thicker—less the absence of noise and more the presence of *listening*. Coyotes didn't sing.

The wind forgot its script. Even the insects paused their night shift.

Up ahead: the trailer.

Single-wide, paint peeling to rust, one plastic chair flipped over in the yard. A wind chime of bent spoons hung by the door, but didn't move.

Lucas Santiago stood in the doorway, barefoot, wearing an old T-shirt and flannel pants. His face was unreadable—more shadow than man. He didn't blink. Didn't shift. One hand rested on the doorframe like it had been there for hours.

The porch light above him was already off.

He had seen her coming.

Luna stepped up the three worn steps without a sound. No nails on wood. No panting. Just presence. Her head tilted once—not up at him, but toward the threshold. As though seeking permission from something *older* than the man in front of her.

Lucas said nothing.

He didn't reach for her.

He didn't smile.

He just stepped aside.

And she walked in.

No ritual. No command. But the shape of it—the silent offering of space, the shared agreement—*felt* like something ancient. As if they'd both done this before, in another life, in another language.

Lucas turned and closed the door behind her. Quiet. Not a click, not a slam. Just the muted thump of wood against frame. The porch light stayed off.

Through the thin trailer window, a faint shift of silhouette, Luna moving toward the back room. Her shape passed a cracked mirror on the wall, but didn't reflect. Or maybe the mirror was just old.

Inside, no voices. No lights. Only the sound of breath syncing to another.

Outside, the wind started again.

It carried a smell: dry cedar, road dust, and distant rain.

On the porch, near the door, an old nylon leash swung gently on a nail. Frayed at the end, a Second Leash logo still barely visible in faded blue stitching. It swayed once, then settled. Like it had been waiting.

* * *

Morning came easy.

A soft golden mist hung over Metro Verde, the kind of light that made everything feel cleaned up and lightly retouched—edges softened, colors balanced. Birds chirped in polite sequences, never overlapping. A sprinkler clicked to life down the street. Not a single dog barked.

Ruby sat on the porch of a modest stucco house near the corner of Lucero and 8th, resting in a cushioned chair someone had dragged out just for her. Her tongue lolled, her thick chow-chow-mix coat brushed and gleaming like she'd been to a groomer that morning. A plastic bowl sat beside her, filled to the brim with fresh water, the surface still. Nothing moved unless she allowed it.

Across the street, a young pit bull lay on its belly in front of a toddler who was stacking toy blocks on the dog's back. The child's mother watched from the porch, sipping coffee with both hands wrapped around the cup like she was anchoring herself. Her smile never wavered, not even when the dog shifted slightly and the blocks tumbled. She didn't react. Just smiled.

A man jogged by, earbuds in, sweat darkening his collar. He offered a friendly wave toward Ruby. Not the child. Not the woman. Ruby.

She did not return it. He smiled anyway.

At the Tompkins' house, Gabriela stepped outside with a Tupperware container under her arm and a pair of gardening gloves in one hand. She paused on her front step. Took a breath. The air smelled clean—cut grass and warming concrete.

Ted was in the yard, pulling a few weeds from the edge of the flower bed, sleeves rolled to his elbows, dirt under his nails.

"Hey," she called softly.

He looked up. His smile was instant.

"Ready to feed Luna—" he caught himself. "I mean… ready to feed the neighborhood crew."

He gestured toward the sidewalk. Three dogs sat at perfect distances apart, each equidistant like plotted points on a grid. A golden retriever, a small terrier, and an older mutt with cloudy eyes. None of them made a sound. None moved. They just watched. Calm. Expectant.

Gabriela raised the Tupperware. "Chicken and rice again."

"Fancy." Ted wiped his hands on a towel and stood. "We're spoiling them."

"They deserve it."

They walked together toward the dogs. Ted opened the containers slowly, like a priest handling communion. Each dog approached in order—retriever first, then terrier, then the old mutt. No fighting. No sniffing. Each waited, ate, then sat again.

"It's…peaceful," Ted said.

Gabriela nodded but didn't answer.

Her eyes drifted to the other side of the street. A bone, almost perfectly white, had been placed at the base of a stop sign. It was aligned neatly, not chewed. Not scavenged. Placed. Like a marker. Or an offering.

Ted didn't seem to see it.

Back at their house, Gabriela watered the potted basil on the porch. The sun felt good on her arms. Birds chirped in rhythmic intervals. A breeze lifted the hem of her shirt and sent wind chimes ringing in soft harmony.

She looked toward Ruby's house. The chow hadn't moved. But her eyes were on Gabriela now.

Watching.

Not aggressive. Not threatening. Just… present.

Gabriela smiled reflexively, then caught herself. Her lips fell. She turned to go inside, then stopped.

In the reflection of the glass door, for a split second—

Her own eyes didn't look like her own. They shimmered with something golden, something ancient.

She blinked. It was gone.

From the porch behind her, the retriever gave one soft *huff*, like it had seen it too.

Inside, Ted made coffee.

He moved like he used to, but slower, more carefully. Like someone moving inside a bubble they didn't want to pop.

"Something wrong?" he asked, watching her stir the cream into her mug.

Gabriela hesitated. "No. Not really."

He nodded. "Good."

They drank together in silence, looking out the window.

Four dogs now. One had arrived while they were inside. A husky mix, sitting just out of reach. Watching.

A subtle sense of stasis had settled over Metro Verde.

Not mind control. Not worship. Not exactly.

But something had taken hold. And it was working.

Children walked to school with dogs trailing them like bodyguards. Packages were left on porches and never stolen. Mail carriers greeted every house with a nod toward the watching animals. Conversations were friendly, eyes softer. No one argued in driveways. No one raised their voices.

And Ruby never left the porch.

She didn't need to.

CHAPTER FORTY-FOUR

Bronx, New York

The air was thick with old snow and tailpipe grit, not sharp-cold but a humid kind that worked its way into drywall and joints. On 141st near Willis, most of the brownstones had iron gates and cracked stoops, plastic bags snagged in fence teeth, and Christmas lights still up but fading.

David stepped onto the back landing of his unit in slippers and a threadbare hoodie, holding a lukewarm mug of coffee. He leaned his weight against the doorframe like it held him up more than the coffee did. His scalp itched. His hands ached. The world felt like it needed buffering.

He squinted across the short yard toward the property next door.

There he was again.

The neighbor's dog. Big, black, and still. Sitting near the far fence like he'd been dropped there by God and forgotten.

"Hey there, buddy," David muttered. "You back on patrol?"

The dog didn't move, but something about him looked familiar. Not in the way of recognition—more like déjà vu layered over instinct. Same as when someone says your name and smiles like they've known you forever, but you swear you've never seen them before.

David sipped his coffee. Grimaced. Barely warm. He held the mug in both hands anyway, trying and failing to warm his fingers.

The dog—Sam, he thought the neighbor had called him once—just sat. Head slightly tilted. No barking. No tail movement. No interest in the pigeons flapping off the trash can nearby.

David coughed once and turned to go back inside.

That's when he heard it.

Not a sound. Not a voice.

A pressure inside his skull.

Like a barometric drop, but behind his eyes. His vision trembled, just for a second—color smearing at the edges like someone had pulled focus. His breath hitched.

Then it came again, this time unmistakable:

"Get your gun, David."

He froze. The mug slipped in his hands and thudded against the porch rail. Didn't shatter, just dropped like a body. Coffee puddled at his feet, splattered on his ankles.

He didn't move. Didn't speak. His ears weren't ringing, but his bones were. Something inside him had just been tuned like a radio. The air smelled wrong now—burnt copper and ozone—like the inside of a microwave that had just shorted out after scorching a bag of popcorn.

"It's time."

No echo. Just finality.

He turned. Walked inside without shutting the door.

Not fast. Not frantic. Like a man walking into the ocean because he no longer sees the point of standing still.

His feet knew where to go. Kitchen. Hall. Linen closet.

Behind the bleach and an old iron sat a box he hadn't touched in over a decade. He opened it.

Inside: a snub-nosed .44 revolver. Rust at the seams. Fully loaded.

He took it out with steady hands.

Outside, snow began to fall again. Not heavy, not fast. Just a quiet descent. The kind that muffled sound and erased footsteps.

Sam hadn't moved. Still sitting by the fence. Watching.

David came back onto the landing, gun at his side. His face was blank. Not empty, but unburdened. The way a man looks the moment after deciding to quit his job, or leave his marriage, or drive until the gas runs out.

He looked at the dog.

"Yeah," he whispered. "Okay."

Sam didn't respond. Didn't blink. But his eyes—something in them lit. Not glowing like fire. More like deep water catching a current from underneath. That low flicker of yes.

David stepped down off the porch and into the yard. The snow didn't crunch under his slippers. The cold didn't sting his skin.

And the gate between the yards?

Open. Just barely.

He didn't remember unlocking it. Didn't care.

Behind him, the back door still hung open. Coffee cup spilled, steam rising from a cooling puddle. The porch light flickered once, then died.

Ahead, Sam sat sentinel.

No sound.

No need.

David passed through the open gate, leaving the yard behind like it had never been his to begin with.

9 798218 896034